Swords of Steel IV

Edited by D.M. Ritzlin

Cover art by Bebeto Daroz

ISBN 978-1-956173-24-6

Cover layout by Jacob Calta
Interior illustrations by Eva Flora, Joe Minichino, D.R. Lackner, Jo Gamel, and Sarah Kitteringham

"The Wizard and the Tower Keep" originally appeared in *Fierce Tales – Savage Lands* (Millhaven Press, 2018)

www.dmrbooks.com
Instagram: @dmrbooks
Facebook: www.facebook.com/dmrbooks

CONTENTS

ALSO AVAILABLE

Swords of Steel Omnibus – *Swords of Steel,* with its novel concept of fantasy stories written by members of heavy metal bands, was the most critically-acclaimed sword-and-sorcery anthology series of recent years. Now every story from all three volumes is packaged together! Features Howie Bentley (Cauldron Born), Byron Roberts (Bal-Sagoth), E.C. Hellwell (Manilla Road), Mike Scalzi (Slough Feg), J. Christopher Tarpey (Eternal Champion) and many more.

Karnov, Phantom-Clad Rider of the Cosmic Ice by Matthew Knight, Howie K. Bentley and Byron A. Roberts – Returning from battle, the warrior Karnov discovers his family murdered and his homeland ravaged by vampyres. Aided by witchcraft and sorcerous allies, will Karnov's powers and burning lust for retribution be enough to avenge his loved ones, or will undead wraiths corrupt the earth forever? Classic horror film atmosphere meets pulp-style swashbuckling adventure in this action-packed epic.

The Eye of Sounnu by Schuyler Hernstrom – This collection contains all of Hernstrom's critically acclaimed stories for *Cirsova Magazine,* as well as a few uncollected and unpublished tales. Running the gamut from sword-and-sorcery to sci-fi, these heroic adventure stories will satisfy fans of Robert E. Howard and Jack Vance!

The Godblade by J. Christopher Tarpey - Brakur the Insane God has returned to the world of Arginor. The warrior-smith Rænon must seek the tomb of the dead god Farick for the remains he needs to pyre-forge The Godblade, the only sword that can kill Brakur and stand against the nefarious cult of Arhai. Will the armies sworn to the cult sweep through the lands of Arginor or can Rænon bring the forces of Aelbrond together to stop them? Will cold steel prevail over sorcery and the dark gods?

Introduction
by Schuyler Hernstrom

I've gotten old enough to know how ridiculous I am. I've paid enough bills, raked up enough leaves, and spent enough time at the dentist to really understand the mundane nature of most of our existence. I don't mean to sound bleak. It isn't a bad gig, raking up leaves on a beautiful fall day with the kids running around. There are red-tailed hawks where I live. You can look up from the leaves and see them flying in lazy circles like they have done since before history. It's much harder to romanticise the dentist. As an adult I've learned that a little pain and discomfort now will save you much worse later.

All this is good. But it isn't quite enough. It starts when we are young. It burns horribly, the formless desire, the nameless need, the yearning. We want danger. We want blood. We want to see and feel many times more what the mundane world can offer. Our ancestors lived rough. They killed and they were killed. No doubt they prayed for peace. We pray for war. Not to kill or die in a foreign land so some senator in a suit can get rich. The war we want is a chance to feel. To transcend our normal existence. We want to feel the barbarian's heart thundering in our chest. We want to be pushed to the brink of madness by the wizard's secret knowledge swirling in our brains. Our desires take shapes from myth, the secret language coded in our DNA. We want things this world can't give us.

This state of affairs would be completely unbearable without an outlet. Lucky us, the world has given us two. Metal and Fantasy. Two expressions of the thing that burns in us. Some people like one or the other. But some of us need both, a great deal of both, to make it through this world.

I suppose out there somewhere there are people who listen to metal "ironically." Maybe they flip through a Conan story and snicker a little, pretending to recognize the genius even as they tear it down with modern criticism. I don't need to waste time worrying about what people do. If you get it, you get it, and if you don't, you don't. The purpose of this introduction is to introduce this volume to people who get it. They feel the music deep within. They read the stories and lose themselves in the landscapes, the fetid jungles, the stygian dark of the forgotten tomb, the ice-blasted mountain peak, the wind-whipped dunes under a merciless sun, the molten rock that steals the air from your throat as you near it, the lonely tower under a sliver of moon.

This collection is for you. The authors are a rare breed, twice talented. Some are titans like Howie Bentley, an accomplished songwriter and guitarist. As a writer he carries REH's standard in the battle against the gray blob of mass entertainment. And his bandmate in Cauldron Born, grim faced Matthew Knight of Eternal Winter, a vocalist to rival any of the old gods of the '80s. No one who does what he does can be faking it. These are just two of the writers in this volume. We could talk all day about the others, the bands, the stories, the strange journeys you're about to take. But I'm sure, like me, you're impatient when it comes to this stuff. Turn off your phone and turn the page, and let these voyages satisfy some of that nameless need.

Schuyler Hernstrom *spent a great deal of his youth reading and rereading the works of Jack Vance and Robert E. Howard. After two enlistments, an education, and many years abroad he finally found himself ready to make his own contribution to his favorite genres, fantasy and science fiction. DMR Books released a collection of his stories entitled* The Eye of Sounnu *in 2020.*

When the Stars Invert

by Matthew Knight

Illustrated by Eva Flora

I

Candles blazed and incense smoke filled the dimly lit stone chamber. Chanting accompanied solemn prayers as a marble statue gazed from a hazy altar. Gleaming in the torchlight, the carved image of a serpent-entwined, winged youth with the head of a lion stood tall. A congregation of robed men and women reverently bowed before it.

They gathered in support of Othamere, a novice sage of the temple. After spending a year studying the Mithraic rites, the youth had proven his worth to the high priest by healing an afflicted girl with sacred alchemy. As a reward, at midnight he would become a true member of the order. Celebrating his expected initiation into the sacred Mysteries, the faithful mass sang praises to their god, giving thanks.

Women with black braids wearing bronze-plated tunics waved great palms, augmenting the flames of the hanging braziers, and causing shadows to dance eerily around the altar. Raising the hood of his violet robe over his head, Othamere concealed his dark hair and shadowed his tanned face. At his waist hung a book containing ancient texts, geometric sigils, and sacred incantations. From a cord of woven silk around his neck hung an oblong pendant of myrtle wood carved with an image of a hero slaying a bull.

As the hour drew near, the high priest approached the altar. He was a frail, elderly man in a sapphire robe; thinning white hair framed his kindly face. He raised his hands, facing the crowd. The chanting ceased as all kneeled.

"Brothers and Sisters of the Mithraeum," he addressed the

followers with a gentle, uplifting voice, "tonight, we celebrate a great deed. By the grace of Arimanius, our ailed Samira is cured—this being the work of our good brother, Othamere."

From her kneeling position, a young maid smiled sweetly toward the youth. One of the few women in the congregation, Samira had only recently been initiated before falling ill. Now cured, firelight gleamed on a piece of chestnut hair that escaped her hood, falling before her charming blue eyes and dark brows. Othamere returned a quivering grin before quickly turning his attention back to the high priest.

"This pious, young sage has been ever faithful, and proven his worth time and again. I declare the day has come for his initiation. Through the sacred Mysteries, he will inherit the divine knowledge, and serve our veneration to a fuller extent."

Sweat beaded on Othamere's brow as he anxiously awaited his call. He exchanged another glance with Samira, whose eyes watered, emotionally moved by the coming event. The attention only escalated his nervousness.

"And now, by the divine rites of our patron god, I call forth..."

The high priest stopped mid-sentence. Paling, a look of alarm overtook his countenance as he heard the far-off pounding of many hooves. The distant rumbling grew louder. Like demon drums at Samhain it quickened, surging throughout the countryside. The crescendo became unnerving, as the vibrations of the stampede could be felt in the bellies of the flock. The unsettled congregation fearfully beheld one another. Finally, the thundering gallops halted. The wide-eyed priest raised his hand, commanding silence, as he heard the sound of riders dismounting. The tension increased.

The door violently flung open. A knight in full armor and steel helm loomed in the doorway. He wore a white cloth garment bearing the sign of a red cross over his chain mail. Armed with sword and shield depicting the same symbol, he pointed his blade toward the high priest.

"Blasphemers!" the knight exclaimed. "Let us sanctify this place. Have at them, men!"

He ran forward into the temple as a horde of identically clad knights surged through the door behind him. The high priest recognized them as the Caedesiates, a corrupt lineage of renegade knights. Disguised in the garb of the famed Knights Templar, they invaded the land in a crusade to banish the ancient gods. He never suspected they'd find this secret place.

Panic struck the followers as the steel warriors entered the hall. They rose, attempting to flee, as two Caedesiates barricaded the door. One of the knights grabbed a man by his purple garment, driving his sword into his chest. Blood sprayed the attacker's white cloth as the victim fell lifeless to the ground. Another affiliate tried to fight back with an iron candelabra. Disarming him, an infuriated knight struck his head from his shoulders in an arc of blazing steel, painting the stone walls with gore. An elderly woman screamed in horror as the head rolled past her, only to be silenced by having her throat slashed by a broadsword. A spray of crimson gushed from her severed windpipe as an armored pikeman impaled the man beside her from groin to collar bone.

The red wave of carnage swept through the hall as the false Templars mercilessly took the lives of pagan initiates. Swords slashed jugulars and spiked maces bashed skulls, splattering brains upon the wall. The slick floor was littered with corpses and gore as shrieks of the dying echoed throughout the chamber.

As all disciples in sight were slain, the Caedesiates cleared a path, moving bodies out of the way. They stepped aside as their Grand Master entered the chamber. Tall and menacing, he wore an embroidered cloak of ebon and gold. A crested amulet around his neck indicated his supreme rank.

Seizing the high priest before the altar, two knights bore him to the ground.

"Grand Master Malethius, what should be done with the

profaner?"

Unsheathing an ornate, gold-hilted Accolade Sword, the Grand Master knelt over the priest, holding the blade above the man's chest.

"By leading others to worship your false god, you disgrace our master," he said with a deep voice.

As the sword plunged into the breast of the priest, the victim's eyes bulged. Blood surged from his mouth as his rib cage opened. Reaching into the chest cavity, Malethius tore out the still-beating heart, raising it before him.

"For your treachery, you will dine with the Princes of Hell tonight!"

He splattered the pulsing organ on the altar, leaving a crimson stain upon the stone.

Othamere evaded death thus far by cowering in the shadows, reciting prayers during the slaughter. With trembling hands, he rapidly read from his hiding place below the altar. He gasped as an ironclad hand seized him from behind. Lifting the youth in the air by his neck, an armored brute raised his sword to strike.

"Halt!" Malethius commanded.

Striding across the corpse-strewn floor, the Grand Master addressed the knight frozen in mid-sword stroke, holding Othamere.

As Malethius inspected Othemere's book, he noticed the myrtle pendant.

"This one looks like a magician. He might be useful. Spare him for now but keep him tightly bound. Gag him too. We don't want him mumbling curses behind our backs."

Another hulking Caedesiate came forth leading Samira and an auburn-haired initiate known as Elantis by a length of chain. The leash attached to iron bars fastened around their waists. Their shackled wrists bled as they struggled. Samira looked at Othamere with tears streaming down her face. Her garments had been torn and stained with the spilled blood of others.

"What should be done with these, Grand Master?" the knight asked. "They appear to be the youngest and fairest of the lot."

Removing his iron helm Malethius revealed a battle-scarred yet handsome, hawk-nosed face. Perspiration glistening on his chin-length moustache and beard stubble, his shoulder-length dark brown hair fell tousled and sweaty.

"They may be needed in rituals," he replied, his amber eyes blazing. "Keep them alive for now. Find a place out of the way for them, but keep the sorcerer at hand so we can watch over him."

The leash bearer led the captive girls down a corridor to a small shrine and chained them to marble columns. He then bound Othamere, leaning him against the wall of the main chamber.

Crossing his arms, Malethius grinned, pleased with the work his slayers had done. All the initiates were dead save the prisoners. The Caedesiates began moving bodies out of the blood-drenched hall before wheeling in a large wooden cart. Upon it sat strange artifacts, locked chests, provisions, and many flagons of wine.

After clearing the floor and unloading the cart, the knights removed their helms. Some appeared fair with shocks of golden hair. Others red-headed, bearing tribal markings upon their brows. Many were dark like Malethius with sun-browned olive complexions. Regardless of origin, all had a dangerous manner about them, and a mad, burning ambition in their eyes. Othamere noted that the influence of this deadly cult had ranged far and wide.

"Now that these dogs are taken care of, prepare for the ritual!" commanded the Grand Master.

Three knights rushed to the altar. With a large hammer, one of them crushed the statue of Arimanius. The lion-headed stone idol fell to the floor in a pile of rubble. Shuddering at this blasphemous deed, Othamere recited a prayer to his defiled deity.

A knight placed a heavy, silk-shrouded object upon the altar.

Once situated, he lifted the veil, revealing a statue of a bearded head. The realistic carving resembled the head of a corpse. With a death-like paleness, the statue's eyes were closed and its grey-blue lips grimly set. Othamere found it grotesque and disturbing to behold.

On each side of the altar, the knights assembled brass thurible stands loaded with black, aromatic herbs. Once ignited, the incense filled the chamber. The musky, fragrant scent inebriated Othamere as he breathed the fumes.

Upon the ground the knights drew runes within a circle with white chalk. Then from an ironbound chest, three glass vessels were brought forth. One was a large basin, the second a retort with a long downward pointing stem, and the third, a round collection vessel. These they assembled into an alembic. A small dome of stone and mortar was then placed within the circle and the alchemical device was set upon it. After removing the lid from an iron coal scuttle, a knight placed several red-hot embers within the dome using a small spade.

"All is in place, Grand Master," said a knight as he pulled a large brown book from a satchel, handing it to Malethius. Leather-bound and ancient, occult symbols and runes adorned its cover.

"Good. Let us begin!"

Facing the altar, the knights knelt in single file. Bowing, they pointed their swords to the ground. Malethius stood in the center bearing the arcane tome as incense smoke shrouded the chamber in an eerie haze.

"Brothers of the Caedesiate Order," began the Master, "tonight we praise His name and seek council. With this sacrifice and the blood of these profaners, we pay tribute in the hope that He will once again honor us with His presence. Let us pray."

In chorus, the knights recited as Malethius read from the book.

"Lord of the Cosmic Spheres, we call upon thee, Mystery of Mystery. As one sovereign Order, the Word of whose Law is

Divine Will, we commune."

From the chest a dusty bottle of Falernian was retrieved. This rare and ancient wine was poured into the apparatus. The deep ruby liquid splashed into the bottom basin just above the burner. Steam began to rise as it warmed.

From a sack, a Caedesiate revealed a large black asp that hissed and thrashed in his grasp. Carefully holding the deadly serpent in his iron-gloved hand, the man firmly pinched the back of its skull. Placing the snake's fangs above the alembic, he extracted a small amount of venom that was mixed into the wine.

Next, a large, oblong glass jar was taken from the chest. Inside the reflective glass loomed an exotic squid pickled in brine. A knight opened it and pulled the sea creature from the jar, yellow liquid dripping from its long tentacles. The squid was held above the alchemical still and squeezed until a black ink issued from it, mixing with the wine and snake venom. Once completely milked, it was discarded.

The mixture bubbled and churned as steam rose to the top of the vessel. As it did, an alchemical substance, purple and vibrant, slid down the glass shaft and into the collection vat. The elixir was poured into an obsidian and gold libation vessel and handed to Malethius.

"Partaking in this Alchemical Mass, we confess one baptism of Wisdom whereby we accomplish the Miracle of incarnation. Let us drink of the cup that ye drink of and be baptized with the baptism that ye are baptized with."

Raising the vessel to his lips, Malethius drank before passing it to each of the Caedesiates who did the same. Othamere shuddered in disgust.

"By the Bearded Head we confess our lives individual and eternal—that were, and are, and are to come. Amen."

The basin returned to Malethius. Tilting it back once more, he drained the final drops, savoring them. Facing the altar, he raised his sword above his head, a violet stream leaking from his mouth.

"Lord, we have performed the sacred ceremony and sworn allegiance to you through this alchemical rite. Grant us council. By the wild satyr gods, Dionysus, Hermes, and Pan, let our transcendental magick awaken thee!"

Tension filled the air as the Caedesiates silently awaited a response. With sweat beading down his face, Malethius' cat-like eyes darted back and forth anxiously.

The eyes of the statue opened, redly illuminating the gloom. With a crepitation, its grey lips parted, revealing stone teeth. Its nostrils flared and it seemed alive.

A monstrous, spectral image of a goat-headed humanoid appeared, hovering above the altar. Crimson eyes glowed below two horns on its fur covered head. Muscled as a brawny youth, upon its bosom jutted two full breasts like those of a voluptuous amazon. Its dark green nipples contrasted with the rest of its greenish-gray skin. Its loins wrapped in a burgundy, silk garment, it sat cross legged, levitating above the altar.

The knights bowed in allegiance.

"Great Lord of the Cosmic Spheres," said Malethius, "we are honored thou hast graced us with thy presence."

"My time is short, knight." A deep, resonant voice came from the mouth of the stone head rather than the beast. "Why hast thou summoned me?"

"When we last communed, thou promised to grant me the hidden knowledge to decipher the texts within this book if I slew the followers of the false gods. I have done as thou asked, shedding the blood of thousands of non-believers, banishing their religions. Have I not proven my worth?"

"For this to be done," said the hermaphroditic creature through the mouth of the bearded head, "I must be able to fully manifest on earth."

"And how can this be achieved?" asked the Grand Master

urgently.

"Only by the union of the Goddess, Lilith, and her male counterpart, Samael, may I traverse to this plane. For eons they have been bound and stranded at different ends of the cosmos. Each connected to half of a severed serpent, they can only mate via Tanin'iver, the blind wyvern. He is the intermediary that connects the serpent halves and unites them. Only through him shall the procreation of Samael and Lilith be fulfilled. When Tanin'iver is created whole, through his emanation the union shall occur, and I may manifest upon thy plane. The tome ye possess provides instruction."

"But Lord, I cannot read many of the incantations in this book," replied Malethius. "They are of a language beyond our understanding. I must be granted the hidden knowledge!"

"There is one among you who can decipher it," said the creature. The spectral being pointed at Othamere. "Indeed, he knows the Cykronoshian tongue, and is sufficient to perform the spell."

The knights turned their attention to the bound sage who cowered in fright. Malethius grinned. At that moment, Othamere wished he were an apprentice carpenter or blacksmith and had never dabbled in the magick arts. It would be better to have died with the rest than to perform such evil rites.

"A certain component is required to perform the ritual," the large-breasted figure continued. "Nearby lies a secret treasure—the Grail of Zoa'ulla. It is an oblong glass vial containing the viridescent blood of a future alien messiah from beyond the stars. By mixing the ichor of Zoa'ulla with human blood—perhaps that of these Mithraic followers you've imprisoned—during the proper ritual, Tanin'iver could be awakened. The Grail is sealed by sorcery within the vaults of the Abraxas Temple. A spell is needed to open it which is also contained in thy tome, and can be performed by the sage."

Again, Malethius grinned fiercely at Othamere, pleased with his decision to spare the youth for his magickal abilities.

"I canst tell thee no more," said the spectral image. "My strength on this plane wanes. Seek out the Grail of Zoa'ulla and use it to awaken Tanin'iver. Only then canst I manifest and grant the knowledge you seek."

"But Lord, wait!" Malethius shouted.

The spectral being vanished as the illuminated eyes of the bearded head extinguished.

The knights looked to Malethius. The Grand Master stared wide-eyed in grim contemplation. He walked over and knelt before the sweaty, squirming youth. With his iron-gloved hand, he grabbed Othamere by his shaggy, brown hair, gazing deeply into his terrified eyes.

"We will go to the temple. You will read the spell to unseal the grail, and you will perform the ritual to awaken Tanin'iver. If you disobey me, you and your female friends will be flayed alive. Do you understand?"

So frightened that he could not speak, Othamere trembled. His teeth rattled and his body convulsed as his eyes bulged in fear.

"We leave first thing tomorrow for the Temple of Abraxas!" Malethius addressed his men.

The stress of the horrific events exhausted Othamere, as the pungent incense caused his mind to whirl. As the knights cheered in excitement, his body went limp and he fainted on the stone floor. The last thing he saw before his vision faded was the purple-stained grin of Malethius laughing maniacally.

* * *

Strange music and awful ravings filled his head as consciousness slowly returned to Othamere. Regaining his senses, he peered through the haze, the dense smoke making visibility difficult.

Illuminated in cloudy orange torchlight, the knights had set up more braziers and incense burners. Naked, they reveled, each Caedesiate's body and face painted in earthy tones. They danced wildly around a bonfire that burned more aromatic black leaves, contributing to their intoxication. Chanting and singing, the knights drank wine from large clay vessels. They guzzled deeply, passing flagons to one another, spilling wine upon themselves and the floor.

Four men seated upon the ground played musical instruments. Two banged on drums made of animal hide while another played a lute strung with cat gut. The fourth blew into a long flute of yellowed bone. The exotic music was upbeat and dissonant with melodies of a harmonic vocabulary foreign to Othamere.

Along with the unclad Caedesiates, in the smoky firelight danced naked satyresses. Fair, with lithe bodies and long hair of different hues, horns spiraled upon their heads. Their ears were pointed, and their large eyes glared like those of forest animals. They wore necklaces of stringed flowers and dried mushrooms. Between their legs, patches of thick, green, moss emitted a fragrant scent like that of lavender and honeysuckle.

The painted knights attended them with lust and glee. One burly man poured wine onto a satyress' chest then greedily licked it off her breasts. Another buried his face in the mossy crotch of one, breathing deep of its sweet aroma while smacking her buttocks, reddening them. Throwing back their horned heads, the female Bacchantes laughed wildly above the maddening music. The knights took them to the floor and mounted them. The Dionysian beauties moaned in ecstasy as the painted brutes ravaged them in pools of spilled wine.

Averting his eyes from the obscenities, Othamere looked to the altar. He thought he saw a dark grin creep across the face of the bearded head. The intoxicating incense again overtaking him, he lost consciousness once more.

II

Dim light from hanging street lanterns reflected on cuirass, cuisses, and greaves as a sergeant of the Caedesiates stopped his horse and empty carriage outside a remote tavern. The knight tethered his horse and removed his helm. He was a rugged man with dark hair and a thick black beard. Straightening his cape, he ensured the pendant he wore bearing the insignia of his rank was visible.

Lurking in the darkness, a man clad in ebon robes watched, his hood concealing his black mane and shadowing his green eyes. None would assume by his appearance that beneath those tattered robes rippled lean muscles like those of a panther. He observed silently and unseen with hand on sword hilt as the sergeant strode into the tavern before closing time.

A barbarian from a distant land in search of an ancient book, Erodus had been the victim of the havoc it caused more than once. Penned in the days of Hyperborea, the magickal tome made its way across seas and time. Although he did not practice magick, Erodus understood the power of the book and knew what might happen if it fell into the wrong hands.

He heard rumors that the leader of a band of false Templars known as Caedesiates now possessed the book. By gaining information of the order's secret motives from an inside source, he knew the knights were nearby. He hoped this sergeant would be his key to acquiring the book.

Peering through murky windows, Erodus listened intently as the knight demanded a drink from the innkeeper. Unseen, he watched the sergeant guzzle two large flagons of wine. Loud and boisterous, the knight claimed his authority, threatening anyone who came near. Erodus restrained his urge to intervene as he watched the brute pummel a youth and manhandle several women—all the while laughing and drinking.

After an hour, the sergeant exited the building, leaving men battered and women sobbing on the floor.

Erodus sunk deeper into the shadows.

Stumbling through the street, the knight mumbled to himself, laughing and belching. Stepping into a dark area near his horse and carriage, he removed his groin-piece and lifted his faulds to relieve himself. He closed his eyes, sighing in alleviation.

An undetected sword blade quickly penetrated the back of his exposed neck, grating against his collar bone and sheathing itself in his vitals. Blood sprayed as the man howled, falling lifeless to the cobblestones, his heavy body dragged further into the shadows.

* * *

A misty autumn morning shed gloomy light upon the leaf-covered ground outside the temple as the knights prepared to depart. Men groomed and bridled horses while others reloaded their wagon with items and provisions. The knights bathed at a nearby stream and had a meal of ale and roasted mutton. They sharpened their weapons with whetstones and polished their armor with goose fat. Othamere and the captive women received their morning rations and had their binds retightened.

As the clouds parted, sunlight gleamed on a silver rider rushing down the distant hillside. A lone Caedesiate galloped forth on a white steed pulling an empty open carriage. Crimson plumes flowing from his helm, he traversed the slope winding upward on the outskirts of a forest fringing the vale below.

As he came into full view, it could be seen that he wore a gold-embroidered, crimson cloak similar to the black one worn by Malethius. Also like the Grand Master, he wore a gold amulet, though adorned with a different sigil.

Sweat beaded upon Erodus' brow as he halted his steed, approaching the party. Dismounting, he dropped to one knee before Malethius. He removed his helm, revealing a handsome face framed by a dark mane. His emerald eyes blazed above a small battle scar on his left cheek.

"Hail, Grand Master Malethius," he said. "I received word that you require a means to transport your prisoners. Thus, I have brought this carriage."

"Hail, Sergeant." Malethius regarded the man with hesitant familiarity. "What is your name?"

"Brockmere."

"Ah, yes. We've not met since we fought together at Damascus. I scarcely recognized you, save for your crest. You've shaved your beard, I see."

"Aye," said Erodus, disguised as the sergeant. "The road has taken me through many sweltering deserts since then. Do you require another sword arm? You and your men saved me and mine from Saracen bandits years back. I would return the favor."

"We'd be glad to have your sword with us, Brockmere. The Abraxas Temple is a three-day journey. You will ride at the front with me."

Erodus nodded and rose. The knights ordered the prisoners inside and shackled them to the iron bars of the coach. Malethius and Erodus walked to the front of the procession. Within moments the caravan departed.

Leading the crew on their black and white stallions, Malethius and the feigning Erodus picked up speed as they went. The other knights followed militantly with their wagon and carriage at the rear. Othamere and the captive women were tossed to and fro inside the carriage. Chained to the bow, they gripped their shackles and leaned against one another, fearing they might fall out and be dragged along.

Like Riders of the Apocalypse the brigade stormed through the countryside. From quiet vales and fruitful orchards to poverty-stricken villages with shale tombstones they rode. Wagon wheels churned and dust rose from the pounding ironclad hooves as they traversed field and fen.

The authoritative Caedesiates were met with fear and apprehension in every town. They interrogated and flogged many innocent folk while mercilessly trampling those who did not clear from the road.

Abandoning civilization, the caravan moved into the wilder territory. The surrounding woodland thickened as large mountain ranges loomed in the distance.

Near a dense forest, Malethius ordered them to halt. Turning, he faced the crew.

"Daylight wanes. This is a good place to hunt for our supper before we camp. Draw your bows, men."

The knights dismounted. They placed the prisoners at guard, once again leading them by chains. Entering the forest, they separated.

A dank scent of mushrooms and moldy leaves permeated the air of the still, quiet woodland. Waning sunlight filtered through the autumn foliage, casting a golden glow upon the leafy ground. Moving stealthily beneath boughs of high oaks and locust trees, the knights crouched with arrows ready. Once in their positions, they waited in anticipation of a stag or pheasant bursting through the thicket.

Moving deeper into the forest, Erodus separated himself from the group. His keen instinct told him of something lurking beyond the shadows.

Suddenly, a tusked, grey boar burst from the brush, running at full speed. Shrieking loudly, enraged at this trespass, it charged Erodus. The armored barbarian let an arrow fly, striking the boar in its side. Blood spurted from the wound as the beast screamed, bolting deeper into the woods, the arrow protruding from its ribs.

Following the trail of blood, Erodus, an expert hunter, pursued the boar patiently, analyzing hoof prints and broken twigs.

The trees thinned as the trail led to the edge of the forest. Leaving the woods entirely, he came to a barren moor. Tall reeds rose from pools of dingy water in a field of brown grass. Trekking through the swampy area, Erodus carefully avoided areas of silt and quicksand.

He spotted the boar lying in its own blood by a tarn. The barbarian knelt and cut the dying animal's throat. Removing the arrow, he slung the beast over his shoulder and began trekking back toward the forest. Large enough to feed several knights, he hoped this kill would please the Grand Master, perhaps getting him closer to the book.

Avoiding pools of mire and rotting vegetation, he saw a dark form huddled on the ground near a tarn. A woman of late age shrouded in black regarded Erodus with a cold stare. Grey hair from beneath her hood fell before her filthy skin. She looked as if she had been in the wilderness for weeks.

"Hail, crone," he said. "What do you on the moors?"

The woman eyed Erodus suspiciously.

"Though you wear their garb, you are not one of them," she said in a worn, husky voice.

Erodus looked around, ensuring no knights had followed that and could be nearby listening.

"And how do you know that, wench?"

"They would've tortured me for sport, not hail me as you did. They are a mockery of the true order—fiends who defile the Templar moral code."

Erodus noticed a charm around her neck. Recognizing the symbol upon it from the book he sought, he knew she was more than an ordinary witch.

"I know that sigil," he said.

"You know the Cykranoshian runes?" she asked. Her eyes blazed with new interest.

"No," he replied. "But I know of their power."

"You know of the book, then," she said, staring off in contemplation. "Perhaps we can strike a bargain."

"What mean you?" Erodus asked.

She pulled from her bundle a rectangular piece of vivid green amber, a chunk small enough for a man to grasp firmly in one hand. Embedded within the center of the viridescent resin loomed a carved figure several inches tall. First appearing to be a small statue of a Madonna and child, upon closer inspection, Erodus saw that the beings depicted were inhuman. The cyclopean woman had three breasts and a serpentine lower half. The faceless child she cradled had gills and fins like a fish.

"In ancient times, this fell to earth from the spectral moon of Arcturus. The carved idol inside is Sera'xus, the Blue Madonna. She is the mother of Zoa'ulla and is revered as a Queen of Ævänah."

Erodus' eyes widened at the last word she mentioned.

"Fossilized in the life-giving nectar milked from her bosom, this artifact gives its user the ability to seek a boon from the Queens and be saved from their wrath."

"Why offer this to me?"

"Because I am starving, and that animal you carry would feed me for a week. Furthermore, I wish to see those Caedesiates burn, and I think I know what you will use this relic for." She grinned darkly.

"And you swear by this?"

"I swear by the seven Queens of Ævänah."

"That is an awful oath."

Again, Erodus glanced around to ensure no one had followed. Seeing scars of torture upon the crone's hands and face, he believed her story to be sincere and resolved to trust her. He slung the boar from his back, onto the ground next to her.

"I agree to this bargain, hag. I think the results of it will please you."

She grinned and handed him the brick of amber containing the Madonna statue. Erodus stuffed the fossilized relic in his arrow quiver.

Before returning to the forest, he nodded to the witch who immediately began gutting the huge boar with a shale dagger, licking the blood from her fingers as she worked.

When Erodus reached the party, the knights were already loading their hunted game. They heaped freshly killed carcasses of plump hares, grouse, and deer into the wagon. Their spirits high, they knew they would eat well that night.

"How did you fare, Brockmere?" Malethius asked. "I reckoned you went deeper into the woods. I see there's blood on your hands, and you're short an arrow."

"Aye," replied Erodus, "I encountered a great boar. After a struggle, it got away. I nearly had it."

"Strange for a seasoned hunter such as yourself," Malethius replied, eyeing him suspiciously. "A pity. I would've relished the tender meat of a pork loin. But we have plenty to eat. Let us move now that the wagons are loaded. It will be dark soon and we must make camp. There's a vale just ahead."

The men stashed their bows and arrows in the wagon with the other weapons. Erodus secretly removed the amber-encased Madonna from his quill. Quickly wrapping it in a velvet sash, he slid it into his saddlebag.

With the prisoners secured in the carriage, the knights mounted their steeds and the caravan embarked.

As they rode, Erodus glanced at the ornate, armored figure of Malethius riding beside him. Near the Grand Master's leg in plain sight hung a large, locked saddlebag. Certain it contained the book, Erodus schemed. Even during the hunt, Malethius kept it guarded. He had no doubt it would be closely watched over day and night. To try and seize it would mean instant death. Different measures would need to be taken.

* * *

Smoldering hickory branches hissed as the Caedesiates cooked and feasted around a crackling fire. They ate, drank, and laughed heartily while passing vessels of strong wine to one another. They set up brass thurible stands and loaded them with black aromatic leaves as they had done in the defiled temple. The rich scent of the incense commingled with that of roasted fowl and venison.

Erodus disguised as Sergeant Brockmere ate with the knights. Trying to remain inconspicuous, he laughed and jested as they did. He drank wine, being careful not to intake as much as they.

Othamere and the maidens devoured their evening rations. Exhausted from the journey, the women slept upon the hard ground, their slumber aided by the incense fumes. Lying awake, Othamere pondered an escape plan. He thought that if he could get to the book, he might have a chance at casting a spell to save them. He would need time to practice the incantations. In his current state, and with the tome locked and closely guarded, this idea seemed nigh hopeless.

Malethius laughed wildly at stories of crusade forays while gnawing on a rib bone, his gold-plated armor gleaming in the firelight.

After they dined, the Grand Master arose and unlocked an ironbound chest. From it he presented to his men a leather face mask with a long glass tube stemming from its mouthpiece. At the end of the conduit, a cylindrical opening gaped.

"Let the revelry begin!" he shouted, holding it high.

The men raised their drinks, cheering in excitement.

Approaching one of the thurible stands containing the burning herbs, he donned the leather mask. Grasping the cylinder in his hand, he held it above the burning embers. With a great draw of breath, he pulled smoke from the censer, through the tube, into his lungs. Removing the mask, he exhaled a cloud of purple smog. The knights cheered as the Grand Master coughed and staggered, the escalation of his intoxication apparent.

"By the teats of the Horned One, who's next?" he exclaimed.

One at a time the knights eagerly took turns using the apparatus, inhaling the smoke of the mind-altering herbs with much satisfaction. Erodus avoided partaking and slowly slipped into the shadows.

Soon, all the men had inhaled a great amount of the fumes, except for the two vigilant knights who guarded the book.

"Now, it's time the night got interesting!"

Reaching into a leather pouch, Malethius grabbed a large handful of glittering dust and tossed it into the fire. Flames shot up, turning green and silver, illuminating all in an ethereal glow.

"Daughters of Pan," he called out, "attend us once more!"

Sitting in silence, the knights gazed into the uncanny blaze. Sweet, haunting music emanated from the surrounding woods. Interweaving melodies playing against one another harmonized in counterpoint. It created a hypnotic effect as five satyresses materialized in the firelight.

Naked as before except for their flower necklaces, they played pan flutes. The honey-like fragrance of their moss-covered pubic areas was immediately discerned by the knights. Dancing and whirling around the fire, the satyresses fluted in harmony. Their lithe bodies moved with inhuman grace. With long hair flowing from their horned heads, wild eyes gleamed as red lips wrapped wooden instruments. Prancing to the melodic tune, their empyreal beauty entranced the men.

Ending with a deceptive cadence, the satyr-women ceased piping and stood motionless. Stillness reigned in the silent vale as the audience anticipated what would follow.

With a wave of her hand, one flaxen-haired vixen magickly transformed her flute into a ceremonial dagger, holding it high.

Turning their backs to the knights, the other four faced the woods. In unison, they began a new harmony. A minor dirge, slow and somber but lush and melodic, this mesmerizing piece utilized parallel fifths and voice-leading intervals.

In a flowing dance, the golden-haired satyress swayed side-to-side with the meter of the tune, waving her dagger in the air. Falling to her knees, she made dramatic arm motions toward the woods, flailing her body as if beckoning to something.

From his place upon the ground, Othamere longed to turn away but could not. He watched intently, spellbound by the splendor of the forest-women's song and dance.

With their tune, the maenads lured three forms from the darkness of the woods. Huge, incandescent toads emerged, each of a different color; orange, yellow, and blue. Fat with large, bulbous eyes, they moved lethargically. Stopping as they approached, they squatted motionless before the fire. Measuring several feet wide, their heads came as high as a man's waist.

Approaching the orange toad, the blonde satyress gently slid the blade of her dagger horizontally along its back, steeping it in thick, transparent slime. The luminous amphibian remained completely docile. Scraping the backs of the other two toads, she gathered slime from each onto the blade.

With coated dagger in hand, she approached the seated knights. Each man eagerly opened his mouth into which she let a small drop of toad-slime fall from the tip of the blade. Once each knight ate the slime, they lounged back upon the leafy ground.

Their perception altering, their surroundings became vivid. The forms of the satyr-women wavered, changing shape and color as the toads' heads appeared as laughing humanoids. Planets and comets soared along with swarms of armored locusts, and spectral green lizards crawled upon the very fabric of space and time. An intense feeling of euphoria and enlightenment accompanied these sights.

Othamere averted his eyes from marveling at the satyresses, then closed them. Slipping into a meditative state, he put his attention on the sound codes embedded in the music. With his intention, he transformed the harmonic frequencies into geometric visions within his mind's eye. An overwhelming sense of euphoria overcame him as the energies of the current planetary cycle connected with the celestial forms surrounding his body.

Disrupted from his trance, Othamere tensed as a steel-gloved hand seized him. The abductor lifted the youth off the ground by his garment and covered his mouth. Being forcefully dragged into the woods, the sage struggled in vain. The intoxicated knights as well as the guards remained oblivious to the act, being distracted by the otherworldly scene, and more concerned about protecting the book than the prisoners.

Once out of sight, Othamere's captor forced him to crouch down upon the fern-laden ground. Surprised, the youth beheld the moonlit face of who he believed to be Sergeant Brockmere. Othamere trembled in fright as the kneeling man glanced through the trees, ensuring no one had followed.

"Have you or the women been harmed?" asked Erodus.

"No, Sergeant Brockmere," replied Othamere in a shaky voice, bewildered.

"Brockmere is dead," said the man. "My name is Erodus. I have entered the Caedesiate ranks in disguise because I seek the book they covet. I have a plan to retrieve it, and if successful, I can save you and your companions. I will need your help."

"I'll do anything you ask!" said Othamere urgently, brimming with new hope.

"Then listen carefully," said Erodus, his emerald eyes ablaze. "In the back of the grimoire is a section concerning the summoning of seven alien deities called the Queens of Ævänah. When the Grand Master orders you to recite the incantation to open the seal of the Grail, you must instead perform the summoning spell to bring forth one of these Queens. Not understanding the language, he and his men will be none the wiser. I possess an artifact that provides the ability to request aid from these deities. I will bid it to destroy the knights before returning to its own realm. You prisoners will be freed, and I will take the book."

"Why do you seek the book?" asked Othamere.

"Because I understand the destruction it can cause. What these Caedesiates plan could bring mankind's doom. It must be returned to a safe place."

"You're sure no harm will come to me by performing this spell?"

"Yes," assured Erodus. "The Queen will be used as a weapon against the knights. That is all."

Othamere thought deeply. He could think of no other solution. His only hope resided in Erodus' plan.

"I will trust you in this, though I like it not. I've seen what can be summoned from that book."

"As have I," said Erodus, "but this time they will aid us. Remember, a Queen of Ævänah must be summoned."

"Aye," sighed Othamere, nodding.

"Good. Now it's time to get you back before those blundering brutes discover your absence."

Less forcefully than before, Erodus carried the chained youth back to the camp unnoticed by the inebriated knights. Returning Othamere to his place among the prisoners, he slipped back into the party, feigning drunkenness.

Othamere lay upon the damp grass dreading this deed he must accomplish. Beside him, he saw the beautiful eyes of Samira looking straight into his. Not being asleep as he assumed, she had witnessed him being taken and returned unharmed by Erodus. Her gaze fixed him with a hopeful expression. Tears filled Othamere's eyes as he beheld her innocent countenance. He managed a heartfelt smile and an assuring nod. Samira smiled back then closed her eyes and fell into a deep slumber.

III

Beneath raven-flecked skies the thundering of hooves resumed through the wild countryside. Chain mail clanged and wagon spokes screeched as the party raced along rocky ground. They made an early departure despite the previous night's revels. With the air growing colder as they entered mountainous terrain, the serene forests and picturesque meadows of the preceding day's journey gave way to treacherous crags and dangerous ravines. Riding along a steep, winding pathway through the mountains, they ascended.

Throughout the day they rode. Othamere, Samira, and Elantis huddled together for warmth in the carriage as chilly air rushed over them. Above the roaring of the caravan, they heard the harsh cries and commands of Malethius as he thrashed his horse, driving the crew onward.

As the sun lowered, they stopped to eat. The party dined on freshly killed mountain goat and drank from a freshwater spring. Malethius indicated that he did not wish to make camp, but to carry on through the night. He declared that the full moon would light their path enough to take them beyond the mountains before daybreak. Some knights voiced their concern about travelling through rocky slopes in the dark, but the Grand Master insisted.

After a short rest, they mounted as night fell. Resuming their journey, they held torches high. Aided by the flames and bright moonlight, they could see well, but proceeded cautiously.

As the path narrowed between two high ridges, they stopped at a fork.

"This road leads to the White Gorge," Malethius said to Erodus, pointing to the left path. "The other continues through the mountains for miles. We can save half a day's journey by heading across the gorge. The bridge is sturdy enough to take us over it. Trading caravans used to traverse it regularly."

"But Master," a red-bearded knight spoke up, "what about the legend? You know about the bridge, and on a full moon…"

"Fool! That is gypsy superstition. I should flog you for questioning my authority. We head for the gorge!"

Erodus looked at the man who spoke. The silent knight shot him a fearful glance, shaking his head nervously. Malethius urged his steed into the chosen path, and all followed.

After a stretch of rocky slopes, the road led into a forest of tall pines. The shadowy woods were mysterious in the full moonlight. A fog arose covering the path. Only the Grand Master's hawk-eyed vision saved them. Strangely, it was even colder in this forest than in the mountains. They rode through the dark wood with torches blazing. Othamere shuddered as timber wolves howled in the distance, and he thought he discerned ghostly forms in the fog.

As Malethius focused on leading the caravan through the gloom, Erodus urged his steed to pull back so that he briefly rode beside the red-bearded knight who protested earlier.

"Tell me about this bridge," he said discreetly.

"An old legend of this region," the man replied, leaning toward Erodus. "They are known as the Sisters of the Moon Wolves. Damned souls of two holy nuns who dabbled in the secret arts, the church authorities captured and flung them into the gorge for heresy. Lore has it they offered their souls to some cosmic wolf god as they died. On nights during a full moon, travelers have encountered them at the bridge. Few have lived to tell the tale. There's no telling what awaits us."

Shooting the man a concerned look, Erodus rode onward, resuming his place near the front of the procession.

They continued through the fog-enshrouded woods for nearly an hour before coming to a clearing. Exiting the forest, they halted as they beheld a canyon of shale and granite gaping before them. The moon sat high above the surrounding pines, bathing the gorge in pale luminescence nearly as bright as daylight. All could clearly see the black abyss of the canyon's depths.

A wide bridge of timber, iron, and thick rope spanned the gorge. It was wide enough that two rows of men could ride side-by-side. A sturdy overpass of tightly bound planks, no one doubted it could hold the riders and their caravan. A dense fog obscured the land on the other side.

"Don't just stare at it," Malethius commanded. "Let's move!"

The Grand Master led the knights onto the bridge. They rode slowly, taking care so that no horse slipped off the edge. Othamere shuddered as gravel beneath hooves fell into the dark chasm. Erodus glanced behind him at the red-bearded knight. The man's eyes darted nervously as sweat ran down his brow despite the cold.

Nearing the other side of the fissure, the jade fog came forth upon them, obscuring even the bridge they rode on. They halted as a milky viridescence covered all.

"Damn this fog!" roared Malethius.

Blind and motionless they stood as swirling winds arose from the gorge. They steadied their horses as sudden gales swept against them. Othamere and the captive women clung to the carriage in fear and desperation. The knights drew their swords as the nearby howling of wolves echoed.

As if by sorcery, the fog dispersed. Once the verdant murkiness subsided, they beheld a creature of strange proportions hovering above the precipice at the end of the bridge. The heads of two nuns wearing white bandeaus and black veils sat atop a wide, round, black body. Its shiny form wavered and undulated with ebon tentacles flailing from its bottom half as it floated. At its large bosom, the unknown substance of its being melded into the likeness of a nun's habit, donning a white neckerchief and coif. With faces fair as porcelain, the heads regarded the knights with icy blue eyes and glistening red lips.

Leashes of steel chain spanning from the levitating creature connected to the iron collars of six spectral wolves—three on each side of it. Semi-transparent, and green like the fog, the beasts slavered and drooled, baring deadly teeth. Their emerald eyes radiated in an uncanny glow.

"Why dost thou seek passage across the White Gorge?" asked the right head in a stern, female voice that echoed through the chasm.

"We mean no trespass," said Malethius. "We're travelers seeking a shorter route through the mountains."

"You lie!" the left head spat. "You bear the sign of those we curse!"

"Nay, Sisters," replied the Grand Master, "we have abandoned the old ways. We are Caedesiates—renegade knights seeking vengeance against the very ones who wronged you. Grant us passage and you shall be avenged!"

The two-headed cosmic being stared at Malethius, beating its black tendrils in the fog-wisped air. The right head turned its attention to the prisoners at the rear of the procession.

"Who are the robed ones?" it asked.

"They are of a pagan sect whose lot we slaughtered. We spared them for ritual purposes."

The heads looked at one another and licked their lips with red, snakish tongues.

"You must sacrifice one of the prisoners. The Moon Wolves of Thanator must be fed."

The ghostly beasts salivated, growling in hunger.

"Fine," said Malethius. "Take one of the females. Only the male is precious to me."

"Grand Master, wait…" Erodus started.

"It has been decided!" shrieked both heads in unison.

Lashing one of its tentacles toward the carriage, its appendage wrapped around the torso of Elantis, the auburn-haired maid. Samira screamed in terror as the ebon tentacle ripped her companion from the carriage, breaking the steel chain restraining her. Whipping backward, the shiny tendril dropped the helpless girl to the ground before the slavering beasts. Instantly, the wolves were upon her, rending flesh from her bones and thrashing limbs from her body as they feasted upon her.

Erodus stifled the urge to try to save the poor lass. He knew cold steel would be no use against these supernatural foes, and his true nature would be revealed if he intervened. The girl was doomed.

"Very well," said the left of the Sister-heads. "You have satiated the wolves. If you give your word to avenge us, we will allow you to pass unscathed."

"That I do," Malethius bowed.

"Go forth, then, and claim our vengeance."

The path cleared as the tentacled being and the wolves vanished. Only traces of green fog and the stripped bones of Elantis remained. The knights proceeded across.

Once on solid ground, Malethius looked suspiciously to Erodus, wondering why he objected to sacrificing the prisoner. Othamere and Samira leaned against one another in the carriage, sobbing as the sky grew grey with the coming dawn.

* * *

The sun gleamed upon the Abraxas Temple as they arrived late that morning. A wide grotto of sandstone beneath stout, crimson-leaved maples, it stood since ancient times as indicated by the antiquated architecture. A carved emblem of a whip-armed warrior with the head of a cock and serpents for legs adorned the building's exterior.

Malethius immediately ordered the knights to dismount, storm the temple, and slay all within. After donning their helms and drawing their blades, they positioned themselves outside the ornately carved wooden door. When the Grand Master gave the signal, they charged through the entrance one by one.

To their surprise, the knights found the hall vacant. No incense or braziers burned. Dust covered the altar, and it seemed the place had been abandoned for some time.

"There will be no sword-quenching after all," said Malethius. "Very well. Let us descend to the vaults. Bring the prisoners and the book."

Moving through an alcove, the Caedesiates entered a dark, winding stairway. Here they lit torches. The old stairs crumbled as cobwebs clung to the walls and the scent of mold permeated the air.

Approaching the foot of the descent, they stepped onto the bedewed ground of the temple's catacombs. Seizing old flambeaux from sconces upon the walls, they lit them for additional illumination. The further they travelled, the temperature of the atmosphere dropped. White patches of nitre gleamed along the granite walls. Embedded in them, rare stones and crystals glimmered. Also visible were human bones, making it apparent that the dead were entombed within.

Deeper into the moldering crypt they reached recesses where grey, oblong objects covered by dust and fungi protruded from wooden racks. Upon close inspection, they identified these as age-old bottles of wine. The knights marveled as beneath translucent mushrooms, half-disintegrated, handwritten labels indicated ancient vintages of Vitis Vinifera including Allobrogica, Nomentana, and Falanghina.

Erodus felt the weight of the amber-encased Madonna he secretly carried in a leather pouch. He glanced back at the prisoners. A large knight led them by a length of chain. This man kept not only the keys to their shackles but also the book. He carried the tome in a satchel strapped to his back.

Passing through the vaults, they came to a door through which they arrived in another stone altar room. It appeared to be vacant but lit by torches and braziers. In the center, a marble altar stood. Upon it, held in a gold stand was an oblong glass vial with incandescent green liquid contained inside. The swirling fluid churned, emitting a verdant glow.

"The grail of Zoa'ulla!" said Malethius. "Not interred, but here for the taking!"

As he moved toward the altar, several knights in golden bronze armor unexpectedly emerged from the shadows, blocking his way. Armed with swords, maces, and Morningstars, their shields displayed the sigil of Abraxas. They matched the Caedesiates in number.

As the warriors appeared, the chamber door slammed shut and the sound of latches and bolts clicked.

"What is this?" shouted Malethius as the Caedesiates drew their swords.

A tall knight stepped from the shadows wearing a cloak of jade and gold, and an ornate breastplate of rose-gold. His amulet indicated that he too was a Grand Master. In front of the altar, he faced the enraged Malethius.

"Greetings, fellow Grand Master. I am Gromathar and we are the Knights of Abraxas, sworn to protect the grail of Zoa'ulla. We heard of your coming from watchmen in the mountains. Your intentions to molest the Grail have sealed your doom!"

Forming a wall to protect the Grail, the bronze-clad warriors attacked the Caedesiates as a battle of steel on steel ensued. Clashing with brutal fury and overtly tactical fighting skills, the knights battled in the altar room as white cloths were reddened and bronze hilts became grimed with gore.

Charging Erodus, a mace-wielding foe struck thrice, each blow being blocked by the Templar shield. The barbarian hacked once and dodged another swing before driving his sword through the golden knight's chain mail, into his chest. Erodus turned just in time to block the blade of another Abraxas knight.

Malethius battled Gromathar before the altar. The massive Grand Masters dealt furious blows to sword, shield, and armor.

Sparks flew as the Caedesiate's blade grated on a crimson gauntlet before his rival's Accolade Sword nearly severed his neck.

As Erodus ran his sword through a worthy opponent, he noticed the large Caedesiate guarding the book fighting nearby. Blocking blows while being relentlessly driven backward in a duel with a berserk Abraxas knight, the guardian stepped in reverse toward Erodus. Seizing the opportunity, the barbarian lifted his sword and thrusted it downward through the collar of the unsuspecting Caedesiate into his innards. Retracting the blade, he lunged and slashed open the jugular of the man's opponent. Both knights fell in a pool of crimson.

Removing the book satchel and the keys from the dead Caedesiate, Erodus ran to Othamere who was huddled near the wall with Samira. Unlocking the youth's shackles, he handed him the objects.

"Now's our chance. Remember the plan!" he said before charging back into the fray.

"Surrender the Grail, Gromathar. Your knights are falling!" grinned Malethius as he swung madly at the golden Master before the altar.

"Nay," returned Gromathar, "your Caedesiates will soon drown in a sea of blood. Abraxas wills it!"

Now freed, Samira lurked in the corner hiding from danger while Othamere rapidly scanned through the book, searching for the incantations.

The brittle pages were weathered and stained with blood and other spell components. Coming to a section that read "Queens of Ævänah," he noted descriptions of several deities written above incantations in addition to illustrations. Speeding through the chapter, he shuddered at the hideous and evil-looking depictions of the Ævänah Queens. The book expressed the obscene tendencies of their characters to be extremely dangerous. Dreading bringing forth one of these hellish beings, he began to think Erodus' plan mad.

Reading *Sera'xus*, the final page portrayed a peaceful-looking, alien Madonna holding a child. It described the being as noble and powerful rather than malicious and dangerous. He did not have time to read the entire excerpt, nor to consult with Erodus. He resolved that for fear of losing his soul, and the safety of Samira, he could not summon the other deities. He decided he would bring the Madonna to their aid. Over the clangor of steel, he chanted the Cykranoshian words.

"Yield to the Order of the Horned One!" spat Malethius as he dealt brutal sword strokes to Gromathar who blocked with blade and shield, returning merciless attacks.

Erodus battled nearby, dodging the whirling Morningstar of a rival knight. Striking low with stabbing thrusts, he evaded the deadly ball of steel. Blocking a blow on his battered shield, he lunged, running his sword through the knight's midsection, penetrating his chain mail. As the opponent fell, he heard another death groan behind him. Turning, he saw that Gromathar had suffered the same fate, as Malethius had buried a yard of steel in the Abraxian's chest.

The Caedesiate Master laughed as he twisted the blade. "You should have listened to me and handed over the Grail. Now it is mine and your order will be destroyed."

Gromathar roared and continued hacking at Malethius as he died, falling to his knees in a pool of blood.

Othamere conjured in hypnotic trance. The summoning spell of Sera'xus required the use of sacred geometry. Envisioning specific celestial shapes surrounding him, he recited the incantation. Seated with hands held in the proper mudras, he saw around him whirling light-filled octahedrons, star tetrahedrons, and other three-dimensional prismatic figures while he read intently.

Erodus, the only man aware of the magick-working, urged his opponent backward, engaging him in fanciful swordplay, attempting to block Malethius' vision should he turn and notice Othamere summoning.

Malethius boasted to the dying Gromathar. As the Abraxian leader died, the victorious Grand Master approached the altar. Two knights quarreled before it, blocking his way. Kicking his fellow Caedesiate out of the way, he lunged his sword through the man's opponent. Malethius grinned as the light from the grail illuminated his maddened countenance. Reaching to seize the glowing vial, he quickly recoiled as a figure materialized before him.

Hovering above, a spectral woman, nude and voluptuous, appeared. With blue skin, her silky, ebon hair wisped in the air like tendrils. Cyclopean, the single large eye upon her face glowed sapphire. A luminescent green fluid leaked from large breasts upon her naked chest between her slender arms. A white aura surrounding her head like a cosmic halo, her serpentine lower half coiled. Othamere's magick had worked.

Enraged, Malethius attempted to strike the Madonna. His sword clanged in midair as if meeting a wall. Unscathed, Sera'xus remained protected by an invisible energy field. Reaching for the Grail once more, the Grand Master discovered that it too was shielded within the celestial barrier.

As the final Abraxas knights fell, the few surviving Caedesiates turned toward the altar, amazed by the Madonna's enchanting splendor. Her alien eye blazing an uncanny azure, she gazed at the knights.

Standing before Othamere and Samira, Erodus revealed the resin Madonna statue, raising it in the air.

"Sera'xus, mother of Zoa'ulla, I ask of you to destroy these false Templars, sparing the innocent, and leaving me the book."

Malethius scowled. "How did the sorcerer get the book? You betray me, Brockmere?"

"Fool! I killed Brockmere. It is Erodus you've let into your ranks, and I've come to regain the book."

"I knew something was amiss with you!"

"The lotus fumes have dulled your brain, Malethius. Now you will face Ævänah's wrath."

Running toward Erodus, Malethius raised his sword. Lifting his blade to block, Erodus' weapon met no blow as with a wave of Sera'xus' hand, another protective field surrounded Erodus, Othamere, and Samira. Roaring in anger, the Grand Master's sword once again clashed upon a prismatic wall.

"Heed, followers of the Horned One." Without moving her lips, the Madonna spoke in a musical, multitoned voice that echoed through the chamber, "The Grail you seek to molest contains the immortal blood of my son, Zoa'ulla. Only those with divine grace and pure intention in their hearts may access it. Thou art stained with the blood of the innocent."

"Let's strike a bargain," said Malethius. "We shall slay all those who defy Zoa'ulla in exchange for the Grail."

"Nay. As the bearer of the sacred relic requested, you must die. I call forth the dead within these walls to take you. Knights of Zoa'ulla, awake!"

A loud rumbling emanated as the earth and walls trembled. All looked around in confusion as debris fell from the ceiling. Erodus used his shield to cover Samira from harm while Othamere protected his own head with the book. Large cracks formed along the stone walls in several places. With a loud crash, the solid barriers opened, revealing black holes as crumbling rocks and dust fell to the floor.

From their moldering crypts, six undead knights emerged. They were tall and skeletal with shreds of decayed flesh hanging from their yellowed bones. The cloths of their knightly garments in filthy tatters, the gleam of their once lustrous armor had long since been dulled by rust and ancient blood. Their faces were grinning skulls with orange fire glowing in their eye sockets. From their mouths protruded long fangs. Arms outstretched, they moved toward Malethius and his knights.

"Ready yourselves, men!" shouted the Grand Master.

A weary Caedesiate struck one of the approaching wraiths through the chest with his sword. Penetrating rusty mail, the blade did not deter the assailant. As the man hacked again, the undead knight grabbed him by the throat, lifting him in the air. Tearing off the Caedesiate's gorget, the creature bit down into his exposed neck to feast. The man wailed in agony as gore poured from his jugular. Nearby, unharmed by sword attacks, another cadaverous knight tore open a Caedesiate's rib cage to dine on his innards.

Before the splendor of the blue Madonna, the undead ravaged the helpless knights. Some ran to the barred door before the ghouls seized, dismembered, and ate them. Gore, corpses, and entrails filled the altar chamber.

Erodus watched in amazement from behind the transparent wall, still clutching the amber Madonna statue as Othamere and Samira averted their eyes from the carnage. Despite the efforts of the seasoned warriors, the Caedesiates could do nothing to stop the Knights of Zoa'ulla. Their weapon attacks proved futile against dead flesh and the supernatural strength of the ghoulish knights.

Soon, only Malethius remained standing. He turned once again to the Madonna.

"I beg of you. Spare my life and I will fight for you!"

The Madonna said nothing but grinned as the six vampyric knights approached him at once.

"No! Get back!"

Malethius swung at the wraiths to no effect. Seizing him, two of the creatures forced him against the altar. The struggling Grand Master shrieked as he gazed into their fiery eyes.

Sera'xus once again waved her hand as the slain body of Gromathar twitched. His eyes opened in a blank stare, turning to orange fire as those of the Knights of Zoa'ulla. The Abraxian Grand Master flexed his muscles beneath bronze armor, slowly arising.

Two grisly knights brought forth a long iron stake and handed it to him. Carrying the pike, the reanimated Gromathar approached Malethius. Pinned against the altar by the other undead knights, the Caedesiate writhed as his reanimated foe came near. With supernatural strength, Gromathar lunged the weapon, driving it through groin, torso, and out the screaming mouth of Malethius—impaling him with the skill of an ancient warlord.

Blood gurgled from the Caedesiate Master's mouth. Lifting him on the spike, Gromathar raised the skewered Malethius in the air. He carried him toward one of the recesses in the stone wall from which the undead knights had emerged. The other wraiths followed in single file. The Caedesiate convulsed and moaned upon the stake leaving a trail of blood behind. Entering the crypt beyond the stone wall, Gromathar took the dying Malethius as his prize. The Knights of Zoa'ulla pursued.

As they vanished into the blackness with their captive, the Madonna raised her hand once more. The recesses of crumbled rock sealed, once again becoming solid stone, as the protective field around the humans vanished.

Erodus approached the altar, Sera'xus' azure radiance mixed with the verdant glow of the Grail bathing him as he gazed into her hypnotic eye.

"Thank you for your aid, Queen of Ævänah," he said. "The Caedesiates were a plague to mankind that would've wrought great destruction with the book they coveted."

"The future messiah, Zoa'ulla, will soon arrive from beyond the stars. The wicked amongst mankind will then answer for the violence they have brought upon the earth. Until then, keep the book safe. With the amber encased relic, you may call upon me again when the time arises. Now, I must return to the spectral moon. Farewell."

The figure of Sera'xus vanished, leaving the glowing Grail of Zoa'ulla's blood safe upon the altar, forever guarded by the undead knights within the vaults.

* * *

A carmine sunset burned the skyline, blinding Erodus, Othamere, and Samira as they emerged from the Abraxas temple. Tired and weary, they chose the finest of the Caedesiates' steeds and set the others free. Securing the book and the statue inside his saddlebags, Erodus turned to Othamere.

"There is a small gypsy town two miles north. There you will find an inn where you and Samira can rest before venturing back to your homeland. If you leave now, you will reach it by nightfall."

"Where will you go?" Othamere asked.

"I must return the book to its rightful owner," replied Erodus. "She is the only one I trust with it. Besides, I long for her embrace."

Othamere looked to the leaf-covered ground in disappointment.

"With our Temple razed and our comrades slaughtered, we have nothing to return to."

"Blaze your own path then," said the warrior. "You are the only true Templar I've encountered in these lands. You have a powerful gift, and a lady by your side. That is more than most men."

Othamere looked to Samira who smiled.

Reaching into his saddlebag, Erodus brought forth two skins of wine he found strapped to Malethius' stallion. Tossing one to Othamere, he raised the other.

"I drink to the god in you, my friend. And damn all others!"

He lifted the flagon to his lips and drained it.

Othamere smiled and took a long swig before passing the skin to Samira. They embraced and finished it together, watching Erodus gallop into the horizon, the setting sun gleaming on his ebon mane.

*When not writing tales of savage swords and dark mysticism, **Matthew Knight** can be found wailing away in the bands **Eternal Winter** and **Cauldron Born**. This year's forthcoming **Eternal Winter** release will be an esoteric concept album based on "When the Stars Invert." Knight is the co-author of* Karnov, Phantom-Clad Rider of the Cosmic Ice. *Another of Knight's tales of Karnov appears in the first volume of* Die By the Sword.

The Last Bastion...

by Howie K. Bentley

From the Annals of Thotum-Karr:

Two thousand five-hundred feet up, Castle Valascu sat basking in the rays of the late summer sun. Inside the darkness enveloped us like a pall, save for the Lord Draco Kharn. I looked in on him periodically where he sat upon his jeweled throne bedecked in the Cloak of the Sun and the Moon and the Stars—a map to the Beyond.

Who am I, you might ask. My name is Kyriana. I was taken by slavers led by the scourge of the desert sands, Murka Tarr, in a raid when I was but fourteen winters. My family had been slain, and I was now an orphan. Murka Tarr was a hard man and adhered to the code of the desert marauding Mosuul. Fortunately, that meant I was not to be deflowered until I had been paid for on the slave block in the market square of Tarkambul.

En route to that wicked city, Murka Tarr's caravan crossed paths with Draco Kharn's equestrian order with my lord in the fore. Draco Kharn's Arman Knights were well-practiced in the slaying of desert vermin, and the members of Murka Tarr's band, including himself, were quicky dispatched to the House of Shades by the blades of Draco Kharn and his knights. Having no home, Draco Kharn took me in. I never knew anything but kindness from him, and in time I became his wife.

Now that you know my place in the saga of *The Last Bastion of Draco Kharn,* I will resume my tale of the knight and his deeds of great prowess. Long had been the crusades against the Mosuul for they were desert savages driven mad by the sun, and but a pawn of the Worm from Darkness Eternal. For the servants and satellites of the Great Serpent had made it their practice to pit nations against one another and let their armies destroy each other, furthering the worm's agenda. By his own subterfuge he placed his agents in high positions, and they embedded themselves in the affairs of nations. These were his Nagaina—snake-men. They could easily shift their appearance to go about in the guise of human flesh. As the years went by the Mosuul were brought to heel under a series of successful crusades launched by the Emperor Janos III and the purge of wickedness shifted from the desert vermin to the snake-men. There were assassinations of men in very high places and in their death throes the shift from human to reptilian was shown. For a while there was peace. But after some years went by the Worm from Darkness Eternal raised its head and hissed, and a plague rode the wind. And that plague was the insanity he blew into the minds of the youth of the land. And they went forth and sought the Nagaina and coupled with them. And the seed of the Serpent spread throughout the land. And the Serpent is the Worm that gnaweth at the roots of the tree from which all sprang.

Emboldened were the wicked, and the hideous offspring let their voices be heard even unto the Western lands. The children of man coupled with the Nagaina, and the progeny of that union coupled again with the children of man. They drank the blood of children, and how they tortured them is best unspoken of. They ate of human flesh and rioted and reveled freely in the streets daring anyone to gainsay them. Openly, the signs of the Serpent were everywhere. Rage mounted within the breast of the Emperor Janos, and a new crusade was launched.

Draco Kharn's Arman Knight Order was the battering ram by which Janos would break the Serpent's power. Long was the war waged on the Serpent and the Children of the Serpent, and their children. Draco Kharn's knights were mad with bloodlust as the green ichor pumped by the Nagaina's hearts jetted at the prompting of cold steel. Likewise, the red blood tainted by the snake-men flowed freely from the veins of the children of the unholy union of Nagaina and man. The inhabitants of whole villages were slaughtered, and flames licked the night sky where the temples of ophiolatry smoldered in blazing ruin.

Alas, the cunning of the Worm was great and there stirred within the bosom of the Mosuul again bloodthirst for the Man of the Sun. All of Janos' resources were called upon to quail the Mosuul uprising. The hosts of Emperor Janos clashed with the Mosuul hordes, and the casualties were great for both Mosuul and the Knights of the West. While Janos' armies were diminished his mind began to deteriorate, and more reptilians were seated in places of power. Assassinations of good men took place and more laws upholding wickedness were passed throughout the land. Finally, Janos fell fatally ill, some say by the Serpent's sorcery. There were rumors of grottos sprang up throughout the land where the black arts in obeisance to the Worm were freely practiced without repercussion from local authorities, some of whom openly embraced them.

One by one, judges sworn to the cause of the Worm were placed in high seats of power. First, rumors of war crimes against the Children of the Serpent were sibilantly whispered of. Then the allied hosts of the Mosuul and the snake-men raced forth to break the remaining bands of the Knights of the West and bring those who lived to trial for their crimes against the Serpent's wickedness. Everything became a mockery of all that was good, and just, and right.

Draco Kharn still commanded a small band of Thorkistani knights that swore fealty to the Count. Swordsmen were sent forth on quests to obtain magickal items, for my lord had said, "Armies of men wielding steel are of no use against the cunning of the Worm. The battles must now be fought on other planes." And so, Count Draco Kharn sent forth swordsmen to procure the magickal items he needed to summon the help he needed from realms beyond the ken of man.

A band of snake-men rode forth with one purely vile human, hight Dessa Kroak, he who had a refined taste in the blood of children and a lust for the pleasure he could only find within the coils of the Nagaina. They were on the way to arrest Draco Kharn within the walls of his own castle for my lord's defenses had deteriorated to just a few men and retainers of the castle who had sworn loyalty to Draco Kharn unto the death.

And so sat Draco Kharn bedecked in the Cloak of the Sun and the Moon and the Stars as he had been since the night before. He told me the snake-men would come to arrest him in the guise of men, but they would not take him or any other inhabitant of the castle with them. He said he was drawing on the magic of the Arman that had been the legacy of our ancestors from lands long sunken beneath the ocean. His words were cryptic, but he had said that the fabric of the cloak was spun out by the Nod from the essence of dead gods that the Guardian of the Rune Realm himself had hunted.

Before Draco Kharn sat a large, opened tome upon his stout oaken desk. His mouth moved as his voice, now hoarse from chanting for hours on end, intoned strange rune sounds and bits of song in a language I did not understand. He said the book he read from was *Oag Sloteth Ryge* (translated, *The Slain's Shade Hath Risen*); it was primarily a work containing procedures for Necromancers to talk to dead warriors who had fallen in battle, but with a brief and strange account of thaumaturgical works dealing with long forgotten rune magic comprising the last and incompatible third, or so, of the grimoire.

Draco Kharn had instructed us to hide in the hidden antechambers connecting the series of labyrinthine corridors once the snake-men had been sighted approaching the castle. The snake-men, along with Dessa Kroak, Defiler of Innocence, swaggered into the castle.

Disobeying Draco Kharn's orders, as I was wont to do, I watched from the shadows as they filed into the great hall. Curiosity got the better of me and I could not bring myself to avoid looking in on my lord as they came to take him away. Pacing swiftly down the long corridor I heard their sonorous voices filled with boastful menace when they entered the room, but the noise of the sinister snake-men was cut short.

Quickly, I slipped through the secret door leading into the hallway, directly behind where Draco Kharn had sat reading aloud from the book of magick. But Draco Kharn no longer sat or read, nor could I detect his presence in the room. Instead, I saw a tall figure, much taller than my lord. His head was thrown back wherefrom horns thrust, curving down like a ram's and jutting back up to stab skyward. Long hair the color of blood fell down his back. He wore the Cloak of the Sun and the Moon and the Stars, holding it flung wide open, showing the interior of the cloak. An eerie moaning emanated from the garment and there were bits of horrible song and terrible melodies hummed. I covered my ears and started to scream but refrained as large blocks of air pulsed in the room and pushed forth a force that was like a burst of wind but was not wind. The men all lay dead on the richly woven rugs on the floor of the chamber. In death the glamor showing them as men instead of Nagaina had disappeared. Their dead eyes showed madness, and their stiff forked tongues protruded, frozen in time. Aye, Draco Kharn had warned me not to look upon the scene in the great hall, but I had disobeyed him. Now I know why, for as I turned to go, I caught a fortuitous glance of the inside of his cloak. I can hardly describe what I saw, but I will try. On the inside corner of his cloak I saw a horrible face screaming, one which I fear will drive me to madness to fully recall, and I believe my mind to have skillfully and mercifully blocked out some details of the thing's visage in retrospect. And I presume it was one of many faces of dead gods, for there was a horrible cacophony that filled that room like a symphony of the damned. I saw the horned creature extend its mighty milk-white arm and lay a demoniac clawed hand on the head of Dessa Kroak. As I slipped from the shadows at the back of the great hall, I heard the demon say, "I restore in you just enough sanity to serve me as messenger." Dessa's eyes looked wildly left and right with the demon's hand on his head. The tall figure continued, "Who is your master?"

Dessa Kroak's mouth fell open like a dumbfounded poppet, and then he spake: "Lord Slythar, second only to the Worm..."

The horned giant, whose name is Thorn, tore a battle axe from the wall, and with one mighty stroke followed by another, hacked away two of the snake-men's heads where they lay dead upon the floor. Green ichor dripped from the gored heads as he shoved them into Dessa's arms and said, "Take these to Slythar and tell him the Guardian of the Rune Realms is coming for him, and the worm he grovels before on his belly."

Howie K. Bentley *has been a contributor to the* Swords of Steel *series since its inception. Howie is the author of the sword-and-planet novella,* Under a Dim Blue Sun, *as well as the co-author of* Karnov: Phantom-Clad Rider of the Cosmic Ice. *In addition to these DMR titles, he has tales appearing in the* Die by the Sword *series, volumes one and two. Howie is the founder of the heavy metal bands* ***Cauldron Born*** *and* ***Briton Rites*** *as well as the guitarist and sole songwriter. He has been a full-time guitar instructor since 1989 and is the author of the guitar instructional book,* Heavy Metal Guitar Scales.

The Fall of Karynthos Keep

Written and illustrated by Joe Minichino

Chapter I

The Black Talons Enter Karynthos Keep

The twilight of Nyktis loomed ominously, its bruised sky painted in hues of crimson, gray, and violet. Beneath this eternally shifting dusk, the Black Talons moved as shadows against the barren landscape, their footfalls muffled by dust that seemed to

whisper with every step. The land, riddled with fissures pulsing faintly with arcane energy, seemed alive, shifting subtly beneath their boots, and the air hung heavy with the scent of ozone and something faintly metallic, like old blood. Somewhere in the distance, a Riftspawn howled a monstrous and unnatural cry that sent a ripple of unease through even the most battle-hardened among them.

Cassian Darios led the warband, his gaze fixed on the horizon, and a subtle frown betrayed the unease he fought to conceal. His hand tightened on the hilt of his longsword, the leather creaking softly under his grip. Though the Talons followed him without question, their trust blind and unwavering, Cassian felt the cracks in his own resolve widening with every step toward Karynthos Keep. The visions had begun again—brief, disjointed flashes of places he did not know yet felt he had walked before. Burning cities. Shadowed figures. And the oppressive sense of being watched. He had said nothing of these visions, choosing instead to bear their weight alone. And what perplexed him most is that those images did not feel like visions, they felt like memories.

"Another fissure ahead," Selene Varia called, her voice sharp and clear. She was a lean figure moving effortlessly ahead of the group, her scouting instincts honed to a razor's edge. "Wider than the last. We'll need to find a crossing."

Cassian nodded but didn't answer. His silence, once a mark of measured command, now felt heavy, uncharacteristic. Selene glanced back, her brows knitting briefly before she turned her attention to the terrain. Whatever was eating at him, she trusted he would speak of it when the time came. For now, her focus was survival.

Trailing near the rear, Aelion Nestor clutched a scroll bound with blackened leather, his fingers trembling slightly. The young acolyte of the Ordo Nihilum was a stark contrast to the seasoned warriors around him—nervous, unsure, and radiating the unease of someone carrying secrets too large for his frame. He muttered quietly, fragments of doctrine slipping from his lips like prayers.

"The fractures... demand... sacrifice..." He trailed off, then whispered, as if afraid the very air might hear, "The Maw... widens..."

"Keep moving, Aelion," Selene snapped, her voice cutting through his whispers like a blade. Startled, he obeyed, quickening his pace to match the others.

The Ordo Nihilum had been clear in their request. The Rift Maw beneath Karynthos Keep was an abomination, a festering wound, threatening to tear further and expand. The Talons had been paid handsomely to ensure it was sealed—or destroyed. But Cassian knew better than to trust men who spoke of purity in the same breath as annihilation. The Ordo did not seek to mend; they sought to erase.

That alone made this mission feel like a mistake.

The fissure ahead was as Selene had warned, its edges crumbling into darkness. Energy crackled faintly along its rim, a warning to those foolish enough to stray too close. The group navigated carefully, finding a narrow point to cross. Cassian paused mid-step, his breath catching as another vision struck him—a city, its spires aflame, its streets crawling with figures too distorted to be human. He staggered, catching himself on a jagged rock. Selene turned sharply, concern flickering in her eyes.

"Cassian?"

"I'm fine," he muttered, brushing her off and continuing across the fissure. The weight of the vision lingered, pressing against his thoughts like a vice.

Karynthos Keep rose from the landscape like a gigantic headstone, its towers leaning at precarious angles. The blackened stone bore the marks of siege and sorcery, its walls etched with sigils that appeared to shift continuously. The gates stood ajar, splintered wood hanging limp on rusted hinges. A faint hum radiated from the keep, a vibration that thrummed in the bones of those who stood nearby. The air within the keep smelled of damp stone, dust, and a faint metallic tang.

Selene approached the gates first, her gaze sharp and calculating. "Claw marks," she murmured, running a gloved hand over the gouged wood. "Recent. Riftspawn, most likely."

Cassian joined her, his expression unreadable. "Then we're not the first to pass this way." His voice was steady, but the unease behind it was impossible to miss.

Aelion lingered behind, his eyes fixed on a half-eroded sigil above the gate. The One-Eyed Sword, a sword with an eye depicted where the hilt met the blade, surrounded by a circle with eight uneven rays. These symbolized the chaotic nature of the "fractured universe," the belief that the universe had been split by a cosmic Cataclysm, resulting in multiple realities. The Ordo considered these realities to be a corruption of the original universe energy, Veros, and they fanatically dedicated their existence to the destruction of all manifestations of such parallel worlds. Hence their urgency to seal the Rift Maw. Aelion stared at the mark of the Ordo Nihilum. He clutched his scroll tighter, his muttering growing louder.

"This place… a nexus… convergence…"

"Speak clearly and when you are asked to do so. Or keep quiet!" Cassian snapped, the edge in his voice silencing the acolyte. He stepped through the gates, his sword unsheathed. Selene cast one last glance at the sigil before following.

Inside, the keep was a shadow of its former self. Dust choked the air, settling thick on the shattered remnants of furniture and debris. The walls were lined with mirrors, their surfaces warped and rippling faintly, as though alive. The indistinct whispers that had followed them across the landscape now seemed to emanate from these mirrors, growing louder the deeper they ventured.

"We'll split up," Cassian said, his voice firm despite the unease clawing at his mind. "Selene, take two and scout ahead. Secure the path to the throne room."

Selene nodded, motioning for two Talons to follow her. Cassian lingered in the entry hall, his attention drawn to one of the larger mirrors. Its surface shimmered as he approached, rippling like disturbed water. He hesitated, a cold dread pooling in his stomach.

And then he saw it. A reflection that was not his own.

Kaelion.

The figure in the mirror was him, yet not him. The same worn leather armor covered his torso, but a cruel smirk twisted his lips, and his eyes, the same shade of grey as Cassian's, burned with an unsettling intensity. It moved independently, its gaze locking onto his with a forcefulness that rooted him to the spot. There was no malice in Kaelion's expression, only a calm that bordered on predatory. Cassian felt a shiver run through him, not from fear of Kaelion but from the sickening realization that there was no separation between them. This was not an enemy. This was himself—a fractured piece of his being staring back at him.

"Captain!" Selene's voice cut through the moment, snapping Cassian back to reality. He tore his gaze from the mirror, his breath uneven.

"Throne room is clear. For now."

Cassian forced a nod, shaking off the encounter as he joined the others.

The throne room loomed vast and silent, its high ceilings swallowed by shadow. Banners of Ordo hung torn and tattered, like executed criminals depending from a death tree. It was as if Karynthos Keep had been its own entity that had prevailed over its invader, the Ordo Nihilum, and it now laughed at the futile attempts to tame the ageless fortress.

A massive cracked mirror stretched above the throne, jagged edges refracting the dim twilight into chaotic patterns. The whispers had not faded; if anything, they had grown more distinct, more knowing.

Cassian settled onto a broken stone bench, pressing his fingers to his temples, reviewing and regretting the deal with the Ordo Nihilum. All had seemed clear at the time—seal the Rift Maw, take the gold, move on. But now, standing at the edge of something deeper, something ancient, he wondered if the Talons had just delivered themselves to a force far worse than the Rift itself. And why did he accept? It was a great amount of gold, admittedly, but he was not driven by gold. Something more inexplicable and subconscious had led him to accept the job.

A whisper slithered through the chamber, sneaking through the air like a mocking breath against his ear.

In the fractured mirror above the throne, Kaelion's shadow flickered faintly. Watching. Waiting.

Chapter II

Whispers in the Mirrors

A shiver snaked down Cassian's spine. He could now see his breath misting in the air, a stark contrast to the humid warmth of the corridor they'd just fled. A stillness settled over the Black Talons, thick as the dust hanging in the air. Their lanterns cast flickering light, but the darkness beyond remained unbroken, swallowing the edges of the chamber. Somewhere in the keep, the wind whistled through cracks in the stone, a hollow sound that almost seemed to form words.

Outside, the Riftspawn stirred. Their presence was a weight pressing against the walls, a quiet threat lurking in the deepening twilight. Their claws scraped against the outer gate—slow, deliberate. They were waiting, testing, learning.

Cassian Darios sat apart from the warband, his back pressed against a cold pillar. His sword lay across his knees, but his grip was loose, absent. His mind was elsewhere. The mirror, the reflection…

Kaelion.

The memory of it clung to him, coiling around his thoughts like smoke. His own face, staring back at him—but wrong. Not a mere reflection, but something more. A fracture given form. He recalled meeting an old man once whose mental sanity was so far beyond utter madness nobody took his screams and mutterings seriously, and yet Cassian Darios recalled his nonsense about fractured worlds, mirror twins, alternate versions of the self living in dimensions across a thing he called the "multiverse."

Across the room, Selene Varia worked her whetstone along the edge of her blade. The slow, rhythmic scrape of steel on stone was the only sound in the chamber besides the distant wind. She studied Cassian through the firelight, her expression unreadable.

"You're slipping."

Cassian looked up, his eyes sharp. "Say what you mean."

Selene kept her focus on her weapon. "You saw something in that mirror."

He exhaled slowly, forcing himself to hold her gaze. "It was nothing."

Selene gave a short, humorless laugh. "Liar."

He didn't answer. Instead, he shifted, pushing himself to his feet. "Take two scouts," he said, his voice steady despite the weight pressing on his thoughts. "Secure the keep. Check the eastern halls. Make sure there are no other breaches."

Selene hesitated, then nodded. She motioned for two Talons to follow, disappearing into the darkness beyond the throne room.

Cassian turned to Aelion Nestor, who crouched beside the crumbling mural at the far end of the chamber. Ancient sigils twisted across the stone, their patterns resisting understanding. The young acolyte had laid out his scrolls, his quill moving feverishly across parchment, his lips forming silent words.

Cassian approached. "The inscriptions. What do they say?"

Aelion flinched at the interruption, his hands tightening around the edge of his scroll. His eyes darted toward the mirrors lining the walls, their surfaces rippling faintly, as though reacting to his words.

"This place isn't just a ruin," Aelion murmured. "It's a scar. A scar called Erethys." He hesitated, then gestured toward the sigils. "The Ordo Nihilum tried to close something here. A fracture. But the Rite wasn't completed. Instead of sealing it, they only—" He swallowed. "—wounded it."

Cassian's jaw tightened.

The Ordo had sent the Talons to finish what they could not, to destroy the Erethys Rift Maw before it spread further. But the Ordo Nihilum did not act out of mercy. They saw fractures as an impurity, a corruption of existence itself. Their mission was not to heal—but to erase.

Cassian had known this, even before he struck the deal. He just hadn't thought about what it might cost.

"What happens if we fail?" he asked.

Aelion hesitated. Then, quietly, "The wound tears open. And whatever's on the other side steps through."

* * *

The Talons sat in uneasy silence, barely touching their meals. The fire burned low, its embers pulsing in the dark.

The scratching at the gates grew bolder, interspersed now with guttural, wet sounds. The Riftspawn were growing impatient.

Cassian forced himself to close his eyes. For a moment, his mind settled—

Fire. Screams. A city collapsing under the weight of its own destruction.

He was there, standing in the inferno, his sword slick with the lives he had taken. The dead littered the ground at his feet, but their faces—they kept shifting. His soldiers. His friends. Himself.

And then—Kaelion.

Not a reflection nor an echo in the glass, but a real, whole, smiling figure.

"You look tired," Kaelion said, his voice soft, amused. "Carrying the weight of their trust. Their blind faith. It's exhausting, isn't it?"

Cassian's breath came sharp, unsteady. "You're not real."

Kaelion's laugh was wrong. It was broken. A voice carried across too many fractured realities.

"Aren't I?" Kaelion stepped closer. "Or are you finally realizing what you are?"

Cassian's eyes snapped open.

The throne room was different. It had grown darker, the air heavy, pressing against his chest. He turned, his gaze drawn to the nearest mirror. Its surface rippled like water, and then—a perfectly clear reflection of Kaelion stared back at him. Cassian went still. The reflection frowned.

"You cannot lead them," Kaelion whispered. "You can barely lead yourself."

Cassian's pulse thundered in his ears. His grip tightened on his sword. "Leave me."

Kaelion's smirk deepened. "You can't leave yourself behind."

Then the mirror shattered. A sound split the silence—real this time, then a crash, and a scream. Selene burst into the throne room, blood streaking her face. "Riftspawn," she panted. "They've breached the side passage."

Cassian was already moving. "Hold them off! Protect Aelion!"

They met the Riftspawn in the eastern corridor.

The creatures had changed. No longer just twisted things of flesh and bone, but something else entirely. They blurred at the edges, shifting, warping, as if their forms had not yet decided what they should be. One lunged, and Cassian saw not just claws, but tendrils of shadow extending from its fingertips, dripping with a viscous, otherworldly fluid. Their mouths gaped too wide, their fingers stretched into impossible lengths, like shadows refusing to hold shape.

Cassian cut one down. His blade severed its throat, or what looked to be a throat, but it did not bleed—it collapsed inward, folding into nothing as though it had never been.

Selene's sword flashed, cleaving through another, but it barely staggered before reforming, the wound knitting back together like melting wax.

A Talon cried out as something dragged him into the dark, his body disappearing before he could reach for help, while another screamed as a winged figure merged with him and resulted in a new monstrous creature that shrieked in agony as if existing alone caused it unguessed pain.

"Fall back!" Cassian roared.

The Talons retreated, slamming the doors behind them.

Selene braced the entrance with a shattered beam, her breathing ragged. "We can't keep this up," she growled. "They'll break through eventually."

Cassian turned toward Aelion, who knelt at the base of the sigils, his hands trembling.

"The inscriptions," Cassian demanded. "Tell me the truth."

Aelion's voice was thin, trembling. He clutched his scrolls tighter, his knuckles white. "The mirrors… they don't just reflect. They—" He broke off, then whispered, as if afraid the mirrors themselves might hear, "They draw power from what's broken. From people. From time." He swallowed, his gaze darting nervously towards the shimmering surfaces. "The Rite that was supposed to close them, but… it failed." He hesitated. "It made things worse."

Cassian's stomach twisted. He turned to the largest mirror, the one looming above the throne. To his horror, it was no longer cracked, it was whole, and in its depths Kaelion watched him, pulled him.

The scratching at the doors grew louder.

This day was far from over.

Chapter III

Descent into the Crypts

The air grew heavier as the Black Talons descended into the depths of Karynthos Keep. The spiraling stairwell seemed to stretch endlessly, the stone slick with moisture, the scent of damp earth and something metallic—blood, old and stale—clinging to the damp air. Their boots echoed in the confined space, the sound swallowed too quickly by the pressing dark.

Cassian led the way, his sword drawn. The weight of Kaelion's presence had not left him. Even now, he felt the echoes of that encounter coiling in his mind like a living thing. The mirrors had shown him something real. Not an illusion. Not a simple distortion. A fracture given form.

Selene moved at his side, torch held high, the flickering light casting deep shadows along the stairwell's walls. She hadn't spoken of what she saw in his face before the Riftspawn attack—but she had noticed. Her brow furrowed with concern, but she kept her silence.

Behind them, Aelion clutched his scrolls, his eyes darting nervously to the passage around them. The Ordo Nihilum had hidden something beneath this keep. Something they had deemed too dangerous to leave unchecked, yet not strong enough to destroy.

What had they sealed?

Cassian's grip tightened on his sword. He meant to find out.

The stairwell opened into a narrow corridor, its walls lined with mirrors.

Unlike those above, these were untouched by dust. Their surfaces shimmered faintly, as if disturbed by something unseen. The air smelled wrong here, thick with an acrid tang, like burnt metal and old incense. The scent of rituals long since abandoned.

Selene exhaled slowly. "I hate this place."

Cassian said nothing.

They advanced in silence, the Talons tense, their eyes flicking toward the mirrors. Reflections moved sluggishly, their shapes trailing just behind their real counterparts. The delay was almost imperceptible—but it was there.

Then, a whisper.

Soft. Faint. Not from the mirrors. From the air itself.

Cassian's breath stilled. The whisper was not words, not truly. A presence, brushing against thought like a ghost of something long buried.

Aelion shuddered. He wrung his hands, his eyes wide with apprehension. "The Rite was attempted here," he murmured. "The Ordo Nihilum meant to close the Rift Maw, but… something went wrong. The mirrors should be inert." His voice faltered. "But they are not."

Cassian's eyes flicked toward the largest mirror at the corridor's end.

It stood taller than the rest, its surface smooth and wrongly clear. A reflection should have waited there, but instead—there was nothing. Just empty glass.

"Keep moving," he ordered.

They passed the mirror carefully. Cassian did not look at it directly but out of the corner of his eye, he saw movement. And not his movement or reflection.

The corridor opened into the ritual chamber.

It was vast—too vast for what should have fit beneath the keep.

The architecture was wrong, angles that should not have existed, walls that stretched too high yet seemed close enough to touch.

At the center lay the sigil.

Etched into the blackened stone, it pulsed faintly with a sickly blue light. Veins of Veros energy branched outward from it, their glow uneven, erratic, as though the keep itself was struggling to contain whatever lay beneath.

Cassian took a slow step forward. The sigil had been used—not just once, but many times.

This place had not simply been abandoned. It had been left knowing that something remained.

Selene crouched beside a set of brittle bones near the sigil's edge. She lifted a rusted dagger from the remains, its hilt still stained black. "Someone bled for this."

Aelion had gone still, his face ashen.

Cassian turned. "What is it?"

The young acolyte's face was pale, his breath coming in short gasps. "The Rite was meant to sever the Rift's connection. But instead… it called something through." His voice dropped to a whisper. "The Ordo knew this. They knew and left it buried."

Cassian's blood ran cold. His hands went numb, a chilling premonition settling in his gut.

Of course, the Ordo Nihilum had not destroyed this place. They had chosen to wait.

Wait for what?

The mirrors lining the chamber shuddered.

Then, from the largest, Kaelion stepped forward and the Talons moved instantly, swords drawn and shields raised. Selene positioned herself between Cassian and the thing that had emerged from the glass.

But Kaelion—no, the thing that wore his shape—did not attack, nor acknowledge anyone's existence but Cassian's.

“You came looking for answers,” Kaelion said, his voice smooth, edged with amusement. “And now you’re afraid to hear them.”

Cassian held his ground. “You are not real.”

Kaelion’s smirk deepened. “Still clinging to that? We both know that’s not true.” He gestured to the sigil at their feet. “You came to finish what the Ordo Nihilum started. But tell me, Captain—do you even know what that means?”

Cassian’s grip on his sword tightened.

Kaelion stepped forward, unhurried. “The Rift Maw is a scar on reality. It does not simply consume. It reflects.” He paused. “You have felt it, haven’t you? The pull. The fragments of yourself that do not quite fit. The doubts. The dreams.”

A flash—the city burning. The sword in his hand. The choices that had led him here.

Kaelion’s voice dropped lower. “Tell me, Cassian. Do you really believe you are whole?”

Cassian said nothing.

Kaelion smiled, but there was no mockery in it this time. Only certainty.

“The Ordo did not send you to close the Rift Maw,” he said. “They sent you to test it.” His gaze burned into Cassian’s. “Because you’re already fractured. And they knew you would not be able to resist the pull.”

Aelion inhaled sharply—he had pieced it together at the same moment Cassian had.

The Ordo Nihilum did not just hire a random warband. They had chosen Cassian for a reason. Not because of his skill, and not because of the Black Talons, but because he was already a part of the Rift Maw’s wound.

He had always been a part of it. Maybe he came out of it.

The mirrors began to ripple, the reflections in them shifting, breaking apart. Shapes moved within the glass, countless versions of himself, all wrong in some way. Younger. Older. Scarred in places he was not. Eyes filled with recognition—and hunger.

"All you have to do," Kaelion said, "is step forward."

Cassian's breath came shallow. His sword felt heavy in his grip.

Behind him, Selene was tempted to move closer, but she knew that whatever was happening was beyond her understanding, or simply beyond her.

Cassian knew then—he had no choice. The weight of that knowledge settled in his stomach like a stone. He felt a strange sense of inevitability, as if he had been walking towards this

moment since the day he was born. The moment he had seen Kaelion in the mirror, the moment he had stepped into Karynthos Keep, the path had already been set.

His feet carried him forward. Selene shouted something—a warning, a plea—but the words were lost as Kaelion widened the mirror.

Kaelion reached for him—

And the world collapsed inward.

Chapter IV

The Rite of Ascension

The moment Cassian stepped into the mirror, the world ceased to be what he knew.

A wrenching pull, deep as bone, twisted through his form, dragging him through the glass. The air turned to liquid shadow, thick and suffocating, and his pulse roared in his ears. He was no longer in Karynthos Keep.

He hit the ground hard, but the surface beneath him was not stone. It was smooth—too smooth, like glass stretched thin over an abyss. When he pushed himself up, his own reflection stared back at him from below, shifting, rippling, as if the world itself was breathing. But it was not just his reflection.

Shapes moved beneath the surface, countless versions of himself. Each one subtly different. A younger Cassian, his face unmarked by war. An older one, his body broken by time and failure. A shadowed figure in armor unlike any he had ever worn, eyes hollow and knowing.

And standing at the far edge of this impossible space—Kaelion.

Cassian rose to his feet, his grip tightening on his sword. "Where are we?"

Kaelion stared at Cassian and replied, "Where we are does not matter, but we are going where we are meant to be."

The mirror beneath them shuddered, images bleeding together. The Erethys Rift Maw flared in his mind, the ritual chamber flickering in and out of focus. He saw Selene, blades drawn, fighting against Riftspawn that should not exist. He saw Aelion, hunched over the sigil, trying desperately to understand something that was never meant for him.

And beyond that—something more.

A vision.

A city not of Nyktis. Towers of marble and gold. A world untouched by the fractures, a world whole.

A world he knew.

His world.

Cassian inhaled sharply.

He remembered.

Kaelion watched him carefully, his expression unreadable. "It's coming back, isn't it?"

Cassian's fingers trembled against his sword hilt. He had not always been Cassian.

Before the Cataclysm, before the multiverse shattered, before he was broken into fragments of himself across a thousand reflections—he had been something greater.

Something whole.

"What… were we?" Cassian asked, his voice quiet.

Kaelion took a slow step forward. "The same being. A single existence, before the fractures tore us apart. The Cataclysm splintered reality, and we were divided, scattered like shards of broken glass." He gestured to the countless reflections beneath them. "Every version of us has wandered, searching. But now, we are here." His gaze locked onto Cassian's. "And we are ready."

Cassian exhaled, his mind swimming. "The Ascension Rite."

Kaelion gave a slight nod. "A reunion. The final step."

The weight of it crashed down upon Cassian. The Ordo Nihilum had not sought to destroy the Rift Maw. They had sought to complete this Rite.

And they had chosen him because they knew what he truly was.

He had walked the battlefield of countless worlds. He had always been searching.

And now—he was here. At the threshold of what was lost.

The mirror beneath them cracked.

Outside, the ritual chamber burned.

Selene drove her blade through the throat of a Riftspawn, the creature dissolving into a heap of black ash. The keep was collapsing around them, trembling under the strain of the Rite.

Aelion staggered backward, his breath coming in frantic gasps as he stared at the glowing sigil beneath him. The markings had changed, shifting even as he tried to comprehend them.

"This isn't a sealing ritual," he gasped. His throat was dry, his vision spinning. "It's something else."

Selene turned sharply, her face streaked with blood. "What are you saying?"

Aelion swallowed. "Cassian… he isn't fighting the Rift. He's becoming part of it."

Selene's fingers clenched around the hilt of her blade. She turned to the massive mirror at the far end of the chamber. It had grown dark, its surface rippling with impossible colors, light bending inward.

"Can we stop it?" she demanded.

Aelion hesitated. His lips parted, but he did not know the answer.

Because deep down, something in him suspected that this was always meant to happen. Inside the mirror, the Rite was nearly complete.

The cracks in the glass deepened, running like veins through the fabric of this place.

Kaelion raised his hand. “One final step, Cassian. No more halves. No more fractures. We become whole again.”

Cassian’s heart pounded.

He had spent his life fighting, resisting the pull of something he never understood.

But now—he understood.

This was not a battle to be won.

It was a return.

He closed his eyes.

And he let go.

The glass beneath them shattered.

The reflections surged forward, coiling, merging, pulling, until there was no longer Cassian and Kaelion—only one.

The True Form.

A being of light and shadow, its form shifting and coalescing, hinting at a power that dwarfed even the Rift Maw. It was a being both familiar and utterly alien, a remnant of a time before the world was broken.

The void around them erupted in light.

Outside the mirror, Selene watched in horror as the glass ruptured.

The chamber shook violently, the energy of the Rite collapsing in on itself. The Rift Maw let out a final, keening wail before its form imploded, pulling shards of reality inward.

And at the center of it all—

Cassian was gone.

Selene ran forward, slamming her hands against the shattered remnants of the mirror. Desperately piecing them together as if recomposing the mirror would do something. Nothing. No reflection. No trace.

She turned on Aelion, fury in her eyes. *“What happened?”*

Aelion barely heard her. His gaze was fixed on the sigil, the remnants of the Ordo Nihilum's script burning into his mind. He saw a pattern, a connection he hadn't noticed before. A terrible, impossible idea sparked in his mind, an idea he knew he could not yet share.

Selene grabbed him by the collar. *"Where is he?"*

Aelion took a slow breath.

And for now, he lied.

"I do not know."

The ruins of Karynthos Keep settled into silence, the Rite complete.

Cassian Darios—or whoever he had once been—was gone.

Chapter V

The Rite's Price

The ruins of Karynthos Keep lay still.

The Erethys Rift Maw was gone. The ground where it had festered now bore only a hollow absence, a wound in the world that had finally sealed itself shut. The air still shimmered with the last embers of Veros energy, dissipating into the twilight.

Selene stood in the remnants of the shattered mirror, her chest heaving, her sword still clutched tightly in one bloodied hand. Her gaze burned into the empty space where he had been. It was impossible. Cassian did not fall. He did not die. He had simply—ceased to be.

The Black Talons stood behind her, their expressions wary, exhausted, but no one spoke. They had seen men slain, torn apart, devoured by the Rift Maw—but they had never seen this.

Aelion stood apart, his gaze fixed on the sigil that had completed the Rite. His hands trembled, his mouth dry. He understood more than the others. Not everything. But enough.

Selene turned on him. "What happened?"

Aelion swallowed.

"Where is he?"

Silence.

Selene seized him by the collar, shoving him against the nearest broken pillar. "Talk. Now."

Aelion gasped, struggling against her grip. The force of her anger hit harder than her hands. But the words he needed to say—the ones she wanted—were impossible.

"I…" His throat closed. He could still see the sigils, still feel the echoes of something vast and unspeakable pulling at the edges of his mind.

Selene's grip tightened. "Say it!"

Aelion closed his eyes.

And finally, he spoke.

"He's not dead."

The words hung between them, alien and heavy.

Selene's breath slowed, but her hands did not loosen. "Explain."

Aelion licked his lips, struggling to gather the impossible into words.

"The Ordo Nihilum… they told us the Rift Maw needed to be destroyed. That this place was a scar that had to be sealed." His voice wavered. "That was a lie."

Selene's grip finally released, but her eyes remained locked onto him, burning with something colder than anger.

Aelion pressed on. "This wasn't a battlefield. It was a… a threshold. The mirrors, the sigils, the Rite—it wasn't meant to destroy Cassian." His voice dropped. "It was meant to restore him."

The Talons stirred, exchanging uncertain glances. No one liked the word *restore.*

Selene's expression darkened. "Restore him into what?"

Aelion's breath hitched. "Into what he was before the

Cataclysm."

The silence in the ruined chamber was absolute.

Selene barely whispered. "Before the Cataclysm? What is the Cataclysm?"

Aelion took a breath "Let me explain… the world, this world, Nyktis… it's not the only world. There are many versions of reality… but they were not always there. The Cataclysm created them, it fractured the original energy of the universe, Veros, into splinter worlds. Everything fractured. Even people. Splinters of beings exist across different realities."

Aelion's gaze flickered toward the last remnants of the sigil. "Cassian and Kaelion… they weren't meant to be separate. They were one being. Before the fractures. Before the multiverse shattered. This Rite—it was never about sealing the Rift Maw. It was about reunification."

"So, he is not dead. He is whole again? Where is he now?" Selene interrupted.

He took a slow, unsteady breath. "Yes, Cassian did not die. He Ascended. And when he did… he returned." Aelion's voice was barely above a whisper. "To the world he came from. The Ascension Rite is taught to us in the scriptures, but I always thought it was a legend… we just witnessed it."

The Black Talons had no words, because there was no name for what had happened.

They had fought beside Cassian. Bled with him. Lived under his command. They had never imagined a world where he simply was not. To Selene, Cassian was the closest thing to a father.

Selene stared at the ruins of the shattered mirror. Her fingers curled into fists.

"You're telling me," she said, her voice dangerously low, "that we came here, fought, bled, lost men—and Cassian just… left?"

Aelion hesitated. "If what I know about the Ascension Rite is true, then he has left this world."

Selene snapped.

She moved faster than anyone could react, grabbing Aelion by the throat, slamming him against the stone once more. This time, her blade was at his ribs, just beneath the armor, where it would slide between the bones.

"You knew," she hissed.

Aelion gasped, but he did not beg.

"No, I did not! Not at first!" he choked out. "But I suspected, when the mural showed the Ascension Rite. And even then I could not know who was to… ascend."

Selene's grip tightened—then faltered.

Cassian had always walked toward something none of them could see. A destiny that did not belong to Nyktis.

Aelion's voice was hoarse. "He was never meant to stay here."

Selene staggered back, as if the weight of the truth had struck her physically. The fire in her eyes burned just as hot, but now, it was not anger, it was loss, and she did not know how to fight that.

* * *

That night, as the Talons made camp, Selene found Aelion sitting apart from the others, staring into the dying embers of the fire. She approached, but for a long time, neither spoke. Her fingers curled around the shard of glass she had taken from the ruins—the only thing left of the mirror Cassian had vanished into. Its edges were jagged, its surface fractured, yet within it, something still stirred.

Selene crouched beside Aelion, revealing the glass shard cool in her palm. "How do I bring him back?"

Aelion's shoulders tensed. His eyes flickered to the shard, to whatever movement lurked within it.

Aelion let out a slow, heavy breath. In his fanatical devotion to the Ordo and their cause, he also realized the institution to which he gave his entire life had sacrificed him, maybe even light-heartedly. He was nothing but negligible collateral damage, an acceptable price to pay for the closing of the Rift Maw.

In that moment, he ceased to be Aelion, novice of the Ordo Nihilum, and was simply Aelion, and spoke calmly, but with a new sensation in his heart, something like vengeance.

"He is gone. But… there is someone," he admitted. "A man named Ulpius. A priest, a scholar—he's in… a place, no—" Aelion shook his head. "Not a place. A world. A world called Gaya. One of those worlds of which I spoke today, worlds that are splinters of the original world from which we all come from. I know he is the Nemesis of the Ordo. There."

His voice grew quieter. "He knows more about the fractures than the Ordo Nihilum ever admitted. If there's a way to undo what's been done, he might know it. Or else, he might know a way for you to reach Cassian."

Selene's fingers tightened around the shard.

"Then we go to Gaya," she said.

Aelion's expression flickered with hesitation. He knew the journey to Gaya would be dangerous, perhaps even suicidal. But he also knew that Selene would not be deterred. And a small part of him, a part that had begun to doubt the Ordo Nihilum, wanted to know the truth, no matter the cost. He did not protest.

* * *

Somewhere beyond the fractured worlds, beyond and before the echoes of the Cataclysm, a man took his first breath in a place that had long forgotten him.

The air was crisp, the sky vast, untouched by Rift-light.

He lay on his back, staring upward, the weight of a body both familiar and entirely new settling into him. His hands curled against the earth, feeling its cool, solid reality beneath his fingertips.

Somewhere nearby, a distant horn blew—a low, sonorous call.

At his side, strapped to his belt, lay a short, sturdy blade. A weapon he did not need to see to know.

A gladius.

The scent of war filled his lungs. Not of sorcery, not of Veros.

Of steel, of sweat, and battle.

The voices reached him—speaking a tongue he knew, yet had not heard in an eternity.

He rose, the shape of his form fully real, fully whole. He moved with a fluidity he hadn't possessed in centuries, the echoes of his fractured selves finally coalescing into a single, perfect form. He felt a sense of… rightness, as if he had finally come home. He did not bear the name Cassian Darios, nor Kaelion.

He was who he had been before the Cataclysm, before the fractures, before the worlds tore themselves. And he smiled, with battle joy.

***Joe "Deathmaster" Minichino** is a vocalist/guitarist, and the founder of Italian epic Heavy Metal band **DoomSword**. Born in Lombardy, Italy, he has a life-long passion for medieval history, fantasy and Heavy Metal.*

The Shrine of the Six-eyed Avatar

by Byron A. Roberts

Many were the dire threats faced by the globe-spanning British Empire during the tumultuous closing years of the nineteenth century. The perfidious machinations of covetous foreign states and the dangers posed by insidious insurrections are today well documented by learned scholars, but history does not record the innumerable perils of a far more arcane and otherworldly nature which beleaguered Queen Victoria's expansive realm. Ancient and malefic forces stirred unceasingly during the era known as the Pax Britannica, as the iniquitous acolytes of malign demigods plotted tirelessly to resurrect and enthrone their chthonic overlords once more. And yet, there were certain intrepid agents within the vast and labyrinthine imperial bureaucracy tasked with the investigation and eradication of such eldritch menaces. The mandate of these valiant men and women took them far and wide across the Empire's myriad frontiers…

Northern Egypt: 1894

Chapter I

Steel in the Shadows

The strident clangour of clashing steel shattered the silence of the benighted desert as Attalus Grimwood parried a furious blow from his shadow-clad assailant. The Englishman's sword glittered in the cold light of the gibbous moon, forcing his foe's curved blade down in a grinding and pitiless test of martial might. A scant second later, both combatants leaped lithely free of the deadlock to resume their desperate duel. The cloaked man dropped suddenly to a crouch and his notched sword swept forth in a vicious arc which Grimwood deftly knocked aside, instantly following the parry with a lightning riposte. The blow snaked above the night-swathed figure's guard like a rivulet of quicksilver and the Englishman's keen blade promptly opened a gaping furrow in his adversary's pallid throat. A viscid gout of oddly-hued blood bubbled from the lips of the vanquished blackguard and he crumpled silently to the sand, dark freshets surging forth from his riven neck.

With the speed of a ravening wolf, Grimwood spun, his imbrued sword poised. Twelve feet away, he witnessed his sole traveling companion, a white-robed Egyptian he knew only as Hisham, engaged with a second darksome foeman, their blades flickering in the lunar refulgence. The Moslem desperately countered a frenzied torrent of sword-strokes, his ornate scimitar agleam, rutilant sparks blossoming from the cold discourse of steel. Ultimately, the Egyptian's superior swordcraft prevailed and the aphotic figure's raiment and flesh were slashed by a velocious lateral strike. Abruptly, the cowled warrior's knees buckled, his cloven abdomen yawning wide and disgorging its viscera to the dusty ground.

"Well fought, old man," growled the Englishman as he crouched to examine the twitching remains of his own fallen adversary. The ethereal moonlight seemed to imbue the grisly corpse with an even more unnervingly malefic aspect as Grimwood cast his scrutinous gaze upon it. The dead man was swathed in a voluminous black robe not unlike muslin in its texture, while a tattered cowl adorned his depilated head. The flesh of his cadaverous face was ashen-pale and adorned with strange sigils, evidently the result of some manner of ritual scarification. Thin, bloodless lips revealed yellowed teeth filed down to wicked points and the corpse's glazed eyes were dun-white and disquietingly devoid of pupils and irises.

Gathering up his foe's sword, Grimwood studied the archaic weapon intently, paying close attention to its peculiar blade and the coarse snakeskin which bound its hilt. The sword was not unlike an ancient khopesh in its aspect, having the appearance of an artefact recently excavated from some hoary, long-forgotten tomb.

With a scowl, the Englishman cast down the implement and proceeded to clean his own sword with the cadaver's ragged vestments, noting with a morbid fascination that the noisome blood appeared to possess a decidedly inhuman, vaguely greenish hue. Then, he rose to his full imposing height, his scarred face a graven mask of consternation. Attalus Grimwood was hard-muscled, with prodigious breadth of shoulder, his alabaster flesh long since bronzed by the interminably harsh sun of the Empire's far-flung southern climes. The man's steel-spring thews bore a skein of old battle-scars and a handful of long-faded tattoos. His ash-blond hair was close-cropped and a flaxen beard adorned his chiselled, granitic jaw.

Grimwood was clad in a frayed shirt of white linen, trousers of blackened canvas and a pair of calf-length buffalo-hide boots begrimed with the incessant dust of the arid desert. His corded neck was encircled by a silvern chain from which hung an array of protective talismans representing various faiths and esoteric traditions. A broad cartridge-bandolier and a leather satchel crossed his barrel-chest, while at his hip was holstered a Webley Mk. I service revolver with textured walnut grips. Secured to Grimwood's bronze-buckled belt was a black scabbard boasting a steel locket and chape, into which the Englishman presently rammed home his yard of whetted steel. That brass-hilted backsword was some thirty-five inches in length and sported a fullered blade, an ornate bronze pommel and a ribbed grip bound with shagreen and copper wire. The fearsome weapon's robust guard and ricasso were bedizened with an array of acid-etched devices and ciphers, and it had served him unfailingly since his acquisition of it some five years ago.

At length, Grimwood fixed Hisham with his cold, blue eyes. "These devils are passing strange. What do you make of them?"

The Egyptian shook his head grimly, his breathing laboured, his ivory-hilted scimitar still clutched tightly in his calloused hand. The man's gaunt face was weathered and rugose, and he sported a pointed black beard which was heavily flecked with grey. He was clad in an ankle-length robe of white cotton and a headdress secured with a black cord of braided goatskin. A narrow belt at the man's waist sported a sheathed *jambiya* dagger and a purloined Enfield Mk. II revolver. His dark eyes narrowing, Hisham regarded his befouled blade, a grimace of disdain creasing his swarthy countenance. "They are vile, inhuman things," he spat in heavily-accented English, kicking contemptuously at the disembowelled body before him with the toe of his camel-skin boot. "The spawn of Iblis! May their unclean carcasses glut the jackals!"

Grimwood's reply abruptly died on his lips as a faint whisper of sound abraded his already tautened nerves; the soft scuff of lightly-shod feet upon shifting, bone-dry sand. Simultaneously, a shadow suddenly loomed from the deeper darkness behind Hisham, its tenebrous contours akin to a man, the pale moonlight striking glints from the steel in its veiled hand. In the span of a single heartbeat, Grimwood's revolver had cleared its holster and roared like a baneful thunderclap in the semi-darkness. The figure at Hisham's back reeled violently, a black crater manifesting between its nacreous eyes. Silently, the wraith-like assailant fell dead to the sand and the Englishman holstered his smoking pistol, the sound of the single shot still echoing throughout the desert. Hisham spun to regard the fallen attacker, then turned warily to Grimwood and nodded his wordless thanks before moving to recover a hefty burlap sack of sundry supplies which he had dropped at the commencement of their skirmish.

"Regrettably, our attempts at stealth seem to have come to naught," muttered the Englishman. "Be wary."

His brow furrowing, Grimwood proceeded to reflect on the events which had led him to his present locus. He had rendezvoused with the man Hisham at the settlement of Kasr-el-Heyet a day ago, the seasoned albeit somewhat truculent guide having been appointed to him by the mysterious patrons of his current expedition. Their journey into the desert frontier had been largely uneventful, marked by scant little conversation, and at length they had drawn near to their remote destination. The party's mounts had been left half a mile to the north, picketed by a jagged outcropping of rock while the men advanced on foot, cautiously scouting the barren expanse with as much furtiveness as they could muster. Their hardy, heavily laden steeds were bred from Arabian stock and carried a variety of supplies and accoutrements in and amongst their saddlebags, including the Englishman's own desert robes and the large leathern holster which housed his Martini-Henry Mk. II rifle and its twenty-two-inch sword-bayonet. The trusty old breech-loader had seen many years of service, but it was still deadly accurate; an assertion lent cold credence by the myriad of fallen foes which sprawled in the Englishman's far-reaching wake, from the mountainous Khyber Pass to the sun-seared veldt of southern Africa and beyond. Twenty minutes into their trek, as the moon had glowered ever brighter in the ebon vault, the disparate duo had been waylaid, their assailants leaping from the gloom like baleful phantasms.

Grimwood promptly emerged from his dour reverie and uncorked the iron canteen which he carried slung across his shoulder. After swallowing a draught of tepid water, he tersely addressed the Egyptian. "How much farther?"

"The ruined temple which you seek lies yonder," Hisham responded, pointing to the southwest. "Beyond those dunes."

"Then let's not tarry," said Grimwood, his mien one of steadfast resolve. He reached into his shirt pocket and produced a small, engraved case fashioned of sterling silver containing a number of phosphorous matches, which he tossed to the Egyptian. "Light one of those torches in your gunny sack, will you?"

Some minutes later, the two men briskly ascended a sabulous rise and upon attaining its summit, gazed out upon the benighted vista before them. The desert stretched for miles in every direction, the moonlight lending the expansive sea of sand an oddly ethereal quality. Far to the south, barely visible in the distance, a line of low, asperous hills brooded at the darkling horizon. But the focus of the duo's unalloyed attention was the object which squatted forebodingly upon the sand some twelve yards ahead.

The crumbling stone shrine was roughly twenty feet in height and possessed a disquietingly incongruous aspect, its fissured exterior entwined by skeins of undulating shadow. Its sand-wreathed base was not entirely unlike that of a ziggurat, but its upper reaches displayed outlandish architectural features the likes of which Grimwood had hitherto not witnessed during his extensive travels across the globe. An array of slender, cracked columns girt the outer surface of the fane, carved in such a fashion that they resembled nothing less than the chitinous, multi-jointed legs of a monolithic crustacean clutching the cyclopean structure in a vice-like grip. Strange carvings encircled the cleft capstone of the temple; hewn creatures of a strangely batrachian nature, some of which sported the remnants of fractured, vaguely chiropteran wings. The Englishman could scarcely guess what hoary hands had fashioned those shuddersome effigies, or what fell beasts they were intended to represent.

The two men exchanged uneasy glances before warily approaching the ruin, the flickering light of Hisham's burning brand casting a rutilant aura about them. As he drew nearer, Grimwood descried an arched cavity in the sanctum's east-facing wall. The doorway's perimeter was flanked by an array of engraved hieroglyphs which the men could neither identify nor comprehend. A riven slab of sandstone partially obscured the black threshold, its upper section bearing a small, heptangular aperture somewhat reminiscent of a keyhole. The lithic barrier had evidently been partially wrenched aside at some point in the past, creating a narrow entranceway which led to the shrine's stygian inner reaches. Grimwood peered guardedly into that atramentous abyss, the hairs on the nape of his neck bristling as he suddenly discerned a faint, chilling sound emanating from the depths. The rhythmic chanting was guttural and sonorous, uttered in a tongue both indecipherable and vaguely unsettling. He turned grimly to Hisham. "Tell me what you know of this monument."

The Egyptian's voice was scarcely more than a whisper, his expression pensive. "A month ago, this profane temple was revealed by a great sandstorm which raged for many days. The folk of the settlements to the east are superstitious by nature and have shunned the site, believing it to be accursed. The local elders claim that this ruin is extraordinarily ancient, older even than the heathen religion of the ancestors and the pyramids of their long-dead Pharaohs. Of late, there have been whispers of the peasantry disappearing from the villages nearby. I believe those devils we encountered are responsible, and I believe they emerged from this unholy place. So, kaffir. The British wrested control of this land from the Ottomans, and as such are now responsible for the safety of its people. Will you summon your army and fulfil this mandate?"

Grimwood's craggy brow arched. "I'm here to assess the situation, and take whatever action I deem necessary. But rest assured, if I find something beyond my capacity to deal with alone, the Consul-General of Egypt has authorized me to request assistance from the Major-General at Cairo. Now, shall we proceed?"

"I am not going in there with you, Englishman," rasped Hisham, his fervid eyes reflecting the light of his brand. "I was paid to guide you to this temple, not to delve into its foul depths. I have had more than I bargained for on this journey already."

"Come on, old horse," said Grimwood with a wry smile. "We've both got places we'd rather be. I'd love to be languishing back in

Shanghai, chasing the dragon in Madam Lai's opium den, but we play the hands we're dealt in this bloody game. Aren't you curious as to what might lie within?"

Hisham set his jaw defiantly. "Mark me, I am no stranger to the denizens of the dark realms. In my time, I have encountered the djinn and the ifrit, but I do not seek conflict with their diabolical ilk. You are brave, but foolhardy. I wish you good fortune, but you are on your own henceforth. Farewell." Without another word, he handed the torch brusquely to the Englishman, spun on his heel and strode swiftly off towards the north.

Grimwood sighed wearily as he watched the Egyptian disappear into the darkness. After several ruminative moments, he reached into his shirt and brought forth two pieces of folded paper. One of the heavily-creased documents was a sun-bleached map of Egypt which he promptly returned to his pocket, while the other was a letter written on grandly embossed paper, which he carefully unfolded and commenced to peruse by the undulating torchlight. He had read the correspondence twice since receiving it, but now felt compelled to once again study the spidery, hand-written script which bedizened the paper's surface…

From the office of Ms. Elspeth Hargrove (Department of Preternatural Affairs, Aldwych, London.)

Greetings and salutations, Sergeant Grimwood,

I pray that Major-General Forestier-Walker's couriers will facilitate your timely receipt of this hastily scrawled missive before you depart Cairo for Kasr-el-Heyet. The head of our clandestine cabal, the inscrutable and taciturn Scotsman we know as Lord Knightbourne, has recently apprised me of the circumstances surrounding your somewhat peculiar covenant with the Department of Preternatural Affairs and the nature of the mission with which you have been entrusted.

Firstly, allow me to say that your encounter with the acolytes of iniquity deep in the heart of the Raj sounds positively abhorrent. The resurgent Cult of Kali, of which you so memorably fell afoul, remains a dire threat, and their vile mind-altering magicks will be countered accordingly. I'm told that it was only the timely intercession of Lord Knightbourne himself which spared you the fusillade or the gallows. While I fully appreciate that you were all but conscripted at gunpoint to join the Department, I nevertheless remain confident that your unique experiences undoubtedly qualify you to spearhead the somewhat unorthodox investigations which we undertake. For my part, I was inducted due to my extensive knowledge of what may be termed the arcane arts. In common parlance, I am a witch, and my coven has been working ceaselessly to safeguard the realm from mystical threats for some years now, as the danger posed by malign sortilege and diabolism simply cannot be overstated. My tenure has afforded me the opportunity to add to my growing collection of sorcerous tomes and grimoires, if nothing else! Forgive the brevity of this introduction, for time is short and I must proceed to the matter at hand.

Allow me now to enlighten you as to what has transpired here since your last correspondence with our illustrious benefactor. As soon as our Sect of Scryers sensed the emergence of the temple which is your avowed destination, as well as the surge of dark sigaldry which surrounded it, I was tasked with learning more of the site's origin and the danger which it potentially embodies. By uncanny happenstance, both the seasoned Egyptologist Sir Flinders Petrie and the noted occultist Samuel Liddell Mathers grudgingly recommended to Lord Knightbourne that I seek the counsel of the mercurial and somewhat nefarious Doctor Ignatius Stone, a specialist in the more esoteric and cabalistic aspects of archaeological research. Therefore, at his behest, I promptly paid a visit to the ominous Grimm's Hold Sanitarium, where the ill-starred Doctor Stone has been ensconced since his return from the ruins of the ancient Sumerian city of Ur two years ago. I shudder to think what malefic, primal horrors assailed that erudite man so pitilessly within those benighted catacombs, but they were evidently dire enough to abrade his sanity to the very abyssal precipice of madness.

At any rate, I was informed that Stone's earlier and more covert expedition to the hoary tombs at Karnak had apparently uncovered extensive cryptic lore and occult artefacts suggesting the existence of advanced antediluvian civilizations and sinistrous avatars far older than even the vaunted monuments at Luxor; shunned and long-forgotten chthonian pantheons and their votaries which evidently have a direct bearing on our current quandary. Thankfully, my visit coincided with one of the good Doctor's increasingly rare periods of lucidity, and although the institution's decidedly odious director Gustav Hildebrandt was initially quite reluctant to grant me access to his patient, Stone was nevertheless able to impart to me a great deal of knowledge concerning those malign cults and their likely connection to the site which you currently seek.

Incidentally, he also bade me avail myself of the expertise of his scholarly colleague Professor Caleb Blackthorne III, an indubitably eccentric prehistorian and anthropologist possessed of an unassuageable preoccupation with the occult. In truth, I had heard much of Blackthorne's roguish exploits through my elusive contacts within the Hermetic Order of the Golden Dawn, specifically his belief that he is a direct descendant of an Elizabethan privateer who once communed with the famed astrologer Doctor John Dee and sailed the tempestuous seas in the service of the realm, his Letters of Marque authorizing him to hunt down and eradicate threats both natural and supernatural. And yet, I fear it was my sad duty to inform Doctor Stone that Professor Blackthorne had mysteriously disappeared only a year ago during an expedition to the forsaken Andean city of Tiahuanaco in Peru. All contact with his meagre albeit well-provisioned coterie was abruptly lost, and regrettably, a rescue party has yet to be dispatched to investigate. The Doctor took the news rather badly and promptly lapsed into a state of agitated delirium, and I was duly compelled to leave the poor gentleman to his fraught ravings, cursing the cruel nature of his insidious malady. But I digress.

Know that I gleaned enough information to arrive at a disturbing conclusion regarding the deathless sect which once venerated the desert shrine. According to Doctor Stone, this particular cult worshipped an obscure and repugnant chthonic deity, believing that their oblations, if performed before an exceedingly rare stellar conjunction, would facilitate the dark god's awakening and enable it to rise from its earthly tomb, the exact location of which remains unknown. Sergeant, I am quite convinced that the primeval edifice recently disgorged by the sands represents a credible threat to the security of the Empire. Consequently, I implore you to exercise the utmost caution when investigating the site, and to take no unwarranted risks in the execution of your duty. Finally, I am formally obliged to ask that you burn this letter once you have read it. I wish you a safe return from the veiled protectorate and remain your stalwart friend and confidant,

Elspeth Hargrove
Vigilantia Contra Malum!

Grimwood passed the letter over the torch-flame, watching sombrely as the paper blackened and burned, swiftly becoming nothing but embers and ash to be carried away by the gentle desert breeze. The enigmatic Ms. Hargrove intrigued him, and he found himself hoping that he would be afforded the opportunity of meeting the loquacious sorceress at some point in the future. At length, the Englishman cast a grim glance skyward, descrying the coruscant stars which glittered like diamonds in a vast, vespertine tapestry. Then, he strode resolutely across the fane's breached threshold and into the foreboding darkness beyond.

Chapter II

Carnage in the Depths

Warily, Grimwood traversed a caliginous passageway, descending a rough-hewn set of stone steps, his burning brand keeping the oppressive shadows at bay. Ever deeper he delved, slowly becoming aware of a shift in temperature; his environs growing markedly colder with each guarded footfall. The discordant chanting grew inexorably louder, the minacious words still beyond his ken, the sepulchral tones reverberating throughout the tunnel. Long moments passed and the passageway gradually widened, the writhing darkness beyond his brand's aura beginning to yield grudgingly to another, unknown source of light some yards ahead.

Presently, Grimwood discerned a cloying, sickly-sweet odour wafting from the depths, vaguely akin to the pungent scent of exotic incense; and yet something else lurked behind that redolence, a mephitic stench not unlike death and decay. He slowed his pace, his senses honed by trepidation. A heartbeat later, he beheld an array of burning torches secured to the furrowed stone walls by iron sconces, the brands evidently having been recently placed. The light became so refulgent that he stowed his own guttering torch in a vacant bracket before pressing on, his thews tensed for danger.

A shadow loomed abruptly before him and Grimwood instantly halted his advance. Twelve feet ahead, another of the black-garbed figures stood, his back to the Englishman, apparently unaware of his presence. The man seemed to be in some sort of trance, his body swaying rhythmically to the cantillation which emanated from the deeps. Deciding against employing his Webley in the interests of stealth, Grimwood slowly began to his free his sword from its scabbard. As the blade all but silently cleared the locket, the robed acolyte spun, a sibilant snarl on his scarred lips, his khopesh glinting in his grasp. Instinctively, Grimwood lunged forward and thrust his sword brutally into his foe's midriff. The blade clove the body like a silvern prow rending a bitumen sea and the man's lungs expelled an effusion of foetid air, his weapon falling from his nerveless fingers. For several gravid moments, the pair stood frozen in that grisly tableau, the Englishman's sword protruding a full twelve inches from the figure's back, its steel glistening with viridian ichor. Then, Grimwood wrenched the blade free and let the corpse crumple to the stone, whereupon it convulsed for several seconds before becoming still. Uttering a whispered oath, he stepped over the quiescent form and continued his journey undaunted.

Finally, he reached the passageway's terminus. Before him loomed a large subterrane, ostensibly a naturally formed cavern, its entrance screened by a range of jagged stalagmites which jutted from the rocky floor like blackened, broken teeth. Grimwood swiftly concealed himself behind the petrous palisade, his eyes widening as he peered at the cave beyond. The shrine's inner sanctum was roughly circular, its walls adorned by an array of carvings and bas-reliefs depicting a plethora of horrific, squamous creatures spawned of madness and nightmare; aberrant, scaly entities sporting tentacles, talons and veinous wings, gaping jaws studded with hooked fangs and rows of tiny concentric teeth, their amorphous heads crowned with crests and great membranous fins.

Abruptly, Grimwood's breathing quickened, a cold sweat beading upon his brow. Before his mind's eye there suddenly flashed unbidden an array of shadowy images; nebulous apparitions exhumed from the vaults of memory, akin to the half-remembered hallucinations born of a fever-dream. For a harrowing moment, the Englishman was once more trapped within the sweltering, labyrinthine jungle of India, facing the blood-ravening cult of a malefic goddess, his mind addled by envenomed draughts, opiate vapours and baleful magicks. Before his fraught gaze there blazed a pair of amber eyes sporting the narrow, elliptical pupils of a serpent, and those loathsome ophidian orbs burned with an ancient malice.

With a supreme effort of will, Grimwood dispelled the insidious vestiges of his delirium, banishing the eidolons back to that shadowed corner of his mind where he kept them shackled. His knuckles whitening about the hilt of his sword, the Englishman briskly recovered his wits, his respiration and heartbeat slowing. A moment later, with renewed fortitude, he once more surveyed the eldritch chamber. Huge stalactites jutted forth from the cavern's ceiling, casting unnerving shadows which did nothing to dispel the feeling that the entire hollow was nothing less than the toothsome maw of some colossal, ophidian beast. The cracked and mosaicked floor of the grotto bore a mass of scrawled occult pictograms, the significance of which Grimwood could not fathom.

The sanctum was illumined by a huge, green jewel embedded in the eastern wall, its crystalline heart emanating a steady viridescent glow. Surrounding the lustrous gem was a skein of slender veins composed of an otherworldly, bioluminescent mineral, the sprawling pattern imbuing the rockface with the aspect of a huge, lucent spider's web. Directly beneath the crystal were arrayed ten sarcophagi of graven granite, their embossed lids askew.

Six figures stood in the chamber, all of them garbed identically to the fiends which the Englishman had previously encountered. Five of the acolytes were the source of the canorous chanting, their guttural voices booming throughout the cavern. The sixth individual stood apart from his brethren, his arms outstretched, a carcanet of bones about his sinewy neck. In his left hand he grasped a gnarled staff engraved with vaguely cuneiform symbols, while in his right was clutched a huge, curved sword. The weapon was somewhat akin to the khopesh blades wielded by the other cultists, save for the dark shards of crystal which encrusted its denticulate edge. The man's face was partially hidden by a crude mask of blackened reptile-skin and he was hunched before what appeared to be a low altar hewn from obsidian, its scored surface heavily stained with unnameable ichors.

Several corpses lay strewn upon and around the ensanguined altar-stone, their emaciated remains having the appearance of empty husks, as if the bodies had somehow been drained of their very life-essence itself. The Englishman guessed that these were the abducted villagers of which Hisham had spoken, and he found himself wracked by a bitter pang of regret that he had not arrived in time to spare them such a gruesome fate. The sight was undeniably disquieting, but it was the abhorrent statue which squatted upon a glyph-etched dais behind the altar which finally sent an icy chill coursing down Grimwood's spine.

The effigy was nearly eight feet tall and hewn from glistening, pitch-black stone. Its oddly-jointed limbs were ridged and scaled, its body clad in a chitinous exoskeleton studded with a myriad serried spikes. Hooked talons, seemingly fashioned of jade, tipped its slender fingers, and its vaguely squamate head was crowned by a ring of serrated horns. Six jewels, evidently emeralds, were set within the creature's carven face in an apparent approximation of eyes, and the golem's distended jaw was bristling with a plethora of crooked, crystalline teeth. Gazing at the effigy, Grimwood found himself musing uneasily as to what primal, chthonic deity it was intended to represent, then he swiftly banished the thought lest he find a sudden, unfortuitous answer. Finally, the Englishman descried an ebony plinth to the left of the statue upon which rested a large grimoire bound in something which resembled scabrous leather, its cover adorned by embossed sigils, the precise nature of which he could not discern from his current vantage point. As he watched, the chief cultist gestured with his staff and the chanting abruptly ceased. The robed figure then proceeded to speak in the same guttural tongue as his disciples, the tone and cadence of the oration suggesting that it was most probably some manner of ireful invocation.

"Aia, Zul'tekh! Z'xulth kura zaktara! Zagha-ratu! Zagha-goru! Xi-kura namta! Xi-kura kanda! Malku niru, zagthoth q'raa! Kantaru'nazathoth! Xiku kanzu zia rak'ta! Xiku kanzu kiu raamu! Ki'garutha! Ki'makanda! Z'xulth na diha! Z'xulth na kura! Kazuraa-tana-kilkara! Ku'ragon! Aia, Zul'tekh!"

Grimwood's mind raced as the incantation reached its frenzied crescendo. He had been tasked with investigating the shrine and evaluating the threat which it posed. Based on what he had witnessed thus far, he was compelled to agree with Ms. Hargrove's deductions. Clearly, this was some manner of invidious cult devoted to that six-eyed abomination, and as such it embodied a danger to the people of the protectorate and the greater empire. Setting his jaw, the Englishman duly reached his decision. The investigation was over. To hell with reconnoitering the temple and reporting his findings; instead, he would eradicate the threat himself, here and now, with hot lead and cold steel. Drawing his revolver and hefting his sword, Grimwood strode boldly forth into the wan light of the chamber.

"Heed me, you black-hearted devils!" thundered the Englishman. "Throw down your weapons and I'll afford you the mercy of ending this swiftly!"

The assembled cultists spun towards him, brandishing their curved blades. The figure before the altar began bellowing furiously in his unfathomable tongue, yellow sputum flying from his lips. Suddenly, the green jewel embedded in the wall flared momentarily brighter, its luminous heart aflame with an eldritch radiance. Grimwood squinted against the harsh glare, and astonishingly, when the light dimmed once more, he found that he could comprehend the glottal language of the chief acolyte.

"Infidel!" the man barked in vexation. "You dare defile the sanctity of this sacred place? You profane the temple of our glorious god with your presence! You will pay dearly for disrupting this rite of adulation! Your life is forfeit!"

Grimwood smiled mirthlessly. "That's not quite how this is going to play out, I fear."

Cruel laughter welled in the acolyte's throat. "Fool! Soon, the true gods will rule once again; the exalted divinities who were already ancient when the primitive peoples of this land still worshipped Horus and Ra! Praise the dark ones who waged war with the accursed servitors of the light! Praise the denizens of the primordial night!"

The Englishman edged silently closer to the altar, his blade glimmering in the viridescence.

"Hearken, interloper," grated the masked man, hefting his staff. "The malefic gods of the Z'xulth slumbered serenely throughout the ages, dreaming their deathless dreams of vengeance as their vigilant disciples beheld the rise of the accursed monotheistic faiths which now hold sway. But the time of awakening is at hand, when the stars shall at last align, heralding the resurrection of the true overlords of this azure sphere! When the sun burns black, these new faiths shall be swept aside and mankind shall bow once more in obeisance to the inviolable monarchs of the outer darkness!"

Grimwood's eyes narrowed and he levelled the barrel of his Webley at the ranting figure. "A fanciful tale indeed," he muttered mordantly.

Unheeding, the diabolist continued his declamation. "Hail the infernal king of the benighted abyss, scourge of the empyrean, father of demons and lord of the chaosphere! Hail the squamous and fecund sea-mother who birthed the progenitors of Man, exulting as her amorphous children slithered forth from her briny womb! Hail the ravening scion, devourer of suns, he who scarred the very face of the void with his searing sword of retribution! Hail they who lurk and breed in limbo, hail they who watch and wait at the threshold, hail the Z'xulth!"

Instantly, the five cultists surged forth, their black cloaks billowing. Five times did Grimwood's revolver buck in his grasp, and five ear-splitting shots reverberated throughout the shrine. The attackers were cut down like wheat before the scythe, bullet-holes gaping in each of their ashen foreheads, their quiescent forms littering the tesserae tiles like peccant detritus. The fane was filled with the acrid stench of gunpowder, its odour temporarily supplanting the mephitic miasma of the depths. Wordlessly, Grimwood holstered the still smoking Webley. With the five blackguards dispatched, along with the one he had gunned down outside the temple, the revolver's six shots had been spent and he had no time to reload. The remaining acolyte abruptly threw down his staff and leaped forth like an esurient panther, his notched blade awhirl. Grimwood parried a flurry of wild blows, one of the strikes breaching his guard to open a red furrow in the hirsute flesh of his chest. Cursing, the Englishman counterattacked, his sword flashing like a storm of silvern steel. The cultist was hard-pressed to defend against the torrent of mighty sword-strokes and was forced steadily backwards, eventually stumbling on a loose fragment of broken rock. Seizing the opportunity, Grimwood unleashed a savage left hook, his iron fist hammering against the man's jaw with a sickening crack. The acolyte fell as if smitten by a thunderbolt, his serrated blade clattering to the stone.

"Where are your vile gods now, miscreant?" rumbled the Englishman, looming over the prone body.

"Still the stark truth eludes you!" the disciple hissed through his broken teeth, struggling dazedly to his knees. "The rite is complete. You shall perish here. That which is fashioned in the semblance of our exalted god shall now stir and wreak glorious havoc! The first of many such avatars! They will be the heralds of the purifying storm to come!"

Grimwood scowled. "Dispense with the riddles. What do you mean?"

The man spat a gout of glaucous blood from his lips. "There are shrines such as this concealed throughout the world! We are the harbingers of the final days! Since before the oceans rose to devour ancient Atlantis, we have waited! When the spheres spin at last in trine, heralding the great cataclysm, more undying sentinels shall rise from their slumber as I did to summon the deities of the elder dark!"

"And they too shall be exterminated like the vermin they are," growled the Englishman, the point of his sword pressing into the kneeling man's sallow throat.

"Wretched heretic!" rasped the acolyte vehemently, doffing his cowl and tearing free his mask to reveal his scarred and malformed skull. "The forces you aspire to stand against are eternal! Abandon your delusion! Forsake your vain hope! Your kingdoms and empires are doomed! The aegis of the light is sundered! Ours is the power of the darkest reaches of the cosmos, ineffable and sublime! Not all your false gods, damnable spells and accursed weapons can save your pitiful souls!"

"Is that so, sirrah?" hissed Grimwood, hefting his trenchant blade exultantly. "Well, this is English steel, and it will be more than enough to put an end to you." And with a single stroke, he swept the cultist's head from his shoulders amidst a welter of viscid green grume. The nodulous skull rolled away into the shadows as the body slumped heavily to the begrimed, tesselate floor.

Grimwood afforded himself a moment to reflect on the fanatic's febrile tirade, but that respite was fleeting. The grinding scrape of stone against stone suddenly drew his attention and he spun to regard the dais upon which squatted the darksome, chitinous statue. To his astonishment, the effigy's head was turning languorously to fix him with its sixfold, crystalline gaze. As he watched aghast, the carven devil then rose to its full height and stepped ponderously down from its pedestal, its jade talons gleaming.

The Englishman gave vent to a litany of sulphurous oaths as the colossus lumbered towards him, its heavy tread trembling the tiles beneath its stone-shod feet. Ducking beneath a sudden vicious swipe of the avatar's claws, Grimwood swept his sword forth in a mighty arc, only to see the blade rebound from the fiend's acicular hide with a strident clang and a shower of sparks. A glancing blow from the effigy's fist then struck his shoulder, sending him reeling to the sanctum's floor. Grimwood scrambled desperately to his feet as the black golem descended upon him, barely avoiding another ruinous strike of its spiked hand. Thrice more did the Englishman evade such deadly blows, but finally a pulverizing fist found him, hurling him bodily twelve feet across the chamber to carom from the fissured wall.

Blood stung Grimwood's eyes as he regained his feet, his sword unwavering. A sudden surge of righteous rage supplanted the pain which wracked his lacerated body and the Englishman vaulted at the towering aberration, his sword hewing ebon fragments from its sculpted haunches. But the hexocular horror then seized him about the torso, lifting him effortlessly from the floor, its multifaceted eyes glowing with an eerie, emerald radiance. His corded thews straining, Grimwood strove to free himself from that unyielding grasp. His muscles rose in ridges upon his bronzed frame, the veins in his neck swelling. His blade rang repeatedly from the behemoth's horned head, to no avail. And the graven monster's vice-like grip tightened. Slowly, inexorably, the effigy's crystalline fangs inched ever closer to the Englishman's throat. Suddenly, a single gunshot reverberated throughout the grotto. One of the statue's six pellucid eyes abruptly shattered into spicules and the creature reeled backwards, releasing Grimwood from its clutches. The Englishman landed lithely and cast a fraught glance at the sanctum's entrance to see Hisham crouching in the shadows, plumes of pale smoke swirling from the barrel of his Enfield revolver, an expression of unalloyed shock on his face. "Good shot, old man!" Grimwood bellowed, vaulting clear of the temporarily thwarted fiend. "See if you can hit another one of its accursed eyes!"

Hisham took careful aim at the stygian horror before squeezing the Enfield's trigger. There came a stentorian crack, but his shot was wide of the mark, and instead of hitting the lurching effigy, it struck the huge viridian gem embedded in the wall behind it. With a blinding blossom of green fire, the crystal abruptly exploded, sending emerald shards cascading across the chamber. Instantly, a juddering tremor shook the cavern and the viridescent veins in the rockface began to gutter like dying candleflames. The reverberations swiftly grew in intensity and fragments of stone began to tumble from the grotto's ceiling, great serpentine cracks simultaneously appearing in its walls and floor. Grimwood scabbarded his sword and made for the rocky palisade. On a whim, he swept up the arcane grimoire as he passed its gnarled plinth, tucking the hefty book under his arm. Then he was at Hisham's side, wiping blood from his brow, struggling to maintain his balance amidst the chamber's incessant quaking.

The Egyptian's eyes suddenly widened in terror. "Damn this black sorcery!" he barked above the growing cacophony. "That thrice-cursed devil is unrelenting!"

Grimwood turned to see the aphotic avatar once again lurching forwards, its movements paroxysmal, black smoke billowing from its shattered ocular socket. Muttering maledictions under his breath, the Englishman ejected his Webley's spent shells before briskly reloading the revolver with an ingrained dexterity honed by countless gunfights. Suddenly, another violent tremor shook the sanctum and one of the huge stalactites which jutted from the shadowed ceiling began to yield to the conflagration, a latticework of cracks manifesting upon its surface. An instant later, the giant needle of stone fell, plummeting languidly downwards. With an ear-splitting din louder than a cannonade, it struck the lumbering effigy, piercing its carven shoulder and wrenching the limb brutally from its body before shattering into a myriad black fragments. The statue's knees buckled and it crashed to the ground, thick runnels of green ichor oozing from its sundered shell. A score of enormous shards then tumbled from above, effectively interring the fiend in an impenetrable tomb. A further barrage of tremors shook the shrine and the lambent veins of crystal finally flickered out, plunging the hollow into darkness.

"Time to get the hell out of here!" roared Grimwood. Requiring no further impetus, the two men scrambled desperately towards the mouth of the tunnel which led to the surface, fragments of stone falling about them as they ran. Swiftly and wordlessly, they pelted along the torchlit passageway, clambering through clouds of choking dust, pursued by a harrowing sound akin to rolling thunder which boomed relentlessly at their heels, along with a ceaseless avalanche of crumbing stone which at any moment threatened to entomb them before they reached the distant exit. Finally, they cleared the shrine's threshold and emerged into the desert night scant seconds before the tunnel collapsed behind them. A great pall of acrid dust billowed forth from the ruin, but the tremors did not cease, rather they increased in magnitude, shaking the very ground which surrounded the hoary edifice. Grimwood and Hisham continued their mad flight until they had reached what they considered to be a safe distance from the shivering sepulchre, whereupon they finally turned to regard the beleaguered site. The temple was swiftly sinking like a breached hulk on a storm-wracked sea, its rent and riven walls crumbling to be devoured by the undulating sand. The tumult continued for many moments, and only when the last sundered vestiges of the fane had disappeared beneath the churning expanse, swallowed forever by that abyssal maelstrom, did the rumbling cease and the swirling dust begin to settle. At length, silence once more held sway over the moonlit desert and the two men stood unspeaking, drawing breath in laboured gasps, each lost in their own sombre thoughts.

Grimwood inhaled deeply, savouring the cool air of the desert night. He cast his gaze to the east, where the sun was just beginning to crest the distant horizon, painting the sky with burgeoning, rutilant hues.

Finally, Hisham turned to the Englishman and summoned him from his reverie. "That abomination will haunt my dreams for the rest of my days," he rasped.

"Damn right, old man. What compelled you to come back?"

"I contemplated the matter extensively, and ultimately decided that I could not allow you to plunge into that accursed vipers' nest alone. You saved my life after all, and I had to repay that debt. Besides, leaving you to perish in that godless place would no doubt have brought me interminable bad luck."

"You're right, I'll warrant," assented Grimwood wryly.

"You look like a butcher," muttered the Egyptian, glancing at the welter of crimson which anointed Grimwood's body. "Those wounds will require a surgeon's hand, lest your blood becomes poisoned."

The Englishman nodded silently. He was perusing the grimoire which he had liberated from the shrine, noting the bone-dry, rugose leather of its binding and the corroded bosses which encased its corners. An elaborately embossed heptagonal sigil adorned the centre of the cover and the entire tome seemed strangely cold to the touch. He released the tarnished clasp and proceeded to conduct a cursory examination of the book's worm-eaten pages, marvelling at the array of cryptic symbols, arcane ideograms and indecipherable glyphs which were inscribed upon the crumbling vellum.

"You should burn that vile book," gnarred the Moslem. "It is an affront to all that is holy; a blasphemous thing that should not be permitted to exist."

Grimwood snapped the hefty volume shut. "Alas, I cannot. Let's just say that I know someone who would find this tome remarkably interesting."

Hisham shook his head disdainfully. "Do you think we dispatched all of those *shayatin* devils?"

"I imagine so. But if there are any more of them skulking in the shadows, we've got the measure of them now. Our blades are still sharp, and we have plenty of ammunition."

"Well spoken, sahib!" exclaimed the Egyptian. "You are a rogue and an adventurer at heart. A man with your talents could live well as a soldier of fortune, owing allegiance to no king or nation. I know this from experience."

"The thought had crossed my mind," replied Grimwood. "But I've sworn an oath, and for now, I am honour-bound to abide by it. At any rate, somebody has to undertake these onerous tasks. The Empress commands, old man."

Hisham scowled. "Bah! All empires fall. Such is the way of things. History has taught us this. Many once mighty dominions are now gone, forever lost to time. The empires which today vie for control of the world will one day be naught but memories. Yours will be no exception."

Grimwood pondered the Egyptian's words for a moment, then shrugged his broad shoulders. "Perhaps," he finally replied, his tone solemn. "But be assured that our bones will be dust long before then. Now, let us return to our mounts and leave this blighted place behind us. The sun is rising, and we have far to travel."

Attalus Grimwood will return.

Byron A. Roberts *is the vocalist, lyricist, and founder of the UK extreme metal band* ***Bal-Sagoth****. An English Literature graduate,*

Roberts conceived Bal-Sagoth as a symphonic black metal project built upon an elaborate fantasy and sci-fi oriented lyrical concept, inspired by the novels, short stories, comics, and movies he grew up with, particularly the classic pulp stories of Robert E. Howard and H.P. Lovecraft. The lyrical mythos of his Bal-Sagoth universe goes far beyond the band's six album discography, encompassing novellas and short stories, most notably the sword & sorcery series The Chronicles of Caylen-Tor, *published by DMR Books. In addition to his musical and literary pursuits, Byron has long been involved in historical battle reenactment societies and is proficient with a variety of medieval and Dark Age weapons. For more information on Byron's work, visit www.bal-sagoth.net and www.byron-a-roberts.co.uk.*

Shadows from Night Eternal

by Peter Salatellis

Illustrated by Eva Flora

The ill-lit inn boomed with raucous howling and carousal as early dusk fell over the heart of Koranth. Mead and ale circulated ceaselessly while drunken thieves and scoundrels made crude gestures at the serving girls who passed. No one seemed to acknowledge the entrance of the robed figure over the wild bedlam, nor did anyone heed him as he paced through the crowd and around the tables like an inky shadow.

A wide hood was pulled over his gray-banded hair which loosely framed the wizened yet weary face of a man entering his sixtieth winter. His long black robe, trimmed in wavy, streaking patterns of gold, enveloped the entirety of his lean figure in the finest jet-black silk that could have only been spun in Koranth. He wore a thin shirt of black leather and a sleeveless black gambeson fashioned with golden buttons, over which hung a bright golden pendant in the shape of a sun.

The shadowy figure sighted a young man, roughly twenty-five winters old, at the far corner of the inn. He was stoutly built and sported a circlet of iron around his head. His clean-shaven face indicated his youth, yet he showed the hardened look of a man who fought many battles. He wore high buckskin boots, and vambraces of toughened brown leather adorned his sinewy forearms. A dark mane cascaded in long waves over his mail hauberk, and the hide of a lion hung from his shoulders and draped his broad frame. Seated in solitude with a scabbarded broadsword at his side and his chin resting on his fist, he sat back and gazed broodingly into the dancing autumn flames of the fireplace.

The robed figure walked up beside him. "Good evening, warrior," he said placidly. "It is quite lively in here tonight and I noticed the unoccupied seat. Do you mind if I join you?"

With a light nod, the warrior gestured at the empty chair with his open left hand.

"Your lion's hide and broadsword are remarkable," continued the man in the robe. "You are Aivas, are you not?"

"Indeed, I am," replied the warrior, somberly. He raised a flagon of ale to his lips for a final drink, all the while maintaining an unbroken gaze into the flames of the fireplace. "How did you come to know my name?"

"You are he who led the opposition to Sanatan's advance at the borders of Koranth. The bards have written of your earned triumph." Inquisitively, the man noticed the warrior's disconnection from the lively revel to which he had his back turned. "Why don't you celebrate your victory?"

"I do not view the death of my fellow men as a cause for celebration," replied Aivas levelly.

"A truth I cannot argue with. I apologize for my impudent inquiry."

Still, the warrior's gaze was fixated on the flames.

Gingerly, the robed man continued, "They say the battle was long, and you and your men fought valiantly."

"Indeed. Steel rang on steel ceaselessly throughout the night and carried into the waking hours of the morrow. Sanatan, that foolish tyrant. He thought his numbers would give him the advantage in a narrow vale. They came relentlessly in scores, and our men cut them down as they gasped their final breaths." Hesitantly, Aivas continued, "The blood of men and devils alike paints the ground in that accursed vale."

Apprehensively, the robed man moved back in his seat. "You speak of demons?" he asked the warrior, eyes widening.

"Aye. Sanatan's ranks were not entirely… human."

A mist began to dissipate in Aivas' mind's eye. Vaguely, he recalled the horrible events of that battle. Things descended from the moon. Inhuman things. At mere sight of these beings, the mercenaries hired from neighboring Aethenea fled the battle in a frenzy of horror. He shuddered at the thought. Blood ran like ice through his veins as the sound of demonic screeches thrummed in the dark crevices of his racing mind.

"And Sanatan. I caught sight of him before his retreat, in the foray. His armor was caked with blood and entrails, and his scimitar swung in crimson arcs. He screamed as I have heard no sane man scream before, and in a guttural-sounding tongue that I could not recognize. There was an unnatural aura about him. I saw his eyes. They burned malevolently, smoldering with an abhorrent fire viler than any human bloodlust."

With a tremble in his voice, the robed man spoke. "Such is what I feared. It is said that his mind has been steeped in the realms of black knowledge. What he has given himself to I know not and dare not speak of, for I know that the gods of Earth gave their mortal lives in sacrifice so that we may never find ourselves face to face with such atrocities."

The warrior averted his gaze from the fire and noticed the ornate pendant borne by the robed man. His eyes narrowed as he spoke. "You are a priest," he remarked.

"Aye. I am called Addamathus, a priest in the temple of the prophet Valkka. There are shadows spreading over these lands, warrior. My mind has been plagued with images of their enshrouding tendrils. Long I have tried to rid my mind of these images, but to no avail. In sooth, that is why I sought you."

The warrior looked at the priest, perplexed.

"It is believed that, right after the gods of Earth sealed away The Unnamable Ones, their prophet, Valkka, inscribed the secrets of living free from evil in the form of prayers on a monolith," continued the priest. "He hid this monolith in the mountains of Koranth, in hopes that the most devoted of men would seek it. It is my hope that these secrets be the spark that rekindles the breaking faith of my fellow priests following the spread of Sanatan's poison."

"I admire your consideration for your fellows, holy man. But what role shall I have in this affair?"

"Venturing inside the mountains without guardianship does not strike me as the wisest of decisions, and thus I would be willing to pay good coin for your sword-arm."

"Gold is one thing, priest, but Sanatan will undoubtedly amass his armies anew at the border, and I am not fond of putting the fate of men in the hands of sell-swords."

"I have observed the shifting of the stars," continued Addamathus, his voice unsteady. "Sanatan is somehow beginning to open gateways to what the priesthood calls Night Eternal—the darkness betwixt the stars. It is my belief that Valkka's scriptures will aid us in closing these gateways and will bring us closer to purging the lands of Sanatan's poison."

Aivas considered the priest's proposition. He recalled the grisly image of Sanatan atop his war steed with that unholy gaze in his eyes.

"I do not know which forces possess Sanatan, but by Aeres, my sword will not rest until the lands are freed from whatever pit-spawn he brings forth. Let us ready our steeds for the mountains."

* * *

Dusk had fallen by the time the two men had ridden out across the vast plain. The falling sun painted the sky above with gradient hues of brash crimson against a depth of dark violet, with golden light streaking and spiraling in myriad shapes. The heavens were alive, pulsing with fiendish strangeness and overwhelming beauty, like the ethereal, droning chant of a siren which plunges the mind into spirals of marvel and darkness alike. The waning of the golden sun met the ascent of a full moon, the two astral companions radiating and reflecting their light onto each other.

Aivas' mail gleamed majestically in the eerie glow as he rode forth with his eyes fixed on the stygian mountains ahead. With his left hand, he gripped the ornate broadsword at his side, its pommel resembling the shape of a silvern crescent. Addamathus rode beside him, the golden etchings of his cloak becoming one with the light and his sun-shaped pendant gleaming more magnificently than ever. His eyes turned to the warrior beside him who sat unmoving atop his steed with gaze unaverted.

"Something troubles you deeply, warrior. Your spirit writhes in agony. Your eyes tell it. I can sense it."

The sound of the priest's deep and level voice began to rend the haze in the warrior's mind, and the light of the moon shone on the image of the battle.

"Demons. They came down from the moon. With teeth and talons, they ripped out the throats of warriors. At first sight, I thought them to be nothing more than the hallucinations of bloodlust and delirium, until one bore down upon me. It dropped me and held me groundward with taloned feet. Its screeches were piercing, and its breath reeked of vile decay. I hefted my blade and brought it down with all the force in my arms, brought it down upon its head and cleft the thing to the breastbone as putrid ichor sprayed the soil."

The priest grimaced at this grisly mental image.

"They were few in numbers," Aivas continued, "but their screeches filled the night air. Sanatan has called up things from the pit, things incomprehensible to me. What do you know of these things, priest?"

"I admit that I do not know of these vile things. Such knowledge is against the will of the gods of Earth."

"But as a priest, is it not your role to command the powers of the metaphysical planes?"

"Many believe that to be so, but the command of these powers is what corrupts the mind and soul. It is the whim of black conjurers and necromancers alone.

"You see, the relation between Man and the gods of Earth is one of parentage. We view them as our mothers and our fathers, while we are their children. They know all that is to be known and are aware of the knowledge that we should not gain. Out of love and protection, they keep such knowledge from us, and to serve them is to not betray their love."

"Should not the acquisition of knowledge come with growth and maturity? For how else would a man learn to live among the beasts and face the terrors of the world?"

"That is true only through the perspective of a human parentage. The parentage of the gods is quite different, warrior. On the cosmic scale, we are eternally their children, and they bleed, suffer, and sacrifice for us."

The warrior reflected upon the priest's words. "Mayhap you are right, priest," he said. "But the perspective of my people differs greatly from that of yours."

With respectful inquisitiveness, the priest listened.

"In the clans of Koranth, it is said that the gods of Earth once ruled this plane. Ultimately, it was unfit for them, and they departed. Yet evil still reigned in the shadows. They raised Man from out of the primeval mire to be conquerors. They imbued within us the Warrior's Spirit to be fostered through trial and tribulation. It was this endurance which led Man to rule his domain, erecting great cities of iron and marble."

"Your devotion and spirit are admirable, warrior. Perhaps we will know the truth when we gaze upon the ancient writings of the elders."

Aivas pondered the words of Addamathus and a thought escaped his lips.

"Although we may not know of the nature of the gods, tell me who is truly freer of evil: he who averts his gaze at the mere sight of shadows, or he who looks into evil's myriad faces and severs its many heads with flaming passion and a will of iron?"

Addamathus' eyes widened. "Your reasoning is robust, warrior, and you pose a question which I also seek an answer."

* * *

At the base of the hill, the two men tied their steeds. The ascent was arduous; the night was chill and dark, and the rough black basalt proved to greatly tire the legs. And yet, the pair endured, for the fire of determination overpowered the sensation of burning thews. Anon, they reached the top of the hill and were greeted with a cavernous maw, vast and gaping, down from which protruded scores of hoary, fang-resembling stalactites. The unusual daemonic strangeness of the cavern's orifice sent a wave of coldness down their spines and up their necks, yet at once beckoned them to enter its tenebrous depths.

Addamathus fashioned a crude brand from a thick log and a bundle of oil-drenched cloth which he set ablaze with a spark produced from the rubbing of stones. Aivas' steel chimed as he liberated it from its scabbard. The light of the stars and the moon danced along the surface of the great silvern blade as he gripped the hilt tightly with both hands. The warrior's face was stoic and showed little sign of discomfort in spite of the fatigue that began to overtake his thews and the feeling of unease that found its way into the apertures of the mind and soul. Implacable, the two men pushed on, descending ever deeper into the obnubilating depths of the cavern.

The cavern's interior was bizarre and labyrinthine in nature. Crooked passageways terminated in acute angles and led the pair through a network of dwindling corridors and oval-shaped chambers. Since their entry, Addamathus had been sprinkling the ground with a phosphorescent powder as they advanced, allowing them to trace their path. The brand he held crackled and caused uncanny shadows to flicker and quaver along the walls, yet the two pushed on, paying them no heed.

The sudden sound of quickly flapping wings echoed through the cavern and startled the priest. With tiger-like quickness, Aivas pivoted on his heels, sword upraised. He saw only a small, black blur behind them.

"A simple cave bat," he said, his breath quickening.

"Aye," replied the priest. "Yet I feel another presence in this cavern. Its unseen eyes are gazing upon us."

Again, the sound of wings cut through the silence like a knife. They now sounded… different. Quicker. Louder.

From out of the darkness, something violently bore down upon the pair, knocking Addamathus groundward. He turned to face a screeching humanoid form with wide leathern wings. Four bulbous, verdant eyes protruded from the front of its horned head, and its maw gnashed two rows of dripping, rotten fangs. A monstrous, taloned hand grasped for his throat, but Aivas' steel swung upward in a well-aimed arc that cleft the thing in twain, severing the torso from the legs. He heard the sound of splintering bone as he drove the blade deeper and deeper into the chest of the shrieking wyvern. Dark crimson ichor gushed all around until finally, the fiend expired.

"Devil-spawn!" muttered the trembling priest, panting.

Aivas' mind raced back to the scenes of the battle at the border. He shuddered, remaining silent.

A narrow corridor led the pair into a circular antechamber, yet this one bore little resemblance to the ones they had previously traversed. Along the room's circumference, torches in sconces were nailed to towering columns of cyclopean ebon stone. They burned with emerald fire, bathing the room in a gloomy, viridian light which starkly contrasted with the amber flame emanating from the priest's brand. Each pair of columns framed a pointed archway. In the middle of every frame stood a different idol, each one crudely hewn from a singular fragment of slimy black stone so massive that it dwarfed the combined size of both men. One such carving depicted a bulbous, multi-winged mass with the hind legs of a goat; another showed a batrachian head with a sharp-fanged maw atop a scaled, humanoid body. Seven idols loomed beneath seven arches as their abhorrent forms reflected the preternatural amber-green light. The gruesome eidolons depicted amalgamations of fish, tendrilled wyrms, squids, octopi, and goats, suggesting a far more archaic and incomprehensible nature.

"These… things," spoke Aivas with a haphazard attempt at hiding his dread. "By Aeres, what are they?"

"They are beings forgotten by Time itself," replied the priest with a tremble in his voice. "They would shatter the minds of all who would gaze upon them, and grind Man to dust were they ever to trample and crawl upon Earth." He suddenly directed his attention to the center of the room and spotted a rectangular structure which, at first glance, appeared to be a stone altar. "The gods only know what these walls have seen."

As the two men approached, it was made evident that the structure lacked a top. They peered inside, gazing upon a horror that could twist the souls of the maddest of madmen.

There was a cadaver in the box, barely discernible at first glance. Writhing tendrils enwrapped the shape of a man. The blanched face of the preserved corpse displayed a pair of wide, dead eyes, and a yawning mouth from which a scream of pure horror echoed throughout the cavern as the man's life had left him. Furthermore, the cadaver's throat had been ripped out, likely by talons, and rather crudely from the looks of the gaping hole in the neck.

Addamathus was on the edge of sanity. He recognized the man in the tomb, and the truth was grisly. There was a word on the edge of his tongue, a name that his trembling voice struggled to utter, until finally…

"Valkka!" he gasped. And it was not a curse.

Like a maddened animal, Addamathus darted toward the threshold leading to the adjoining room. Aivas ran behind him, but the pair halted suddenly when they saw what lay beyond.

They came into a wide, open space framed only by three walls. The cave floor abruptly terminated as the two men stood on what appeared to be a cliffside. It jutted over a seemingly endless body of wine-dark water above which coalesced hues of myriad colors in an unbroken void of cosmic blackness. A structure speared up from the water just beyond the promontory: a massive onyx obelisk, some sixty feet in height, and carved all around with runic sigils.

"The monolith!" exclaimed Addamathus.

"By the gods of Blood and Thunder," gasped the warrior. "The words you spoke were true!"

Wide-eyed, the priest gingerly approached the monolith with his free hand upraised. There then came a sound which lifted the priest from his trance-like state and sent the coldest of chills down the warrior's spine. The waters below churned and erupted as two serpentine necks with dragon-like heads shot up violently. Their cosmic roars shook the cavern, revealing a score of hoary, decaying fangs.

Aivas gripped his broadsword with oaken might. His eyes were stricken with primeval horror as his chest heaved rapidly beneath his mail hauberk. Only a madman would not accept fear had he been in his place.

A head violently plunged toward Aivas. The warrior attempted to strike sideways with his sword, but it was too close for him to connect with the blade's edge, causing him to strike its side with his forearm. The warrior stumbled as he sent the wyrm's snout crashing into the rightmost wall of the cavern as the other head shot downward, mouth agape. Aivas held up his forearm and felt the maw clamp down on the vambrace he wore. With the quickness of a panther, he stabbed upward with his broadsword, impaling the neck of the fiend as thick ichor sprayed from the wound. When the hydra screeched, he used the opportunity to free his arm from its maw. With both hands, he shoved the blade forward, severing the neck halfway before bringing it down anew in a violent arc that hacked off the head completely.

The fiend rolled back; another piercing screech undulated from the remaining head as two additional heads emerged from the decapitated stump.

"Devil! Vile pit-spawn!" Aivas' roar reverberated through the cavern as crimson rage dominated any sensation of fear.

"Aivas!" shouted the priest. "The heads must be cauterized! Sever them and make way for me!"

There was no time for Aivas to contemplate the priest's request. Another head shot toward him. With malevolent fury, he swung his blade and cleft the head right down the middle. His sword arced upward again, sending it spiraling into the waters below as he swiftly retreated to fend off the remaining two. The priest then held the brand an arm's distance from his face and blew into the flames, sending a fiery mass lurching from it. The fire left the shrieking hydra with a charred, blackened stump from which no new head emerged.

"Ha! Cold steel and fire still prevail!" Aivas roared as his soul was filled anew with preternatural strength.

The remaining two heads lashed down upon the pair but were swiftly intercepted. A single, wide stroke from Aivas' bloodthirsty blade cleft both wyvern heads at once while Addamathus' breath of fire charred the stumps.

The long, scaled necks of the fiend writhed spasmodically and wrapped themselves around the titanic monolith. The priest yelled in terror as they shattered the structure, and the remains of what was believed to contain the wisdom of the elders sank ever deeper into the cosmic waters.

A shadow of grief and doom beshrouded Addamathus' countenance. His breath quickened, and his chest heaved with forces of sadness and fury. As if possessed, the priest bolted toward the edge of the cliff, howling.

"Addamathus! Do not!" boomed Aivas. The warrior dashed and threw his arms around the priest's waist, intercepting him mere inches before the edge. The two were sent groundward as Aivas jerked Addamathus back and held him pinned down until the priest's panting subsided. "Not even Aeres knows of the horrors that may dwell beneath those waters," stammered Aivas.

The sudden quaking of the cavern walls forthwith broke Addamathus' trance. Thunderous crashes reverberated as chunks of basalt and stalactites rained down from above. With haste, the pair followed the trail of phosphorescent powder on the ground. They ran frantically through the same dwindling corridors from whence they came, evading masses of crumbling rock until finally, emerging from the stygian depths in the wee hours of the morrow as the great cavernous maw crumbled and closed behind them.

* * *

"I keep well my promise to you, warrior," said the priest. He reached into a bag slung across his steed and produced a leather pouch whose contents rang and chimed as he held it to the warrior.

With a level look in his eyes, Aivas closed Addamathus' hand around the pouch and lightly pushed it back to him.

"It is my belief that I have gained something more valuable on this trial than a pouch of gold," he said placidly. "Use it to rebuild your shrines, for evil still reigns in the shadows of this world."

"I owe you my life. And my faith. Evil will cry and writhe beneath your sword, warrior. Your fate is written as such."

These were the words that echoed in the dark caverns of Aivas' mind from then on to eternity as the priest rode off into the golden light of the dawning sun.

Peter Salatellis *is a Greek heavy metal musician hailing from Montreal, Canada. A lifelong metalhead and avid reader, he has long been immersed in the thunderous rhythms of classic heavy metal and the heroic and mystical tales of Greek mythology and traditional sword & sorcery. Peter aspires to merge these two worlds as the co-founder, guitarist, and primary composer and lyricist in the true metal band* ***Bloodstone****. He also formerly contributed music and lyrics for the melodic death metal band* ***Divine Bloodline****. In addition to his artistic indulgences and esoteric delvings, he studies mechanical engineering at McGill University.*

Wraiths of Pongus Maw

Written and illustrated by Jo Gamel

An October sun moved towards the horizon, slowly sinking over humanity's final battle fought entirely with sailing ships. Father Time had come to terminate the Age of Sail.

From the upper deck of the HMS *Mosquito*, the engraver sketched the sight of the doomed HMS *Genoa*. Upon the unlucky ship, a splinter ripped through the face of Captain Bathurst, followed by a round shot that buried itself in him, killing him in a drawn-out agony. Twenty-six more souls died violently aboard *Genoa*, but that was nothing in the face of the thousands who would die in the Ottoman and Egyptian ranks.

For four grueling hours, the navies of the French, British, and Russians were allied against the navies of the Egyptians and Ottomans. All were locked together in a sudden and explosive sea battle over the only charted trade route between the empires. The Eastern forces were suspicious of the fleet of warships that entered the waters as protection for the transport and supply that crossed through their world. One mischievous lot sent adrift a lit fireship, a vessel similar to a hellburner, loaded with slow fuse explosives. It was a tragic mistake, for although the Europeans and Russians were greatly outnumbered and in foreign waters, they were not outgunned.

Neither side was prepared for the outburst. To get into formation, the Western ships needed to drop their anchors off the bow and the stern, all with their broadside aimed at the Eastern sailors. If any war had been declared, hours would have been dedicated to preparation: the use of a leadline to measure the depth of the sea before dropping anchor, the furling of the precious sails, and the rolling of the hammocks that would have been lined along the decks for added protection against shrapnel and deadly splinters.

The ships hurried together to form an arc on the surface of the sea, making a murderous crossfire as cannon volley wrought explosive ruination to any vessel it ensnared. These line formations were difficult to outflank. Once stabilized by dual anchors against drifting or heavy rocking on the waves, the ships could be oriented by releasing or increasing tension on the massive anchor ropes, building maximum coverage and improving the effective use of various ranges of cannons.

The young boys hired as powder monkeys flew across the lower decks within the ships. In haste, they delivered the naturally insulated, lightweight, and waterproof cow horns filled with gunpowder from the copper-lined grand magazine to the gun crew. There one named Tawney rushed between men. His horrified soul took the terror. Decades later he would retell: about the hatchways it looked like a butcher's stall; bits of flesh sticking in the ring bolts. There below deck, the most chaotic and dangerous scenes unfolded. A shot entered one of the portholes and dashed dead two-thirds of a gun's crew.[1]

Each time a gunner had to access the barrel in order to reload the cannons, he had to lean outside the gunport on the broadside aimed at the enemy. In less than one minute, he worked with long poles tipped with tools; first a worm, then a damper, and finally, a rammer, all while the burning metal beast was his only means of keeping a grip on the ship. Splinters and gunfire showered around him. As soon as he pulled himself in, the deafening ball of iron ripped through the brine and smoke, and the cannon recoiled, in the wild kickback of several stallions combined, the metal death machine lassoed in place by mere rope and wedges.

As the Western forces wrought merciless havoc upon the sick man of Europe, the Eastern sailors would not let these vultures impress their imperial ships as loot. So, the failing vessels, one by

[1] Tawney, (n.d.). *Description of a battle* [Plaque]. Independence Seaport Museum, Philadelphia, PA.

one, were lit from within and blown to smithereens, with all souls aboard, be they Balkan Janissaries or Muslim conscripts.

A cluster of smaller ships crept towards the HMS *Jupiter*, a Leda-class frigate at the left tip of the allied arc. From one ship of the cluster, one hundred Egyptians aboard slammed their axes into her hull and began to pull themselves up towards the gun ports and rails. Captain Martinus Grey unsheathed his cutlass and knew there was no time at all to crank the ten thousand-pound anchors from the seafloor, so he ordered the anchor ropes cut for escape and ran towards the creeping enemy. The dangerous shoreline, guarded with huge *chevaux-de-frise* spikes beneath the waves, became a new danger to the HMS *Jupiter*. Captain Grey and his disparate soldiers of fortune could no longer hold the line as another enemy squadron from the eyalet of Tunis had forced the frigate into an unseen swell—a swell that seemed to have sprung from oblivion. The ship was suddenly expelled from out the cannon smoke on a rapid current, the Egyptians lost their grips on their axes, and the HMS *Jupiter* went spinning adrift.

Several hours later, when the whirling masses of water had leveled, the men aboard the frigate found themselves alone at sea. The crew began to repair the torn sails and bolt the loose cannons. They were uniformed in matching monkey jackets, simple and loose, and pants that closed at the waist with buttons. Most kept their hair cut short, and they covered their heads with hats that had been waterproofed with tar. Their salty discipline prevented them from panicking about the change of course as each rolled the belled legs of his pants in preparation for work.

The fateful mechanisms of circumstance crewed the HMS *Jupiter*. After Napoleon's War, the sea swam with Australian convicts, various governments' privateers, organized press gangs, and the men unchained by the British Slave Act. The vastness of the Majesty's empire and the auspiciousness of the Ottoman

Sultanate turned like gears in the lives of humanity, weaving its iron teeth through the entire globe.

An endless horizon surrounded the frigate, revealing no indication as to where land might lay. The sky was vacant of birds, not even a sleeping albatross gliding through its months-long flight span. The surface level of the water showed no sign of the sort of marine life that would have indicated a nearby coastline. Captain Grey consulted the navigator, Aquila Giorgadze. The navigator was a mystic Christian man, an astronomer from the East who had narrowly escaped religious persecution and studied the star maps painted on the walls and ceilings of deep, hidden caves. Now an elder, he had been hired to guide countless souls safely home from their exotic voyages. Aquila's eyes were dark as sable, the same as the color of his soft, fine hair, which at every moment twisted up into shapes against gravity as if he had just run his hands through it in deep thought. His face was both generously handsome and emaciated, with a beautiful bowed mouth. He stood over six feet tall, very gaunt, and cloaked in beige Eastern robes that he took great care to preserve.

"Where are we, man?" demanded the captain. "Apollo seems to rise much later than expected, and he retires too soon. How can we be so far north without passing through the straits?"

Aquila sighed with resignation as the most restrained eye-roll shuttered through his black eyelashes at the tone of the captain. "I see we have shifted over many mountains and vast deserts. The salt in these brine waters ought to force the fish to the uppermost strata of the sea, yet there are none. This unknown place should not exist," he replied with a darkly meditative mood.

In contrast to Aquila's dark prophecy, Captain Grey felt lit from within. His most passionate aspiration was to discover the unknown. He had once been aboard a ship that was impressed into the control of pirates, where he heard boasts of their unproven shortcuts through the seas. His curiosity for such powerful knowledge was awoken, and he was doubly blessed by rescue after only a few weeks aboard. He set sail with every intention to forge a glorious legacy in a wild land, akin to the triumphant heroes of his boyhood studies. Titillating visions of adventure and grandeur thrilled his imagination.

At that moment, a singular silver-scaled porpoise leapt from the water closely beside the HMS *Jupiter*. The animal's gaze locked on the crew, with one pupil larger than the other. With the blinding glare of its shimmering flesh, it arced and performed a silent rip entry back into the waves.

Aquila immediately remarked in his deep voice, with a subtle panic and frustration, "We must find our way out of this remote place, Captain. Legends warn of such sinister sights as the silver-scaled porpoise. Beware, such a naturally timid creature coming to us and executing this soundless gesture of an apex predator. I sense this eerie beast is contrived as a cursed omen. I will chart our course when Helios sleeps."

The bold captain, enchanted by the ominous sight, was unafraid and curious. He was unphased by the navigator's fearful rush to leave this untouched realm. He had heard dire tales of sinister mermaids and mischievous kelpies, but never had he been told of an evil silver augury. He was struck by the foggy memory of a passage he once read of in *Il Milione:*

"...And at the edges of empires exists a tempestuous chasm that unites heavy seas, with waves so high they often cover the masts of ships and so great that the ships are turned upside down, and through this gaping danger, lies the almighty wealth of TIME. Alas, bringing spices, silk, and rare gems through this rapid and savage portal can never be done, as are murmured the faded tales told of the frightened Ossetians in their Iron dialect, so many wrecked and lost in the whirl of the straits of the Pongus Maw..."

Intuition whispered to Captain Grey that this mysterious sea was connected to those very straits, a sea lane that would accelerate the voyage by weeks. He peered over the rails and studied the aquatic creatures, which in turn inspected the ship: a school of polychromatic jellyfish floated by, and a few small spiny dogfish sharks lurked. After two hours, he became unnerved. The edges of shadows remained directly beneath objects. The sun had not moved since noon.

His brow furrowed as he entered his chambers. There, the cabin boy, Tursun, presented him with an evening meal. Tursun's lineage was lost and found through the enslavement of women to men. His eyes were blue and narrow, extending upwards like his peaked cheekbones. His nose was small and wide, with round nostrils. His long hair was a warm brown, coarse and strong, and four feet long, kept in a tie at the nape of his neck. He was a youth, yet he was thick and muscular and over six feet tall. His large hands and arms were lined and colored with myths from his grandfather's culture. Tursun placed a colossal cast iron candelabra, brightly ablaze, in the center of the oak nautical table, illuminating the captain's quarters.

"Snuff those candles immediately, boy! Waste not what we have in this distant realm," commanded the captain.

"But sir, 'tis eight bells," replied Tursun, not without due respect, gesturing to the face of the largely unreliable astronomical clock as it tolled midnight. The pendulum mechanism in it hardly kept time on dry land, and under the changing barometric pressure of the sea and its meandering equilibrium, the millimeter gears functioned more precisely as a decoration than as a predictor of the cycles of the cosmos.

"Do not contradict me!" Captain Grey barked as he glanced from his pewter plate towards the blown-glass panes of the skylight, expecting the midday sun.

He was awed by the common sight of the millions of burning

diamonds that shone in the night sky. The frozen face of the moon had waned to a narrow sliver, hanging exactly where it ought to in October. He stood calmly from the table, filled with curiosity, folded his arms thoughtfully across his broad chest, and briskly marched out to the deck, minding not to get the remnants of the battle-bloodied sand on his polished boots. The deck was cleared as if prepared for battle, and stranger still, there was no sound at all. The ropes did not creak, the sails did not luff, and the waves did not slap.

With unfettered confidence, he walked toward the rail. He looked over, and to his dark dismay, the water was as still as the surface of a mirror. He saw his reflection there, illuminated in starlight. The captain was strapping, with a straight spine and white skin. His presence was much stronger than that of Tursun or Aquila, though he stood at five-foot-eight. His brow had a deep, handsome furrow that rose from the bridge of his nose to a soft ending in the middle of his forehead. Silver wove its way through his wavy hair and dense beard. His dark eyes peered thoughtfully from under bushy brows. His navy-blue coat was camouflaged by the dark water in his reflection, creating the illusion that his head floated in the water.

Now, just where he gazed, the water began to bubble. Somewhere deep below the surface, a strange fish with luminescent eyes seemed to watch him. Captain Grey tried to perceive the beast, but it faded before it could be studied. The final motions of the creature were lost as the waves returned to their expected rhythm, and the gods of the wind restored their breath to the canvas sails. The ropes creaked again, and the captivated captain returned to his quarters to log these fascinating occurrences.

The entire crew slept a terrorized and strange slumber that seemed to last too long; each had his own twisted and meaningful dreams. All men had laid writhing and moaning in their hanging cots from the powerful sensations of unconscious hopes and unwelcome longings for home. When all hands returned to toe the line, monkey jackets wrinkled and askew, they stood perplexed in the past night's theurgy. Each one had burning mysteries at the top of his mind; all, except Aquila the navigator, who had tinkered and fiddled with octants and astrolabes until dawn. In the tone of the storm-worn planks, Aquila's breath groaned with consternation.

Bellowing with confidence, Captain Grey announced his plans for the crew.

"Men, the coordinates have been mapped. As you know, we are indeed in strange, unexplored seas. Fear nothing, for this call to adventure was ordained to us by God Himself. We will fulfill His ambitions for us. We will faithfully begin our search for the only possible way out, through the mythical Pongus Maw. Let your souls harden in this truth; a man's life is an undignified curse without mighty storms and steadfast courageousness. Crew, prepare the ship. Destiny awaits!"

Aquila, angered by the Captain's unfounded dismissal of his navigator's wisdom, then began to quake, his wide, dark eyes splitting directions as if locked in a thousand-yard stare. His voice croaked from an unnatural register, and he fell to his knees:

"The Maw calls the fearless and the foolish alike! Your Christian God has nothing to do with this course, for it is the Will of another immortal force which beckons your bold and unbidden souls; all of you to be lost and never to be heard or seen again, even as a corpse."

With undue force, Captain Grey grasped the weak-kneed navigator and stood him on his feet. As Grey stared into Aquila's face, consciousness returned to his eyes, his spine's forward arc straightened, and his thick mustache disguised his self-conscious expression.

"The fool is the coward who allows fear to rule his fate!"

trumpeted the captain. The crew, with a slight delay, cheered "Aye" in unison.

"Onwards!" cried the captain. This time, the crew resounded without delay. The first mate axed open a cask of ale, and the crew toasted to the great legacy they would forge for their brave and ambitious captain.

During the ruckus, Tursun managed to spirit a pint away to his best companion, the nine-year-old powder monkey who was waiting for him in the lookout of the mainmast. The boys toasted to the great adventure which lay before them, each with his own dreams. Tursun had made it aboard after a gritty childhood drifting between besieged desert cities. He had grown wise and distrustful of authority after seeing so many would-be civic leaders rise and fall, including his narrow-eyed father. On the other hand, the trusting powder monkey was a war orphan named Bahram, who was once a traveler on a securely bonded caravan. His ascetic people secretly practiced the persecuted religion of Manichaeism, a cosmic dualism that blended aspects of Zoroastrianism, Christianity, and Buddhism. Bahram had a kind and friendly face, with light brown skin unmarked by worry and untouched by the blade's edge. His hair curled into smooth, half-inch-wide ringlets and hung around his head in a dark halo. He was not tall, but he was not fully grown, either. His black irises were fringed by eyelashes that curled like his hair. Like a symbol of his youthful health, his smile was bright, full of white teeth and pink gums. Now on his own, Bahram sincerely sought another wandering fellowship to anchor him.

"Do you think the captain has gone mad?" the powder monkey asked his companion with a hint of laughter.

The cabin boy swirled the ale in his cup in a manner he thought very mature. He responded slowly, "Mad indeed, with the desire to stand with the constellations in the sky. I'm uncertain of whether or not this journey to the maw will be our collective salvation or the Captain's solitary triumph."

Bahram leaned back on the black tar ratlines, a wide smile wrinkled the corners of his eyes, and he chortled at the idea of a man eternally standing around in the sky. He battled winking, heavy eyelids as weariness and intoxication overtook him.

A quarter-hour later, the first mate meandered listlessly to the stern, swaying with the confidence of brew, to gaze upon the rippling wake that trailed behind the ship. Alas, the wake was nowhere to be seen. He registered now the pin-drop silence. As he approached the wooden rail, he peered down into the mirror-like surface and, to his delight, saw not his own bald, stunted reflection but the beautiful oval face of an odalisque with a small flirtatious smile on her hot pink lips.

The pearl visage gracefully emerged from her Venusian waters. Her smile was knowing, and her gaze was sinister. Her form swayed and shimmered in the indigo water. In a disembodied, metallic voice, she assumed the first role as querent.

"How do you find the voyage, *fine* sailor?" Her words rang like a silver bell beside his left ear as if she were so nearby. Her pronunciation of the word "fine" was drawn, breathy, and subtly mocking. She giggled like a twinkling star. The voice had a long echo that seemed never to end. Even in his intoxicated state, this magic disturbed him, and he began to sweat in the cold sea breeze.

"Good evening..." he slurred loudly, adding a belch from his scared lips, "...you slimy sea witch!"

A minute later, Tursun and Bahram were awakened by the first mate's distressed shouts. He seemed to be losing an argument with his own reflection. The two had fallen asleep in the crow's nest and peered down with sleepy eyes at the drunken sailor.

"Shall we have a closer look?" one amused boy whispered.

"Surely!" agreed the other with mischievous enthusiasm.

The two descended the netted ratlines. At first, they crept

slowly toward the first mate, but in real concern, the boys began to walk upright, and then in a hurry, the cabin boy began to rush to the man.

"Oh, yes, certainly I would have those… the riches of the king, and all the power… and the concubines… the captain's respect… no, the emperor's respect… yes, I do deserve it… yes, I can see it all there, and I shall have it! It is mine! Give it to me!" muttered the now irritated, enraptured, and drooling sailor.

Tursun carried a small dagger and gripped its hilt intuitively. He sensed something was pulling the first mate into a trance. The air reeked of ylang-ylang blossoms, and the floral odor choked the company in saccharine charm. Now, long, silvery fingertips reached over the rail, followed by the strangest beast the boys had ever seen.

The silver selkie rose from the water like an unstoppable lava flow. Glowing like luminescent algae, each scale shone brilliant in hues of emerald, diamond, and sapphire. Her lustrous hair seemed to be endless, like the train of her layered filmy gowns. Her form endlessly shape-shifted, oscillating between a repulsive fish and a lustful maiden, just the way that a faceted stone could look deep and shallow at once. Betwixt her fine fingers were gossamer webs, and each fingernail was a long, clear talon. Her face was sometimes angelic, and just as her audience began to fall in love with it, the eerie eyes would begin to slowly, hypnotically slide aside. The thin, aquiline nose would gingerly recede into her skull, leaving only the holes of her nostrils. The small, wet mouth, shaped like a plush, pink rose, would bizarrely stretch wide with the words she said, revealing long, crooked teeth in a heartless, mad smile. Her form shifted between buxom and lithe and then again reformed as a bony fish. In a blink, all the weirdness would resolve, and once again, man beheld a lustful, angelic maiden.

Tursun and Bahram stood agape in awe and horror. The silver selkie opened her webby palm, and the first mate placed his hand in hers. Her talons closed on his hand like a vicious steel trap. Like a rushing whirlpool, she wrapped her tendrils of hair around him and slowly sucked the sailor from the deck. The cabin boy threw his dagger, and it landed with precision in the forehead of the selkie. She froze in midair, grasping the first mate who yet clung to the rail, and her strange, wide eyes bulged from her skull like a demon from the Far East.

A shrieking cackle broke the stillness all around the ship: "Ho, my lovely child, you have only struck the immortal sea. You cannot stop the healing force of the universe! Yield and sleep, my sweet." The dagger fell out of her skull, where the wound zipped closed as if twenty sea spiders ran across her forehead with silk threads. With her strange, echoing voice, the boy felt utterly enchanted. Then, as fast as a shark, from the sea emerged her tremendous five-lobed tail. She whacked Tursun across his knees, fracturing both legs and propelling him across the deck. Helpless, he lost consciousness, and she wrapped her long fingers around the first mate's head and pulled him from the rails. He went willingly.

The captain rose at dawn, unsure of whether or not a new day had begun or if Apollo had lost control of his chariot. Tursun did not present him with breakfast. He discovered the cabin boy among a circle of men on the deck, where Bahram relayed their tale. Aquila squinted unblinkingly at the captain, gnashing his teeth behind his obscuring mustache. The rest of the crew was engrossed in the tale, except for the gunner, who frowned and glanced with one eyebrow raised between the captain and the navigator knowingly.

As sunset fell, Aquila peered toward the amber sky. The sinking sunlight softly beamed over the crests of swells, casting shadows into the troughs. The dancing patterns began to expose an undulating velocity with some gentle breaks. Ra was casting his light and revealing the secret swells in the water: the frigate had been captured by a deep and forceful current.

Aquila interrupted Captain Grey's dinner to inform him of the change and to alert him that such a swift current was caused only by a narrowing ridge in a seafloor, likely meaning they were sailing into an underwater canyon that would pull them into the Pongus Maw. The captain did not raise his eyes. He took a deep breath and a long sip of his goblet. After a thoughtful pause, he cleared his throat, and with unruffled focus, he ordered the ship to continue onwards into the unknown, evoking the silent fury and frustration of the navigator.

Below deck, the men slept shoulder to shoulder in their swaying cots. The gunner, Antoine, was a true lone wolf and lay pondering what he had observed between the navigator and the captain that day. He was a war veteran who had fought in places so exotic that he didn't bother to mention their names anymore, though if Tursan or Bahram were lucky enough to sit at his table during a meal, their mouths remained closed in wait for one of his poetic and deep reflections. Antoine was six-foot-four and a lovechild of the North African coast. His skin was inked with maps of sea currents, constellations, and shapes of shorelines. His soft curls were dark blond, his broad face a freckled complexion, his eyes a deep brown, his lips wide and full, sometimes parting in a relaxed smirk that held a glittering gold tooth. His hands were large enough to wrap around the thighs of wistful lovers, his powerful arms long enough to catch and capture any elusive maiden. If she resisted his rugged attractiveness, she could not resist the slowly eroding force of his patient passion. His worldly perspectives rumbled deeply and quietly out of his lungs in an unplaceable accent, charming anyone who took the time to listen. And even for all these features of Eros, he chose to remain solitary. And for all these wild scenes of his wide-reaching experiences which colored his perceptions, he was a man without a god.

His first escapade onto a battlefield had been as a fifer alongside his late brother, a drummer boy, and his late father, a foot soldier at Napoleon's Battle of the Pyramids. He remembered them as fearless heroes, though he never allowed himself to reminisce on their days together. He instead carried a twitching gesture in both hands, in the manner that one fingers the tone holes of a flute.

Antoine woke at midnight, restless and disturbed. Wandering to the bow, he rested on the bowsprit, gazing down on the maidenhead. He ran his hand through his curls several times before resting it thoughtfully on his square chin. The silence perturbed him, but so much had been amiss lately that he allowed himself to simply observe the changes. Just then, what seemed like a fog rolled in around the ship. It revealed itself to be gun smoke, however, and a very faint cannon fire broke the silence. The gunner's right hand twitched once, frantically, even as he consciously attempted to control his gesticulations. The metallic smell of blood wafted into his nostrils and rolled down to the back of his tongue, gagging him. Oranges, blacks, reds, greys, and yellows pigmented the smoke at various distances. Sudden sounds of crackling fire on starboard. Cries for help at the stern. A faraway wail of his brother rang like a wicked death knell. Bullets whizzed past his face from unseen shooters, squealing like a high-pitched hell. Then the drums and fifes began. At first, softly, and then with a deafening march. Now, signaling a frantic retreat, then notes of a tattoo, and once again a cacophonous assembly. Ghostly ships of all eras of time began to float out of the haze. Two sailed beneath the waves and rammed together under the ship like massive killer whales. Another soared overhead like a mammoth dragon. All these phantasms encroached dangerously to the frigate, an inch from disaster. As they exploded into shards and shrapnel, new ones would rapidly emerge from nowhere.

A behemoth cannon cast in the form of a hideous roaring lion emerged from beyond natural sight and aimed itself at him, then jutted and tremored in grating steps as it telescoped to within arm's reach of his body. From down the barrel, a projectile was hurled toward Antoine. In a split second before the impact, the searing lethal ball halted in midair and rotated on its crooked axis to show a face; ghastly, and yet familiar. It was the grotesque expression he had witnessed on his own father's face when a mamluk musket had sent an iron ball ripping through his neck. The eyes of the face ballooned out of their musculature, brows ripped high up the face, nostrils wide open as the mouth with curled lip and extended tongue, veins hemorrhaging in pure agony as blood erupted from the ears, eyes, and mouth.

The frozen Antoine couldn't draw a breath to scream as all the visions and sounds faded. He presently became aware of the embrace of another being. He opened his squeezed eyelids to see the pearlescent face of an angel holding him affectionately. Around the gunner, the specters and fiends faded and were blown away by a long balmy, aromatic breeze.

In a silken voice laced with honey, her wide, crooked smile seemed to pantomime a message:

"Dear brother, my son, let me take away all this horror. Do not mind these drifting apparitions of folly-filled men. Come with me forever, my righteous and innocent warrior of justice. You have done so much. All is finished now. All of your fanciful dragons have been slain. Now let us leave here and go beyond to live with awaiting father and brother in eternity." As she spoke, a choir of glass harps suffused the air.

"Get off me, fish!" gasped the gunner as he lifted her with one hand, raising her above his chest by her waist.

Her eyes slid wide across her skull, and her smile snapped upside-down into a grimace. The imperceptible harps seemed to shatter like they had been smashed by a mad queen. The silver selkie's nostrils flared, and the flowing hair sank slickly against her scalp with the weight of natural gravity. Then, her entire form recomposed suddenly back into place.

"You are so brave, my heroic gunner. Why do you tolerate the taunts of those phantoms of war?" she asked, her now lovely face an inch from his. Her eyes shimmered like faceted crystals, with unmistakable mischief smoldering deep within them. One pupil was open wide, and the other focused intensely on him. The irises seemed to be rotating hypnotically around the mismatched pupils. "Let me present you with a valuable secret. Your captain is a selfish, ambitious man who cares not if you live or die. He will never miss you. Not as your loving brother and father have missed you. I can take you to them. It is so easy. You won't feel any pain… just keep your hands wrapped onto me." She giggled a girlish giggle like breathless bubbles rising from the corpses lost in the depths of the lightless sea.

The gunner's mesmerization burst by this sick laughter. The silver selkie perceived this, and her countenance grew nasty. She clenched her pretty jaw and showed her sharp, long, crooked teeth. She gradually began to expand and malform again, cells of her skin sucking into themselves and others bubbling like cancer. Little limbs and facial features seemed to emerge and then wither again as she grew herself into a massive fang-toothed viperfish. She pressed herself down onto him, suffocating him with her wretched odor. The gunner shut his watering eyes tightly—and then spastically jerked himself emboldened again.

"I don't need you! I don't need your mercy or your paltry forgiveness!" Antoine wheezed.

"Suffer then as you wish, you witless air-sucking biped!" she screeched in a horrible, deep, demonic voice. As he attempted to crawl out of her reach with his back toward her, she transformed rapidly again, this time into a goblin shark with bloodshot eyes. Just before her jaws came lunging down, he turned and looked into her eyes, alarming her shark instincts. She loomed over him, stuck in place by the sight of her eyes, and in that precise moment, Antoine reached under her chin and tickled her with his fingertips, wise to the knowledge that it would send the shark into a catatonic state. The membrane slid over her eyeballs, and she rolled onto her back, and involuntarily slipped overboard, defeated and yet still furious at his resistance. Antoine crawled away from the rail painfully. The sounds of the whining shiplap sang his exhausted heart into a redemptive slumber as the brine softly kissed his burnished skin.

For the following week, the sun and moon danced arrhythmically in the sky. The crew tried to keep sane as the supply rations shrank. There was no rain to refresh the cask reserves, and the fish seemed repelled by the ever-increasing velocity of the current. The wide-traveled Antoine had brought dried buckthorn berries, ten times denser with vitamin C than oranges, which he had learned of from a red-haired Nestorian Mongol. Only the somewhat credulous powder monkey trusted the substance, having already been introduced to it in liquid form on the Silk Road. The other men's small cuts and surface wounds succumbed to scurvy over the week as the limey grog dwindled. Their hair grew longer and hung cumbersomely over their eyes. The seams of their jackets wore out as their beards grew wily.

Regardless, the captain pressed the crew onward, even as the strange smokes and wraiths visited them both in their dreams and in the darkest corners of the ship in their conscious visions. Tursun offered Captain Grey a concoction of olive oil and aloe for his now red, once white skin. It seemed to the captain that he was locked in a mocking game of tag with the sun, which made itself manifest in the shadows wherever he sought refuge. Meanwhile, the brooding navigator kept his untold insights secret, as he had long ago learned the wisdom to withhold.

During this week of wildly waning and waxing celestial bodies, Aquila had been using every tool at hand to try to determine the latitude and longitude of the ship, but he was dancing in a mad waltz with the wicked magic of the sea witch. Aquila zigzagged between his useless mechanisms in an attempt to observe the seascape. Exhausted and continuously foiled, he tried again to use his Chinese magnetic compasses, of which he kept two for redundancy. At first, when they pointed in the same direction, he had taken to the upper deck to search the sky for the constellation of seven stars arranged like a plow. The constellation rotated in the sky counterclockwise, pinned in position by Polaris, the North Star, which indicated the Earth's Axis and thus factored into a vessel's coordinates.

On the face of each of his Chinese compasses were four ninety-degree quadrants, partitioned further to eight points, creating thirty-two houses named after the constellations that hung in them. When he looked at the iron magnetite arms of his two compasses, they began to turn away from the lodestar and then face away from each other in entirely different directions. They began to spin, faster and faster, until they became too scalding to hold in his hands. He dropped the red-hot objects onto the deck. In frustration, he kicked them overboard, cursed the selkie, and returned to his laboratory below deck. There, he held in one hand a maritime chronometer, a most superior clock from the royal observatory, made with low friction bearings, steel springs, precious gems and jewels. It lost less than one second of time over a month, set to noon in London. In the other hand, he held another maritime chronometer meant to be set to the sun's midday peak in his location. With these he could calculate the difference of time in the sun's zenith, each hour indicating a fifteen-degree difference of the three hundred sixty degrees of the earth. With this simple math, he would be able to determine how far east or west of London the ship was. However, there were three problems: Aquila had no sense of the shape of the shoreline, he was utterly uninformed of the direction of the wind, and most frustrating of all, the silver selkie was intent on keeping him ignorant.

It would be hours until sunrise was expected, so Aquila went out to the upper deck again to measure the angle of Polaris relative to the horizon with his sextant dividers. As he held them up, they began to jerk. The arms snapped open and closed like a crab, wriggling out of his hands and scampering across the deck and overboard like a crustacean. Aquila had no chance to gather an accurate reading, as his octant behaved the same way. Though he was ready to catch the possessed beastie the second time, he slipped and fell hard on the deck. Not bothering to raise his head, he slammed his fist onto the planks. He drew a concentrated breath and collected himself. He estimated Polaris peaked at forty-six degrees above the horizon. Alas, the information proved useless without accurate context.

In his chambers were two globes; one was pasted with an inaccurate, spherical map of the earth and its oceans, with two rings around it, vertical and horizontal, so that one might line the globe up with the measured latitude and longitude of the ship. The other was pasted with a much more accurate map of the constellations, crossed with the same ruled rings, but neither orb would reveal the location of the frigate without measured longitude or latitude. Not that it mattered anyway, as the twisted magic of the selkie kept the two globes rotating as if water rolled them in their frames like floating glass fountain balls.

Before dawn, Captain Grey and the navigator stood together on the upper deck and waited for the sun to arise. Just as the sky began to kiss rose hues, the silver selkie sent the moon swinging through the sky to eclipse the sun. It was followed by a legion of thunderous black clouds to obscure its last trace. Lighting cracked down around the frightened men. One man lost his senses and screamed, "She wants to keep us in this world forever! She will break each of us and drag our souls to hell!"

"Get hold of yourself! Take that man to sickbay!" barked the captain. He spun on the heels of his polished boots as the lightning flashed around him. He faced Aquila. Dark boroughs hung beneath their sleep-deprived eyes as they scowled at one another.

"Well, what else have you got in those wizard's sleeves?" he demanded, breathing deeply and folding his arms across his strong chest.

Indeed, the secretive navigator was yet armed with science and alchemy against these astral mysteries. He drew his rare *sólarsteinn*, a rhombohedral sunstone composed of transparent calcite, marked with two ebony dots on the broad surface. By the birefringence of this material, light is refracted through twice, creating a double-vision from the light waves of the sun. The navigator lay on his back on the floor of the upper deck and held the *sólarsteinn* over his face. He rotated it laterally until the refracted dots became equally dark in their density; thus at a time which, according to the clockface set for London, he calculated to be forty minutes after sunset, he was able to identify the position of the sun in the sky with an accuracy of one degree. Unfortunately, the silver selkie noticed what Aquila was up to, and sent the sun deeper beneath the horizon to where it could cast no beams into the sky.

The frustrated navigator slapped his hands onto his forehead, pushed his greasy hair off his face, and stared up at the clouded sky. The full moon was now aglow with an orange ring.

"Captain Grey, look there!" he shouted, pointing at the clouds.

"By Jove!" rejoiced the captain, his mouth in an open smile, giving his sun-reddened cheeks the round look of Father Frost. The moonlight was gleaming brightly, ricocheting off the water and illuminating the underside of the clouds. A pattern had emerged in the clouds ahead of the bow. Their underbellies were on the portside pitch dark, and on the starboard they hung blackened as well, but straight down the center, the maidenhead splashed toward the illuminated undersides of a massive orographic cloud, which was being drawn high to form caps. This could only mean the vessel sailed towards a watery break between land masses, and those land masses were high peaks. The Pongus Maw was dead ahead, and they had been going the right way from the start.

The captain announced the news to the crew at once. In celebration, the men ran to the belfry to ring the ship's brass bell, awakening their brethren off watch to the hallowed news.

Space and time seemed to stand impossibly still as they drew closer, and the water casks and supplies dwindled dry. Some crew attempted to break into the bread room, so Captain Grey ordered Antoine to sleep there to prevent food theft. Meanwhile, Aquila and the captain drove each other to the edge of each other's patience. The captain confined the navigator to his laboratory to stare pointlessly at the possessed mechanisms and inaccurate maps. When he could take no more of this maddening solitude, he went to the helm silent and sour. There he lingered and cast his shadow over the captain. Martinus turned and faced Aquila.

"What do you plan for these men, Captain? There are no resources for survival in this strange place. Will you claim righteousness in the Custom of the Sea, and have us draw lots to taste the flesh of our brothers, as the Meduse? To live our lives as monsters forever after? Who shall we eat first, my captain? Shall we cook the injured or the miserable ones dying slowly of scurvy? You must order this ship to retreat. We must not venture further!"

As Captain Grey listened to Aquila, he ground his teeth and remained silent.

"Lock him in his chambers. He is mad and requires much rest," the captain ordered in a growl. Aquila squirmed as two men from the crew placed their hands on his neck and shoulders and led him below deck.

The following morning, a formation of cumulonimbus clouds appeared on the horizon, and the sky began to split down on the ship. A warm, moist breeze engulfed the ship in an updraft. The cold October water collided with this breeze, creating a vortex, and an hour later the weak crew found itself facing a full-force waterspout. Beneath the glass of the skylight, upon the pages of the captain's log, cursive words confessed the odds had begun to feel insurmountable.

The squall thundered overhead as the ship was drawn directly through it by the current. But this time, the selkie seemed to have mercy, or perhaps, the men feared, she just didn't want the game to end yet. Upon contact with the thrashing winds, fish began to rain down from the sky, for they had been sucked up in the cyclone.

"Fish dinner! Fish dinner!" cheered the crew as one and all scrambled across the deck catching the flapping Aral trout in their hands. The cook led the cleaning and skewering below deck, as the famished crew laughed, crumbs dangling from their beards, and smiled with open mouths at their luck. They joyfully argued over which of their gods had delivered the day's blessing. Men pressed their fingers around the eye sockets of the fish and popped the eyeballs into their mouths, as they knew the eyes were sources of precious fresh water. The tough, slimy grapes with a marine flavor were a delightful delicacy. They relished the grilled fish with ale and rum, all eventually finding their proper hanging cot to snore and slumber shoulder to shoulder with brotherly love.

Some men developed vibrio over the next few days, due to the raw fish eyes, but the rain from the cyclone had refilled their water casks, thus they were able to recover from the complex dehydration. They went on to argue which one of their gods was to blame for the illnesses they endured.

The following day, the powder monkey was resting on the lower deck when the sun had again left abruptly. The goddess Luna was unprepared for the summoning and so was absent from her stage when the curtain was drawn. Bahram thus sat alone in the dim light of the stars. The troubling sound of silver bubbles rose from the sea. Worse, the familiar giggle of his lost baby sister, Amira, arose as well. He walked over to the rail and looked down at the sea, afraid to find the likely source of the sounds. The glassy, placid water perfectly imitated the sky as if the frigate were a comet hastily sailing past black holes and asteroid fields.

The giggles rang again, this time from beside the helm. There Bahram ran to find the sight of Amira's curled locks, and her face turned away from him. She was engaged in conversation with the silver selkie in her most charming form.

The silver selkie was spangled with beautiful black, pink, and white pearls, iridescent shells, and fine lacey films in a rainbow of bright foams hued lavender, mint, coral, and cream. Her hair was pinned into an elaborate coif with decorative sea glass pinheads, with silky tendrils cascading behind her, over the rail, and swirling across the surface of the sea, trapping the little reflections of stars in her coils. Her glistening decolletage supported a massive necklace of dazzling diamond-encrusted starfish, and matching cuffs ringed her wrists.

"Oh, my little starfish, how I adore you," the selkie warmly cooed as her eyes gradually enlarged and increasingly shone. Her eyelashes moved in slow trails like the plumes of the extinct Indian ostrich. "You are so lovely and good. Come here and sit with me, and I will share my jewels with you." She held a small bouquet of colorful sea anemones out to Amira.

The innocent child stepped closer. Perplexed, Bahram drew a shallow breath, remembering how he saw the first mate sink into the depths with this fish demon.

"You're so pretty… are you a real mermaid? Can you talk to dolphins? Aren't you afraid of the sharks?" Amira sat down in place, fascinated.

The selkie laughed lightly, her large eyes beginning to bulge, and the eyelashes now seemed to be too many, like a fifty-armed Antarctic sun starfish. Her charm remained mesmerizing, scrambling the senses with warmth and comfort like a stiff, sweet rum.

"Oh, not at all, pretty girl. I am not a mermaid; I am far more important than that." The pitch of the selkie's infectious voice began to dip. As she continued it fell to a rumbling low tone and echoed like hellfire roaring in the underworld.

"I am a silver selkie, sovereign of all the ferocious sharks and the ancient fish monsters. The hydrorions that rip from the barnacles the pearl-laden clams and the kronosauruses that snatch from the sky the delicate parrots. Such beasts are among my devoted subjects. They swim beneath us now, waiting for a little princess who might ride on their scaly spines eternally. Perhaps I shall introduce you to them..."

Amira began to sniffle and wail as she received the meaning of the fearful words. Her brother was petrified and in awe of the demonic sea witch. At hearing his sister's wail, Bahram snapped out of the spell and sprinted towards her. The small girl abruptly turned to face him. Her curls blew away from her small face. Her flesh was bloated, blue, and black. Her little teeth hung from rotting gums and her eyelids had shriveled away, revealing the hollowed pits in her head.

The selkie threw her now gorgeous head back in a burst of loud, hearty laughter and clasped her hands together tightly at her cleavage. She lowered her grimacing gaze and waved her beautiful hand over the child's mangled face, restoring it to lively innocence.

"We can all be together again, brother, in the sea! Hurry, run to us!" Amira cried, the illusion disintegrating as her voice too began to waver in pitch.

Bahram screamed and fell to his knees. Suddenly, the seemingly unflappable selkie appeared startled; her eyes narrowed suspiciously, and her huge grin twisted into a snarl. She grabbed the little ghoul and slipped back into the water. The sun began to rise with haste, coloring the sky in soft shades of pink, yellow, and purple. Captain Grey's boots tapped evenly across the boards of the deck, stopping when he stood beside the boy. His long shadow cloaked Bahram.

"Do not succumb to the pranks of this witch. She is a distraction from our destiny," the captain ordered coldly.

"Amira… my sister… she drowned and she was here again, laughing and smiling… it wasn't a trick! Amira was here! She needed me!" he sobbed, spiraling.

"Listen to me, boy. Whatever the selkie has shown you was an illusion. The selkie wants to break you. Her smile is a veil, and she will twist the knife in when she sees your weakness. Forget that wicked mirage and fight for legacy. It is the only victory that lasts. Make your sister proud."

For a moment, Captain Grey laid a hand on the top of the boy's head, then turned and walked away. The powder monkey picked himself up with resolve. He would make Amira, the captain, and the rest of the men proud. He wiped away his tears.

The crew had acquired some knowledge of the flight ranges of bird species in their time at sea. When one spotted a Steppe eagle soaring alone above them, he and his mates determined that the ship was not more than fifty-four nautical miles from land. Shortly after this sighting, a topman working in the mainmast spotted a wedge of mute swans landing on the surface of the water. The others looked to where he pointed ho, and beheld the lovely white birds. In a moment their eyes peeled and their jaws gaped in horror.

The wind of the swans' beating wings and their splashy water landings created a low-frequency vibration that traveled through the water. From below the HMS *Jupiter*, something mercurial and massive maneuvered towards the birds, approaching them from behind. The ship rolled side to side as a semi-submerged aquatic apex predator with an elongated, streamlined body propelled its crescent-shaped tail up and down, akin to the motion of a shark.

In seconds, a lone hunter, the silver mosasaurus, surged upon the birds. The water burst in red and white as it ambushed them in a rapid accelerating shock. The beast had mutated from an ancient terrestrial life that the sea had long since swallowed and thus was equipped with lungs, not gills. The nostrils, positioned close to the eyes on the top of its stealth skull could breathe at the surface, and its retinas had evolved to sit close to each other, giving it a terrible mastery of depth perception. Hulking, agile flippers had grown where massive limbs once were, and the fractured snake-like cranial bones shifted the shape of the head to expand its jaw.

It swallowed the wedge of white swans whole, except those that were caught in sharp, polyphyodonty jawbone teeth. Verily, all of the teeth were continuously regrowing, ever retaining their needle grip, including the secondary pterygoid jaw teeth on the roof of the mosasaurus' mouth which were oriented inward and downward to the throat, gripping any slippery prey, impaled from above. Every subsequent bite sent the mauled, living victims deeper into the esophagus, towards the hellish stomach acid that dissolved shell and bone.

Turning around, the narrow-set eyes locked on the ship, and the silver monster meticulously performed a rip entry as it passed under the shadow beneath the ship, rolling it side to side once again as if it were a swinging cradle precariously positioned over immense danger. The seamen were too sick with fear to scream, and some fainted on the deck.

As the vessel drew nearer to the maw, a solar eclipse hung in the sky for the span of three natural days. The horizon drew near in a manner uncanny, seeming too swift for the sensation of the wind in the men's now long beards and uncut hair. They looked overboard with a loose sense of dead reckoning. They looked for any debris they could spot in the water, and aloud counted the seconds it took to pass, and then squabbled about how to multiply the time by the length of the ship. They blinked and rubbed their eyes when they each seemed to spot their own affects floating by the ship in the water. One man swore he saw a mate floating face down there, and pointed it out the other men. The frigate's wake rolled the body over, revealing it was the man's own face. He fainted and the others carried him away to sickbay, they themselves not wishing to explore the mystery of the ship's speed any longer. The velocity of the ship had now accelerated past thirty knots as it encountered gale-force winds. Tempestuous, dry hail storms began battering the ship and her weary crew.

The navigator, freed from confinement during the celebratory seafood feast, now stood on the deck breathing deeply in meditation. In a short time, pellets of frozen water began to bounce off the deck around him. His dark hair whipped wildly around his solemn face as he peered out toward the setting sun. To his horror, it seemed to be descending between the jagged peaks of innumerable, translucent, teal mountains. A large raindrop splashed onto his face. The men aboard the deck began to shout, and Captain Grey took to the helm. They were about to enter severe cross swells as the current ripped towards the hidden horizon.

The once limpid sea threw itself into dark masses of water which writhed, rammed into each other, doubled in amplitude and magnitude, formed white peaks like snow caps, and crashed down again at haphazard angles. Returning frantically to his chamber, Aquila hopelessly contemplated his astrolabes and sextants, searching for a hidden meaning in the chaos.

"You heartless, miserable hand of evil! You brutal, psychotic sadist!" he cried out in desperation, nearly weeping as the ship pitched at terrifying angles.

A wave smashed through the porthole. It swiftly wrapped itself around Aquila and soaked the man in ice-cold brine.

"Oh, my Eagle, have I been on your mind?" asked the now lovely selkie as she collected herself from the matter of the wave. She was dressed in a voluminous, scintillating, orchid-hued evening gown constructed of leafy sea dragons. Her two cold, moist hands wrapped lightly around his left hand. "It is a dream to see you again… after you broke your willing promise to come and be with me in the sea." Her voice was tender and full of longing.

"Selkie, you know I wished only to save those men. Your navigational prowess comes at a price too great for any *truly* willing man to pay. Have some dignity and release your false hope!" bellowed Aquila as he ripped his hand from hers.

Incensed, the beautiful sea maiden's skin turned a dark blue, dramatically contrasting her pearly white eyes and their turquoise irises. Her hair transformed into an oil slick entwined with exquisite rainbows. Her lips turned a deep plum and shimmered in the light of the desperately flickering candelabra.

Her pout curled as she whispered hoarsely, "You believe you can release yourself from my spell? Do you intend to sail away from me once again, daring hero?" She ran her hands across her flushed cheeks and down the sides of her thin neck, attempting to control her growing fury and communicate with the mortal. "I have an eternity of time to wait for your submission."

"You'll have eternity to ache in your self-imposed prison then!" the navigator roared as he threw her over his shoulder and hurled her back out the window from whence she had come crashing.

The misty echo of her moisture lingered in the room with him. The wind howled in vowels as the sky released a waterfall of the silver selkie's angry tears. The ship moaned heavily as Neptunian waves washed across the deck and the ship's capacity to displace water began to creep to a critical threshold.

During the surge, Captain Grey's unconscious body swung wildly in the ornate wooden bed that hung from ropes in his chamber. He was ensorcelled in a dark slumber, still as a corpse. He dreamt a long and continuous dream, though he felt the hanging cot swinging tumultuously. In a sudden shock, it seemed the ship came to a halt, and Martinus Grey was at last able to rise from his frightening paralysis. The ship was silent as the grave. He rubbed his hands over his face and eyes and blinked them open. He turned his head to where the skylight would have illuminated the room, but there was no light. He couldn't make out the distance to the floor in the pitch-black room. He trepidly reached his feet down, searching for the floor, further and further until his whole body was extended from the edge of the bed. Still, nothing. In a fit of courage, he released his grip on the bed and fell. He fell and fell as if plunged from the mainmast. At last, he landed with a splatter in the undulating sea. Now able to see again, he discovered he was beside the HMS *Jupiter*, and there in the water was Tursun, floating face down. The Captain wasted no time and began to swim over to the cabin boy. When he suddenly heard the cry of Bahram beside him, he turned and caught sight of a frenzy of dorsal fins sticking up out of the water around the young powder monkey. In an explosion of red and white, they ripped him under the waves. Then sharks began to appear around Tursun, and the captain knew he would be next if he didn't get aboard. The ship moaned with a booming crack, and as if whipped by an unseen wind, it began to sail directly away from the captain. He cried out helplessly as he felt the water vibrate with the movement of beasts swimming beneath him. Something suddenly tore him under and water entered his gaping, breathless mouth.

"Captain! Captain Grey, wake up! To the deck! The storm worsens!" a watchman shouted as he banged on the door. Martinus jolted up from the terrifying, cryptic slumber, washed in sweat, and found all around him water leaking into the chamber. He sprinted from his chambers to lead.

From the helm, the exhausted captain gripped the wheel with sheer adrenaline. Sniffling rain like the selkie's pouting heart took the place of the pouring tears, and the waves now seemed to be calming. Dawn broke through the eclipse, filling the cloudy sky with a theatre of warm, brilliant colors. Captain Grey regained his confidence, and his heart swelled with pride for his brave, disciplined crew. The rain grew sleepy and faded to a mist. The exhausted, malnourished crew operated the bile pumps as best they could to regain buoyancy and maneuverability.

The storm had greatly hastened the HMS *Jupiter* along its predestined course. Captain Grey now saw the strait, the fabled Pongus Maw. His mind's eye was filled with wild dreams of majestic processions under dedicated marble archways. Phantasms of blue velvet ribbons, golden plaques of honor, and the bequeathed nobility of kings paraded through his mind's eye. In the solace of the sun, he allowed his shoulders to drop and his psyche to recover.

"Bravo, Captain Grey," a lustrous voice rang, echoing. The spectacular silver selkie, now glistening in skin-tight, transparent vestments of pink and vanilla hues, wasted no time with charming words for the captain, who she found to be the weakest kind of fool. Thousands of glistening water droplets hung from her fingers, neck, ears, hair, and wrists, reflecting fire rainbows like brilliant-cut diamonds. "Such bravado and courage will be revered for all time… well, as long as you can pass through the maw, of course. It's not so easy, you know, as an ancient sea serpent sleeps there," She curled her hair on her fine fingers and her beautiful brow rose playfully. "The one called Pongus, from which the Maw derives its name. He has no patience for proud men who barge into his tranquil home. And you see, this beastie is my sweet pet. Only I can calm and restrain him. What would you do to reach the other side of the maw, O Captain? Perhaps you could spare a few souls?"

His desire, pride, duty, and dreams twisted and turned curiously inside his heart. Entirely undecided, his eyes took in her ever-shifting and alluring form, then moved to the faces of the men on deck who proficiently bustled about.

"What are these men to me?" he pondered aloud, directed at himself and heard by the powerful immortal.

"They can die in the maw, or they can die in the maw for a cause, Captain Grey. The opportunity for you to choose is slipping away. I expected to encounter a more decisive leader, especially given the state of this crew and vessel. Give their deaths meaning, Captain. You must say the word before your men are discovered by my sweet pet! Hurry, Grey! Tell me now, how would you feel if you had double the reward you dream of? I can give you anything, everything you have ever wished for!" pealed the silver selkie, with an unhinged and dismissive laughter in her voice. Her face twisted into many fishy forms and then back again to a warm, saccharine countenance.

The captain knew now, his eyes opening as wide as his mind, that he had led all these good, loyal men toward briny graves. They had each fought their own demons, brought to vivid reality by this putrid sea witch. Some had fallen to their flaws; others survived through the thin power of humility. Alas, their fate had been sealed since the first sighting of the silver-scaled porpoise, and those repeated warnings of the navigator.

Captain Martinus Grey gave his solemn answer, and watched as the selkie slithered back into the sea again. Then he saw Aquila standing there, lurking insidiously.

"Why did you know of the maw, Aquila? How came this knowledge to you?" the captain asked without thought, overcome with a primal intuition. "What made you recognize that porpoise as evil, when I, who has sailed so many seas, had never heard such a thing from any other sailor?"

Aquila stood glowering at the captain. He was silent. His chest heaved as panic and anger took control of him.

"Tell me, you Christian bastard! How did you know this? You knew her! You knew where she was taking us all along! I'll have you hanged for your treachery! You are the reason we face this danger now, you evil coward!" spat the captain.

"Yes, I knew! I knew we were caught in the terrible net of the selkie from the moment that unnatural swell took us from the battle. She had impressed a ship I was aboard before, but I was able to evade her bargaining, I admit. But you shall not accuse anyone else of casting us into this nightmare oblivion, Captain Grey. Your own evil, selfish vainglory could not be stopped by any one of us. You perfectly acted the role of the fool for the selkie, to the demise of us all!" howled the navigator.

The captain unsheathed his cutlass. "Evade her bargaining, you insidious liar? No, I think it was you she trapped us here for! You're the reason she sent the swell! The damned fool is you, Aquila! Damn you for dancing with a sea demon! Now you will fulfill your promise to her, and rest in her waters, so your mates can be free!"

Aquila snatched a worm, a pole tipped with a double-helix corkscrew, from beside a canon. The men roared at each other as they charged into the brawl. Martinus spun his blade in an overhead flower, accumulating power before bringing the blade down, while Aquila defended himself with a cross-body swing against the blade from left to right without returning a strike. Martinus then swung the blade across his body in another lightning-fast flower, and sent the ricochetting energy back toward center with a twist of his torso. His eyes never unlocked from the target: the navigator's neck. On time, Aquila of the East lunged down on his back leg, with his front leg extended in front of himself, then low to the ground like a cobra he switched the bend from his back knee to the front, and with the flow of kinetic energy he shot his right arm that held the worm forward, the other arm extended above, balanced in a four-fingered expression of a broadsword. He sent the tips of the spiraling helix twisting upwards towards the captain's exposed armpit. The needles sunk into the flesh with a bloody sting. The captain's sword fell in a clamor and went spinning across the deck, as he grabbed the worm with both hands and pulled it out of his wound.

Aquila stood, standing tall over the Captain as a silent truce was called between their eyes.

"You will not survive this, Aquila. When we reach land, I'll have you be hanged for your secrets, for treason against the HMS *Jupiter*," Captain Grey murmured coldly.

Aquila calmly replaced the worm beside the canon and spoke with a groaning sigh, "I do not foresee any of us dying by hanging, my captain."

Now the maw gaped before them like the toothed jaw of an ungodly crocodile. The watching moon was full, washing over the ship in a flood of icy, grey light. The vessel sailed past treacherous crystal shoals that jutted from beneath the water, tangling in straight blades into the narrowing mouth of the maw. Here and there seemed to be the silhouettes of wrecked ships from across the ages. In the water floated the remnants of a wooden head of a dragon from a lost Viking voyage. It stared at the crew with wild, frenzied eyes as if trapped in the eternal nightmare of a vicious death.

"...björg..." rang softly in the air.

The crew whipped their faces around for the source of the disembodied voice. They looked into each other's eyes for answers, only met with panic and terror in the expressions of their company.

A dense umber fog rolled from between the jagged, smokey quartz that barbed the entry in pointed prisms and peaks.

Moonlight strained in rays and ribbons around the spikey walls, otherwise reaching through the minerals and casting colored light not unlike the stained glass of a Gothic Cathedral.

The water glided quietly. The only sounds were of waves lapping gently as the maidenhead cut through them, and a tropical breeze luffing in the sails. This silent aura, like a hallowed crypt, kept the men on edge.

"...azarni..." whispered into their ears, and drifted away on the wind. The men clutched their weapons and began to sweat.

An unseen object splashed down from the cliff ahead of them, and the men jolted and recoiled. Another fell somewhere behind them, bouncing off the crystal walls before landing, echoing along its descent like the ticking hands of a clock. The wind whistled through the cretaceous crevices. It seemed to whisper pleas in Coptic, yet none could understand.

A low bass pop, like the cracking of massive hulking joints, boomed through the maw.

A foul smell of rotting ocean life wafted into the air.

A swelling, cold shadow of a Titan slowly fell over them.

Men looked at each other as the moonlight disappeared over each of them like black sheets over corpses. What it was hung hundreds of feet above the mainmast, consciously positioning itself in silhouette by the moon.

"...ezer... help me... Allah save us..." More voices spoke. They seemed to rise from the water, like a choir of drowned ghosts. "... fire run... fire run... ahhh—" The words began to form nonsensical chants in strange lilts, and the screams cut short as if the speaker were suddenly cut off.

It was a taloned toe that rose from the water, followed by a second. These two mighty sinuous digits hung above the ship and obscured the moonlight. They wrapped around the foremast and pulled it slowly down towards the water, like a babe would palm a new object and draw it to its mouth.

The source of the voice was one being, but the voices were many, and all of them seemed to be spoken from a fleshless face formed of teeth, without the softening closure of lips. The mouth emerged as the frigate tilted and pitched like it rode a waterfall over a whirling cliff. The crew grasped anything. Men slipped. Ropes snapped. Skulls smacked on planks. None could scream.

"hatzilu… hello… peekaboo… my god help me!" thundered through the air, in a merry greeting.

The Pongus had emerged from the depths.

The monster's beak cresting from the murky water, peaking out of the dense umber mist. It now let out a shriek in one hundred thirty-five decibels, a shockwave which resounded against the barren quartz walls of the maw passage, causing the very air to vibrate. All the men's equilibrium was blasted and shot as if caught directly in the crossfire a bombardment of cannons. Their brains rang in confusion as their eardrums frantically tried to recalibrate. Their deaf disorientation was worsened as the ship tilted rapidly back into position when the Pongus snapped off the foremast. The ship thrust with helpless upheaval towards the stern, sending men, swords, and cannons rolling like a stampede of death through the chaotic crew.

With the retreat of the Pongus, the cold, mean moonlight returned and shone through stained glass crystal spikes in bars of dark and light. The bow and stern found balance again in sickening swings like a pendulum clock as the Pongus slipped beneath the ship.

A massive wave slapped on the starboard. Then a thunderous thud on the port. Next a swell again near the stern.

"It is circling us, the unholy vulture!" wailed Tursun.

"This beast is not acting on instinct—it thinks!" cried Bahram.

At that moment, the helm began to spin wildly as if possessed. The Pongus had twisted the rudder and ripped the mechanism of ropes out of the arc deep inside the ship, disabling its prey.

Now, a few yards away, it rose, and it mimicked Bahram.

"It thinks… It thinks…" it parroted nearly perfectly in the same wailing cry.

The crew understood now that the voices that created the macabre choir they had heard in the water were the last words of a world of crews who had been taken into this cathedral of death. The Pongus was imitating them, playfully, mockingly, wickedly, like a cat with an injured sparrow.

All eyes darted to behold the beast. It was mammoth, covered in slick green feathers, like those of a penguin, with a heaving, ruby underbelly. Round, orange eyes ringed in icy blue held the pulsing red pupils that locked onto the ship with chilling intelligence. It charged directly towards the ship, drew its thick black tongue into its mouth, and extended its bony serrated beak, fused with fossilized crinoids and ammonites, towards the ship.

"To the cannons, you cowards!" screamed Captain Grey as his leadership engaged.

Men scrambled to piece together any firepower they could. Bahram ran to the copper-lined magazine with every powder horn he could hold. Tursun slid and slipped across the now bloodied deck in panic and disorientation.

Antoine grabbed a sea service musket, checked if the flint was secure in the jaws of the cock, loaded the powder, rammed the load, and took aim. He fired.

The iron ball whizzed through the air in what seemed to be slow motion. It zipped gracefully past the Pongus, flying like an arrow from the bow of Eros himself, and nested itself in the bosom of the lady who stood on the crystal peaks, her wild smile twisting in dismay and pain. Cupid pierced the steel heart of the silver selkie. She gasped, and swooned in shock.

The Pongus, with its multicolored eyes on the side of its head, saw everything in its periphery. It shrieked ominously at the sight of its injured mistress.

The helpless men cried out and scattered in defenseless terror. Aquila ran, arms opened widely to his sides, toward the Pongus, courageous, unarmed, and resolved. The monster screeched again and lunged down like a guillotine blade. Just as it severed the navigator in two parts, the writhing, wounded immortal selkie, already rapidly healing, wailed a woeful howl that turned the blood of the recoiling men ice cold. The Pongus turned to face her and exhaled a rumbling coo of confusion. The silver selkie rose to her knees upon the quartz cliff and wept with her hands gripping her hair in misery. In sacrificing himself for the greater good and dying without drowning, he had broken her righteous claim to possess his soul. He was now a martyred spirit, canonized for eternity.

She lowered her head, now not like a woman at all, but like a deadly mosasaurus. The Pongus understood her intuitively and turned its focus back toward the ship, which was now racing away. It hastily limped and crawled as men fell over their own feet, desperate to exit the Pongus Maw strait.

The frantic captain cried out to the selkie that he had rejected her deal and she had taken her sailor's soul anyway, therefore she must release the remaining men as promised. But the furious silver selkie didn't care if the balance of the universe was severed for all time. Her womanly, furious vengeance had to be fulfilled. The thunderous Pongus raised its head once again and came cracking down on the trailing stern like a bolt of lightning, pulverizing the ship into splintered wreckage with a sickening boom and creating a calamitous tidal wave that thrashed the vessel out of the maw. Catastrophe and chaos were instant. The bow was lifted from the water, and the maidenhead rose like an angel into the sky, causing all aboard to lose their footing and fly through the air. Every cannon broke loose and rolled like hippopotamuses across the gun deck. The frigate buckled inward, and water rushed in through the severed planks. The powder magazine ignited and the sails were enflamed by the splintering wood as if they were lit by a match. Ropes snapped like taut harp strings and whipped through the air as the mainmast fell, launching the men on the ratlines into the sea. Other sailors held onto the rail or anything they could find while Captain Gray gripped the wheel pathetically as the already useless rudder was thrashed apart by the debris churning through the water.

Tursun gripped a rolled hammock in his arms and wailed a Zoroastrian prayer memorized from his youth, a cry for righteous fulfillment and truth: "Ashem vohu vahishtem asti. Ushta asti, ushta ahmai. Hyat ashai vahishtai ashem."

Clinging to his side, and also bearing a rolled hammock, Bahram chanted an invocation of the Manichaeist forces of light for protection and safekeeping from the forces of darkness. He begged the divine light to triumph over the silver selkie as the hull collapsed under the tons of pressure exerted by the water.

As Captain Grey, still clutching the now-dismembered wheel, sank beneath the waves, the silver selkie appeared before him in all her splendor and her glory.

"Let me impart to you this wisdom, Martinus Grey, as you writhe in your small and meaningless death. The folly you died for in this life was your own insignificant ego. Life is not generous, Captain, but it is kind. In its true nature, it is noble. It is through the ripples of our noblest moments that life reaches outside the small bodies it occupies and gives to itself its own love. Now sleep, and dream of what you could have done, you unimportant insect!" she spoke as her voice sank to a hellish, vibrating rumble, and the captain could no longer distinguish the air bubbles around him from those millions of common twinkling planets, moons, and stars he had seen in the nights of his brief life.

A small girl collected seashells along the shore with her older sister. The pair of children had just discovered a strange astronomical device on the beach, pondering the astrolabe in their hands. As they held it up to the sky, the little one noticed something.

"Look, sissy, a man is sleeping on the beach."

The girls inspected the man, who stirred as they poked him. Softly, they asked if he was dreaming. Captain Gray opened his eyes. He lifted his head and looked around. Nearly three hundred crewmen had washed ashore. They slumbered around him on the beach like a roost of starlings. By the gods, they had survived and lived to tell the tale of the wraiths they had seen in the Pongus Maw.

***Jo Gamel** is an award-winning international artist whose sparkly artwork has spangled the walls of the Louvre and the European Museum of Modern Art. Singer, bassist, and video director of the power-prog metal band **Metal of Jupiter**—a quirky creation Fenriz favored on his podcast—she also sculpts seashell-shaped soaps, hosts the global Rock Goddess interview channel, and teaches the art of spinning your ADHD into gold. A poet, art college instructor, grad school dropout, bookbinder, and pixie, she thrives on the absurd, the whimsical, and the unapologetically useless. Her two colorful parrots shriek in protest when she leaves the house, which is fine because she leans agoraphobic. For more entertainment, find her on Instagram @oracleofjupiter.*

Escape from the Bad Magick

A prequel to "Journey in Somnamblia"

by Jean-Pierre Abboud

To those uninitiated it would seem not to stand on its own, but Weydan's garden fortress gleamed as if suspended in the sky. Blackened spirals of onyx stone twisted on a clifftop as if in perfect harmony with the ground beneath it. Yet there it floated with its towers unrazed; a message, if any, to the bound vassals of the city's power and energy. Its beauty matched by its foreboding godlike edifice told the vassals who ruled and who will continue to wield magick in all its forms for their glorious land. The sun, beginning to descend, chimed the cosmic hour of celebration; an event that to Weydan's elite was both perennial and ubiquitous. In this meeting the Parsimmons of Weydan arrived to meet their guests atop the sprawling high opticon within the city center.

The day of Zora Roch's arrival had been meticulously planned. Their empire existed long before Weydan, but had in the last century grown fond of its gold. Everything from complex spells to clothing and fashion could be seen within its walls; only the highest of Weydan were even allowed to travel there. These were an ancient and deeply disciplined caste, interested in powering the business of Weydan to continue their very real golden age. Of those who dwell within the alleys and grottos of the city, endless stories and legends are told of Zora Roch.

A land of magickal might descended upon Weydan's city stronghold in the form of a horde of blackened spectres atop a floating theatre. Glints of shining green smacked the eyes of the Parsimmons as they marveled at the flying spectres circling the approaching structure in the air. Almost as if buttressed by the physical force of their flight, the people of Weydan knew it was a show, albeit a spectacular one. They weaved and cascaded around the flying structure like bats. Somewhere there were many suffering mage slave beings driving their life force to generate this spectacle. And if there were any major difference at this time between the two realms, it would ring true that the thralls of Zora Roch's mage slavers had been made to love their fate. To be birthed into it and cherish it. Certain higher powers in Weydan envied these wizards' ability to bind.

The shining garden on its impossible cliffside castle, flanked by three gilded towers, glowed brightly in the red-skied evening. The group in ceremonial gowns of white and green were the Parsimmons who governed Weydan brutally, exporting its gold. The opposite group clad in black were the outer city and province nobles and wizards of Zora Roch. They set their emerald theatre in the courtyard to awestruck gasps. From an eagle's view, it seemed a green gleaming chessboard garden party, but this was a rare event. These two groups only congregated twice a year, to man the pieces of the land, to cognitively wield the future so to collect on the present; they were the perennial gods of this world. They were men, like those below them, but in command of magick power they were superior and the masses yielded in dependence.

While shows of strength and boasts of power were not alien to such an event, the main activity was business. There would be no performance of any kind or musical attraction, those were simply for the lower caste to waste their time. Only results and demonstrations of power could count in this place. The Parsimmons met a certain quota in gold every year as their city's engine runs on alchemy; Weydan required this standard to be met with no exception. The wizards of Zora Roch made their play centuries ago that Weydan could function on a draconian, punishment-based model. Magick takes a lot out of a body, so for water to be plentiful and gold to be produced, the machine calls for bodies, more so bodies with no agency. How do you take away agency? By convicting heretics, the treasonous, and bad actors.

Hand them a sword if they're loyal enough. Otherwise? Drain them of their energy to power magick conduits. A noble sacrifice for a life lived poorly; if anything, they saw it as a mercy.

During the celebration, each honoured guest answered only to a number. This tradition dated back from before the days of Weydan: the ancient wizard rite to erase the ego and crude visage of humanity. All that is left is one's enumeration of power and their ability to wield it. To possess a number was only for the Zora Roch and Parsimmons; no common man in Weydan could ever receive such a symbol of status. Mataera Nom, the daughter of twelve, mother not of noble line, would never receive a number.

Suddenly the merriment subsided. Every head had turned to confront a baffling use of magick. There was the grand crystalline bowl, a perfectly cut and balanced piece of enormous diameter meant to rest within a dead mountainside for the country dragon to soak in. It collected Weydan's toxic rain, which, while poison for wheat or drinking water, was perfect for a dragon's scales. But there it was, floating in midair as if on a collision course with the great event. The party began to scatter in panic, running to the outer edges and exits of the castle garden. The bowl, hovering overhead like the point of a giant top, began to descend.

The grand crystalline bowl gleamed with the purest water ever seen, so many millions of gallons appearing out of thin air. Every noble of the outer cities, every emissary of the high order, stared in a silenced gasp. Like Gods of Olympus, there they stood in awe, mystified at the effortless exhibition of the rebellious daughter of Parsimmon lords Mataera Nom. To produce the purest water at such an amount confounded purveyors of high alchemy and elite sorcery.

This power could change the lives of everyone. Water and gold, the base elements of life and magick. Endless water could enable discovery of gold without the draining power of magick, to reorient the practical application of alchemy to serve higher knowledge.

Mataera envisioned a new enlightenment for Weydan, mage slavers no more, vassal and conduit based draconian punishment no longer needed. Did she herself see that such a gambit could potentially end up leading to her downfall? To reveal the extent of her power to all of the nobles and emissaries carried that risk, but the message remained far too important. Tomorrow everyone from the highest gilded palace to the dankest pit would know.

"That they know it's possible is more important than my safety. Everything would simply be the same if I hadn't done it. It's all right if it all changes for me."

Even though she knew, Mataera couldn't face the innocent ones. The ones along for the ride. Her mother, the children of the order, the old avuncular Emissary Hansin who she always confided in before she knew the truth, before she saw the mage vassals. Even during the exhibition of her spell, she saw Hansin's face, wide set and in wonderment, as the world had finally changed. Abon, her lifelong guard and mentor, found her wandering the tower.

"It can't continue, you simply cannot be this way. Do you have any idea? Any idea at all how you're ruining such a momentous event for your most important relations?"

Mataera looked upon the face of Abon, who she thought she once knew. Someone who, recalling the past, would always act in good faith, loyalty, and compassion.

"How could things change so abruptly?" Mataera responded. "How could my spells have caused such a change, outside of their own action and containment? Almost as if they've turned against me, the damned hexes. They wield their power outside of the small space I perceive, their effects lingering, entangling the minds of these weak nobility. They are weak, aren't they? Even so one cannot realistically survive alone. Abon, I meant no harm to the high order or to cause concern."

"The cauldron has boiled over, no way to put it back again."

"Let's drop the panic," she snapped back. "You need to

understand I have trained my whole life. I have seen the trouble we will face if we continue to bind and harness our people. A threshold driven past, where my magick can drive it back."

"They're already talking. They're already making their move."

"Then let them move. Far better than to be frozen in place! Perhaps lifting the crystalline bowl to the top of the castle garden was too grand a gesture, but I had to make it so everyone could see. Everyone down there, Abon."

Any established order faces the risk of change. In truth the exhibition of Mataera's spell did not produce a whisper of mirth. Spells to catalyze precipitation existed for centuries, however this particular unorthodox potion and prayer yielded more water for a month than mage slavers could ever derive. The truth is that was the change, the ideal land of Weydan and its prosperity could no longer shine in Mataera's eyes. Magick cannot be wielded indefinitely without a body as a conduit to carry such charge; the magick required to sustain Weydan's production of gold, as well as production of food and water for its people, necessitated the mage slavers drive the unlucky ones to death. A ghastly fate which usually befell anyone from a petty enemy of the order to a rival mage.

Abon stormed off, resigned to the fact that his position was no longer safe. Mataera's continual stride towards unorthodox magick, to operate outside the confines of established parameters, was unheard of. To Abon, training Mataera as a young daughter of the high order came as another job, another opportunity to prove himself, and not just in Weydan. To be officially selected to exit the confines of the powered walls, to trade and deal with the outer land cities, was a privilege for a chosen few. Abon laughed nervously to himself. "I guess she'll get me beyond the walls one way or another," he said, knowing that it all had changed.

Unsure of the next action Abon would take, Mataera cautiously moved back to her quarters. Without hesitation, she began to undress quickly, favoring her armour and finely engineered effects, anticipating an attack at worst. Tossing her ceremonial gown aside, it skittered on the ground, making slightly more of a sound than expected. "What was that?" she said aloud. Mataera suddenly realized in haste she hadn't lit her lantern or her torch. Unaware of which sense hit first, she reached into the dark, grasping a handful of cloak and trembling shoulder.

"Merrick, you perverted little slime!"

"I'm sorry, Mistress, I happened in here by mistake!"

"You've made a mistake, to be sure. You'll do what I say now. Or everyone knows. Sit down and be quiet," she firmly commanded as she laced her boots and unracked her armour. Merrick trembled in compliance, cursing the error he had committed. Despite his lesser station as a pitch man for moving empty estates, his place put him close enough to the high order to hear the whispers and secrets. *They plan to take her out. What is it if I get a look or two, how is it even wrong? Not any more wrong than what they'll do to her. I can take this and wait; she'll be had soon enough I haaaa—*

Now, not unlike a stroke, the possession suddenly took hold in crystalline bursts through Merrick's mind. Ruminating on his predicament caught him vain and foolish, as he was unaware of Mataera's spell of possession. Her hand now on his forehead, his limbs fell slack, then were harnessed with convalescent energy.

"We'll see who you've been talking to, you little pervert."

"You're the foolish overpowered idealist stealing from dragons. Everyone knows you can no longer be trusted. I'll do with you as I please."

"You'll what?" she spat, pushing the diminutive mage fiercely against the brick wall. "You'll die."

"We'll see who does," Merrick meekly choked.

"No. No, you're coming with me. We're leaving tonight."

"You fool, you expect me to *aaaaahh—*" The crystalline bursts turned into excruciating migraines and hallucinations, completely severing Merrick's mind from his body.

"I can't believe you've reduced me to binding," Mataera angrily lamented to herself, "but this will be all right for the time."

Eyeing Abon in the distance of the great hall, Mataera knew that fast flight was the only option. If a vile creature as pathetic as Merrick could be so bold there was no telling what danger awaited her, and clearly any still friendly relations would turn. The only way is out, the only way to pass through Zora Roch, a suicide to go but surely a suicide to stay. The only way is to die, Mataera remitted bluntly, and she knew Abon would understand.

Since the publication of the first Swords of Steel ***JP Abboud*** *has been busy, having long runs with Canadian bands* ***Gatekeeper,*** ***Traveler,*** *and* ***Syrinx*** *as well as newer stints with US groups* ***Among These Ashes, Viperwitch,*** *and his own solo project LP in the works. Revisiting the world of "Journey in Somnamblia," we find where the exile began and how quickly our heroine falls out of favour.*

For an Unnamed Succubus

by Howie K. Bentley

When I was a young man, I was a peddler of… sweets. I had no qualms about the grief this led to for others, and it afforded me the time to develop my hand at crafting verse. My buyers came at night and were often female, though I let it be known that my preferred customers came without their pimps.

Sometimes, I would even partake of the sweets myself, at least, those of the milder, less addictive variety. For at the time, I greatly admired the works of Baudelaire and Balzac among other famous hashish eaters, and I, being young, dumb, and the other thing I will get to presently, used what they used in a bid for greatness. Eventually, as I recognized my own pretentiousness, I disposed of it along with my affectation. It also became clear to me that cannabis was not only turning my mind against me, but with some distance and clarity I also perceived my efforts under its influence as artificial at best.

Now, a young man, on the surface, is little more than a vessel of flesh *besatt* by a rutting satyr, but I had done plenty of satyring, and about this time C. had come into my life. She had become my best friend, falling madly in love with me, and eventually running all the other women off. And I had allowed it, if nothing else, for the simple fact that she tolerated my frequent absences, though I sat right next to her, entranced, listening to the Secret Radio. She told me my muse would always be my first mistress, and she was fine with being second. Her visits had increased to the point that she was staying at my house most of the time and we eventually got married.

C. was the light that balanced the darkness within me, and I loved her. But the longer we were together, the more our relationship became of a spiritual nature, and less like that of a man and a woman. She longed more and more for the light, and I had gone deeper into the darkness. Simply stated, we were growing apart. I had spent most of my adult life with her, but there had always been fantasies about other women, some I had previously known, some I wanted to know, and some were imagined. My wife was pure of heart, but frankly, rather bland in bed. When one marries Eve, he spends the rest of his life pining for Lilith and vice versa. Despite this, I never cheated on her. Neither of us had betrayed the other except in our own secret thoughts. I longed for a dangerous female companion to go out with at night and commit crimes, and my lust for the otherness continued to grow throughout the years.

C. died a year ago this past summer. She was eight years older than me. I have been alone with my thoughts for some time now, and though I am not too far from entering my autumn years, I have been existing in the perpetual autumn of my mind the majority of my life. What stimulation I experienced regarding any flesh and blood woman lay in memories of when C. was healthy and young. And any "real" woman I saw walk in the daylight only reminded me of the stench of necrot, and I could only think of her as an animate rotten corpse because of what C. and I had gone through at the end of her life. Even then, I sometimes longed for a woman's embrace beyond the corporeal. A month ago yesterday my thoughts went to my wife, and I could feel her again as I spilled my seed under the blast of warm water from the jetting showerhead. She liked to do it in the shower.

As I stepped out of the shower to finish drying myself, a glance at my medicine cabinet mirror caught my attention where it hung slightly ajar. Where dripping lines ran, I read the message, "If you pine for a corpse a succubus will appear."

Even for one who is so common and inspired by nothing in that they cling tightly to the concept of pareidolia for fear of rushing back into the arms of the church they so loathe, it would have been indisputably apparent that those words had seemingly written themselves on that mirror of their own volition.

I preferred to only use the two light bulbs sitting to either side of the mirror and leave the overhead light off in the bathroom. I found it more relaxing to shower in low lighting. I raised my hand to the mirrored medicine cabinet door, pushing it shut to better examine the message. As I closed the door a quick glimpse behind me revealed the imposing figure of a winged being in the shower stall I had just vacated. I sucked in my breath just as the lights dimmed and went out. Something grabbed me around my chest and squeezed tightly, then quickly let go as the lights flashed back on.

* * *

I lay in my king-sized bed with a stack of pillows propping me up and relaxed, waiting for the Secret Radio to come on. The post-coital state would last a long time and allow me to go about my work undisturbed. My pen and notebook lay by me on my nightstand; my arc floor lamp shed soft light on the corner where I lay in my dim bedroom.

At some point I had briefly fallen asleep. Suddenly something prodded my psyche and my whole body jerked awake. Was the Radio coming on?

First there appeared a shadowy presence in the bedroom doorframe. Within the black shapeless form, a solid whiteness moved like smoke, emerging from the darkness and, unfurling, formed into a winged woman. She raised her head, but I could not make out any defined features as her eyes and general countenance were veiled within the chiaroscuro of the mild light emitting from the lamp hovering over my nightstand table.

Time slowed down as she flowed languidly across the room, exhibiting the naked splendor of her milk-white flesh. I felt the blood rush to my groin and a wave of heat surged, opening a path that travelled through my abdomen, chest, throat, and into my tingling head. She crawled across the bed and over me, her long black hair, followed by her ample breasts, brushing my skin, now stinging with ecstasy. Then she spread her membranous wings and straddled me, riding up and down on my lap. I saw myself outside myself, standing in front of us, and she joined me and walked up behind the me outside of me, laying her head on my shoulder. Now, there were the two of us rutting in my bed, and the two of us who had joined the first two in our own private orgy. Standing behind me and running her hands all over my *doppelgänger*, she spread wide her bat-like wings, enfolding me in her embrace wherein we entwined like mating serpents and formed into a cylindrical pole-like tube. She thrust and gyrated her hips rhythmically, and bounced up and down on me as we pounded my mattress with fervor. I raised my hands to clutch at her swinging breasts as she rode me. I still could not see the face of this mysterious winged woman even as close as we were, for what portion of her visage was not obscured by her long raven hair was yet veiled in shadow. But as the cylindrical fetish that was the entwined ethereal bodies of me and my nascent nether-realm lover hummed, it rotated and slowly raised from the floor. As we thrusted into each other on the bed her countenance was revealed to me. For on the rotating object, I saw the face of every woman whom I had ever been infatuated with, even some only imagined, but lost to memory in ages fell past. Her face was all of them. Every one of the faces contorted in the throes of ecstasy. And issuing from their mouths, their moaning and groaning, shrieking and screaming, was a dissonant choir of the damned composed to extol the virtues of the sweet ecstasies of Hell only few will dare to experience.

The second set of us, our distilled essences contained in the cylindrical shaped weirdling, arose into the night sky together, violently unbound, together, an abhorrence like a seedling from beyond the stars that rode on I-know-not-what, and though she was silent, she proudly showed me her demesne. Not one, but two moons burned in the skies of the monochromatic landscape and cast down its stark white witchfire upon a vista that I had known before I could speak. The twin moons illuminated the barren embankments littered with dirt and shale. Gnarled boles with wide bases lined the edge of the embankment on the right and wept, spatting their venomous tears out the ends of branches that reached out and beckoned like the arms of a dead lover.

The tree's tears hissed acid in pools of lament that sent up vapors I dared not breathe. I held my breath. "What's wrong?" she said. It was my wife's voice. She had said it that night that I had to finally admit to myself that she wouldn't be around much longer. That night I had dreamed we were walking down the driveway together holding hands. "What's wrong?" I said. There was an ambulance blocking the end of the driveway. When I woke up, she was gone. The house was redolent of cinnamon and grave flowers barely masking the stench of rotten flesh.

I had briefly forgotten the present and my winged woman, or was it intentional on her part? Had she shown me the memory on purpose?

Now, there appeared human cattle in pens, naked and shorn. They ran to the fences where we passed, pleading in vain with desperate gestures, for they were without voice. Up ahead we came upon lofty structures topped by domes where long, needle-like spires jutted up displaying impaled bodies. The pens enclosing the prisoners I had just witnessed made sense now. I knew she was smiling, though I could not see her inside our strange means of transportation.

She showed me the sorcerers I had been in my other incarnations from epochs I had never known existed. And we had all fallen madly in love with her. She showed me I was Dylactus Sargoth, a withered mummy she had stolen from his tomb and brought back from black oblivion to sit by her side and transcribe her secret alphabet. It was written in a book made of sin and bound in the dried essence of abortions. This was to be bestowed as a gift to those lovers she deemed worthy.

Shullen-Nashob: Then I was a malformed old man animated by the Jinn that possessed me and fueled by my hatred of mankind. She had given me back my youth and power by transforming me into a corpse-like spider the size of a big man, and she allowed me to violently join in her infamous revels.

Questa-Bload: I wasn't really a sorcerer, or anything else, but the sigil of a servitor revealed and recorded by the now-forgotten hand of a shaman who had quickly scrawled the concept hinting at my existence on his cave wall under the influence of some concoction he had ingested containing a poisonous plant. He died later that night leaving me to languish in obscurity until she found me and brought me forth into being.

Dwetchul! Oh, merciful lord, the thought of even the name of whatever that is makes me… My mind can never bury the memory deep enough in my subconscious, even though I can't begin to grasp if it is a creature, a concept, or some other abstract thing that is beyond my human ability to comprehend. Oh Lord, whether you govern from the celestial heights, or the infernal abyss, beyond the stars we know, or the depths beneath the ocean floor, strike this memory from my mind. I don't want to take it with me wherever I am going.

I don't know how I was able to last as long as I did while she imparted to me what she wanted me to know. And there are many more things she showed me, but time is too limited to tell it all and I'm quite anxious about what I must do. So, I will bring this part of my tale to the climax.

"Go ahead. Shoot your seed," she said in a throaty growl. "I won't burden you with a child." I let go and erupted inside her. My emission was so strong that I must have blacked out. When I opened my eyes there was no sign of the winged woman. I got up and took a shower.

* * *

Last night has been a month since my liaison with the winged woman. "If you pine for a corpse a succubus will appear," rings in my head repeatedly like a mantra. In an effort to recreate the experience I've tried summoning her the same way I did that night in the shower, masturbating to the memory of my wife. I've noted the moon phase the first time the phenomenon occurred and implemented that, along with every variation of planetary hours appropriate for such a working. Nothing. I also tried the same ritual with the memory of the winged woman. Nothing.

Occult books of every type imaginable litter the floor of my living room in stacks, some of them very rare, quite expensive, and trucking in the kinds of magic that can get one in serious trouble with the law. I have searched every one of them repeatedly to no avail.

I'm exhausted to the point of desperation, but I will not relent. My .45 lies on the table where I am writing this. I must go into the darkness now for I know it is in black oblivion where I will find her, if I find her at all. I just wanted whoever reads this note to know that I could not live without her, and this is all for her. *La grande mort*... that is all.

The Wizard and the Tower Keep

A prequel to "Beyond the Mirrors of Faellnoch"

Written and illustrated by D. R. Lackner

In misty forests beyond the dungeons of Evermorn did the metal warrior wander.

I

The night was long and cool, casting violet shadows on wise trees of old. He moved through the wood as a beast of the wild, having grown accustomed to this planet alien to his birth. Vines entangled the branches of the maples and oaks, whose bark gathered the dew and glistened in the moonlight which was shattered by their canopies.

He wore the helm of an ancient lord of war, pointed as the Phrygian caps of his home world. He was outfitted as the barbarians of the fantasy tales of his own world. About his waist was wrapped a loincloth of leather and a brass studded belt, from which hung a pouch and ancient bronze dirk. Soft leather boots covered his feet. About his back was slung a sheathed sword of steel and a domed iron shield, bearing the mark of a great winged predator of times unknown. The artifacts which served him now were once the pride of ancient warriors, handed down through generations on this planet. They eventually had come to rest in a burial mound of their fathers, and were revealed by the elements through the passing of ages.

He bore no name on this world, as he had left his own name behind on his home planet: indeed, he had forgotten it. Time moved differently here: it may have been many years since he had tasted the air of Earth.

II

The warrior arrived on this planet as he was born: with nothing to clothe him and with no defense against the harshness of nature. The cold earth he stalked now, as a titan of the woodlands. He bore the scars which were dealt him by both beast and savage. He had learned to sustain himself on the bounty of the wilderness; he knew only of stone tools and the ways of a primitive mind.

He came across a clearing in densely forested lands. In this clearing lay a great mound of earth, in the shape of a coiling

serpent. In the central earthen mound were standing stones arranged in a circle, fallen into crumbling heaps. He ascended the mound. When he entered the circle, he found a disc of stone with the emblem of a great bird upon it: this was the seal of a tomb.

The warrior knelt, and with some great effort, slid the stone away to reveal the entrance to an ancient hall of the dead. The shaft of light leading into the earth did not reveal what riches or horrors lay beyond, and yet, he leapt down into the tomb. There, in the earth, were four sarcophagi, each with inscriptions in an ancient runic language he did not understand. At the far end of the room, barely visible in the light pouring down from the earth above, there stood a carven statue of a great warrior or king of old. Upon its bearded stone head, it wore a pointed iron helm of curious construction. In its folded hands rested a sword of steel with golden hilt and pommel, and at its feet rested an iron shield and bronze dirk. The warrior gazed upon the visage of this line of people, which was of a forgotten past, and as the sunlight above changed, it shone a shaft of light onto the form. The stone statue seemed enlivened by the shifting light, and the warrior felt a call to lift these artifacts back into the world of living men.

With solemn reverence, he lifted the artifacts from the statue and wiped away the dust of untold centuries. As he donned the helm, he felt a power rising within him, both obscure and familiar. Having outfitted himself with the tools which he would require in this world, he ascended back into the world of the living. As he did so, he felt like he understood, perhaps, how the prehistoric creatures of his own world might have as they rose from primordial pools to the dawning of life. He felt that although he had been on this planet, and in this dimension, for an unmeasured length of time, that this was the day of his birth.

From this time, the warrior, whose name had been left behind, entered the world of mankind once more. His adventures led him to the far reaches of this new world. A great many evils lurked within the shadows which men feared. The Earth Warrior became a raider of these dark places, bringing to light riches of ancient lore and relics beyond the reaches of time. The languages of this world became familiar to him as he made his way from village to village selling his mysterious findings. Fear and honor came to him through his mighty deeds. He went his own way in his own time.

III

The dungeons of Evermorn bore their cruel reward, after was slain a demonic entity: a creature which crawled between worlds, eons before the kings forged the sword which brought about its demise. The tendrils and horrors which sought to end the warrior's life now lay in a gelatinous heap on the cold stone of the Romanesque hall.

Heaps of gold lay at the feet of the warrior who owned no name, yet had he no means to bring it all into the cold sun awaiting his exit. All that was recovered were a few coins and a strange blue jewel, which fit neatly in the palm of his callused hand. This stone was unlike anything he had seen before: it was a token which seemed to emanate energy both weird and ancient. The stone did not refract light, it absorbed it. It did not shine like the rubies and

emeralds of common find; a dim glow came from within its uncertain creation. He placed the jewel in the pouch at his belt, which barely concealed its form.

The warrior traveled onward into a vast forest outlying the ritual grounds which lay above the dungeon lair of Evermorn. The trees grew tall and old here. The land itself seemed to sigh and heave, as the breath of nature enlivened the dense growth. The eyes of uncertain predators lay upon him as he traversed the hills and valleys of the wood. As he lowered into a shallow incline, a thin spring bubbled, winding through its trough.

The warrior bent to quench his burning thirst and peered into his own eyes. Long had it been since he had seen his own face. Long had it been since he had seen his eyes. He remembered a time on earth where he as a child sat listening to the records of his father on his turntable: sitting on a carpeted floor, in a house, in an idyllic suburban neighborhood, with homework on his mind, and the coming day at school his only dread. These things were far away now, impossibly far. He remembered listening to albums recounting fantasy tales, weaving their epic spell through time and space. He remembered the dimensional doorway, which had sprung him from Earth. He did not recall exactly what triggered his appearance here; his memory had been clouded by the mists of time.

The last moments he remembered of Earth were on the night of the big thunderstorm that hit his town. He had been watching from his bedroom window, sitting with his guitar. With a flash, lightning struck his house, sending his belongings careening from his shelves as glass shattered all around him. Smoke rose from his guitar amplifier as electricity crackled up through the instrument which he held. He could hear the sound of rain on the rooftop far away in his mind. Electricity leapt from the instrument into the air, and struck the needle of his record player as it bounced between the grooves of a Uriah Heep album. He remembered the strange luminous ball of energy which grew to engulf him, and then he awoke to find himself no longer on Earth. He could not tell whether these things occurred years ago, or lifetimes ago, but the fact remained that he was here now, and must wander on.

As he crested the hill opposite the stream, a vision of civilization did unfold. Outstretched before him lay the dominion of Ardona, a storied realm of wickedness, ruled over by the wizard known as Vael. The warrior had not seen civilization of such magnitude since leaving his home planet. Stone buildings, some in ruins, left by a previous, wiser, civilization formed familiar, yet ramshackle, city blocks. Adorning these buildings were triumphant statues as tributes to great heroes and kings of the past and grotesque, gargoyle-like beasts of legend. Intricate carvings adorned the walls in relief, and their arches were supported by muscular columns. At the center of the city there rose a tower of dark stone, its courtyard walled high. It spiraled upwards, far above the other structures crowded at its foot. About the city there stood a high sloping wall, wide enough for posted guards to walk their charge. A broad, banded iron gate stood at its center, with a horse road leading up to it, curving away from the forest in which the warrior viewed it. Beyond the walled city lay tall craggy mountains, brutish and foreboding in stature and form.

Having no use for the strange Evermorn gemstone but to trade as plunder, the warrior set forth to enter Ardona as a trader, as he was in need of supply after many months of travel. He walked down from the hills of the wood to the city gate. As he approached the wrought iron lattice, he saw that the gate was drawn half open, and two guards lay dead drunk by a small campfire, bottles still in hand. Whilst the warrior stalked past the snoring, sounds of great chaotic revelry abounded from the buildings beyond. The streets were lined in filth, with beggars upon the curb in rags. Shabby carts with wooden wheels were hobbled along by scheming merchants peddling vials of magick potions and elixirs. At this late hour, only the most vile roamed the streets. Mercenaries bearing the scars of battle sauntered brutishly, followed by would-be squires. Strange parlors of evil magick opened their doors to the street, with curling incense smoke wafting upwards, beckoning the desperate in deceit.

The warrior walked past several cross streets and alleys, observing the strangeness of the scene. A song could be heard in the distance, coming from a small tavern, unattached to the surrounding buildings, standing two stories tall with a thatched roof. The warrior walked in through an open door at its center and entered a room with several folk, some clearly of this town, and some fellow travelers from distant lands. As he entered, the bard's song ceased. A fire burned in the hearth, and an unearthly glow arose from candles fitted in ornate metal stands on sparse tables, heavy with oil and wear. The travelers looked up at him; some hid their faces in their hooded cloaks, while some stood with eyes ablaze in silent fury.

At the far end of the room two figures stood behind a long oaken bar laden with bottles and mugs. In the candlelight stood a woman with heavy eyes; she seemed to have seen too much of this strange world in her short lifetime. Further behind the bar top sat a heavy man with crude, untrusting features; his face bore the scars of a brawler. The room felt heavy with silent unease. In a dark corner of the room sat a maiden, beneath a richly embroidered cloak and hood of blue, whose eyes seemed to shine with wisdom of worlds beyond.

To break the silence, the bard by the fireside produced an instrument alien to the warrior, yet one which resembled the twelve stringed guitars of his home. He began to play, and sang a song recalling the deeds of the wizards of a bygone era. He sang of the founding of Ardona by a council of these wizards, and of how they were ultimately overthrown by the dark magick of Vael. The warrior paid for a mug of ale with coin from the dungeons, not hinting at the strange wealth which he held in the glowing stone. Yet, as he opened the pouch which held his coin, he felt the maiden's iron gaze upon it. As he turned to join the travelers by the fire, the maiden motioned to him, and he followed to sit in the shadow as the bard played on.

The dreams of fate are calling me back
I hear the howling of the wind
Shelter now, and weather the storm
And a tale of legend I shall spin

Of demons, wizards, and kings
Swords of steel drawn in the night
A tale beyond the shackles of time
Of those who would stand and fight

Sit now by the fire; quaff your mug of ale
Gather 'round and listen, to this old bard's tale

In the song of swords was forged his path
In the strangeness of magick he did arrive
Tried in battle, and crossed by time

A warrior left mystified

Now, while the fire grows dim, the poet lifts the veil
Rest a while and listen to this old bard tell his tale.

"I have journeyed far, crossing the great sea to the west of the mountains beyond this land. I have sought what you carry now, the bones of my retainer you likely found in your battle in the ruins of Evermorn. The stone you carry is not what you would believe; it has no physical origin." The maiden spoke these words, her voice ringing with prophecy. The warrior produced the stone, having no sensation of trickery: her word was true. He held it out in his hand near the strange glow of the candle, and the light produced by each did not mix, as oil and water. These were things of two magicks.

"The light—it is not of this world," said the warrior; it had been a long time since he had heard his own voice. "This crystal I dug from the mass of gelatinous flesh left by the Demon you seem to know well; its pale light shown through the tainted flesh of the fiend."

"It is the Eye of the Kings which you have recovered from the Demon of Evermorn. This was entombed with Eldrin the Wise in another time, when the deceit of Vael began. Vael overthrew the Wizards who founded this realm, in his deceitful campaign to rid this world of the need for magick. He dethroned the council, with the support of the mob, and as soon as their power was diminished, he cast his own dark magick over the land. This evil has held onto the land for ten generations. The line of kings is lost, ending with Eldrin, who sacrificed his eye in the search for wisdom. The last remnant of this line of kings is in your hands."

The warrior gazed down at the eye, and felt a pulse emanate forth from its core. His suspicion that this object held more than wealth was confirmed. "Vael will know that you are here. He will know that the eye is upon his realm," spoke the maiden. "I come from a line of sages who served the kings of this lost realm. We were guardians of Ardona once, aiding the wizards and kings lost to legend, but in our failure, we can only plot our revenge to set our world to right. The magick in our blood keeps us hidden from Vael's minions, yet binds us ever to our task. There were many once, and now, only I remain. His wicked gaze bears down on this wicked civilization from atop the Tower Keep, where he makes his spells and converses with the demons of time."

IV

The dark wizard peered into a scrying pool laid out in a hemispherical basin of black onyx. About him lay implements of evil magick: dusty tomes, scrolls offering forgotten wisdom, obscure herbs and poisons, and artifacts taken as mementos of fallen civilizations. Robed in crimson, the wizard pointed his black beard as he surveyed the city in its unhinged revelry.

"Warrior, you bring what I have sought for eons. Hidden by the Demon of Evermorn, its dim light had remained obscure to me, but now you have brought it into the cold sun of Eryn for all to gaze upon. Now, I shall take what I am owed," said the wizard in the Tower Keep. Vael set about to poring through a tome of sorcery, from which he spoke the words to summon a troop of dark riders on horseback.

"Darkness shall descend upon you further, warrior. Black magick riders: seize the Eye of the Kings!"

V

The bard played on into the night, as the warrior and the maiden spoke of their travels. The overbearing atmosphere of the tavern grew to be more hospitable as the ale flowed from the tap. The bard paused between songs only for all to find that the noises in the street had silenced, save for the slow trot of hooves on cobblestone. In an open window the patrons of the tavern could see three riders clad in black upon black horses. All around them, a strange smoke-like glow arose, as if their evil could not be contained by their physicality.

"And now, it begins," spoke the maiden in a low voice.

"Warrior!" shouted the lead rider, in a voice lacking the familiarity of humanity. "We come for the Eye of the Kings!" he rasped as he unsheathed his sword. The warrior sprung up from where he had sat bearing his blade of ancient making. He walked out into the street, sword in one hand, the Eye in the other. This was no time to speak, nor a time to hide one's intentions. The black horse in the lead reared up in sight of the glistening blue jewel, and the rider held high his sword, swinging downwards upon the warrior as the horse brought down its inky black hooves. The warrior stepped to the side of the blow and landed a rising cut through the midsection of the rider. Thick black blood spewed forth as the rider was cleaved in two. From within the newly formed chasm in this cloaked entity demonic tentacles writhed, springing forth and flailing wildly before falling to the ground. Each of the other two riders raised their swords, attacking the warrior from the sides. Ducking the blades which whirred past his head, he turned and swung his sword at the neck of the rider to his right, beheading him quickly, and then thrust the tarry black steel into the heart of the remaining rider. From each of the riders burst forth tentacles of the same demonic origin, and an ocean of black blood splattered onto the cobblestone street. The bodies of the demonic riders melted in a disgusting heap and rolled down the sides of their steeds, which galloped off down the street, then up into the sky, dissolving and dissipating as smoke.

The maiden from beyond the sea approached the open doorway, her billowing cloak of azure catching the breeze of the night air.

"Now that he knows you have the Eye, he will send greater demons to find you. These attacks will not end while he lives," the maiden said. "You must ascend the Tower Keep, or die battling the summoned wraiths of a mad wizard. There is no entrance to the tower but for an underground passage which has been barred for hundreds of years. Beneath Ardona, you may enter the sewers, which some say leads to a labyrinth of catacombs which house the founders of the kingdom in which you stand. Through these catacombs may you find the roots of the Keep. To stand against Vael is to accept death, but, for you, there is no alternative. Beneath the foundation of this tavern, there is an entrance to the sewers which you may follow far enough to find the catacombs which lie deeper still."

The warrior followed the maiden back into the tavern as the other patrons stared in silence. He grabbed a rag from the bar to wipe the black demonic blood from his sword.

"I will find the chamber at the top of the Tower Keep, and the wizard will find himself at the point of my sword," the warrior called back to the maiden. "If this blue stone carries with it a great power, perhaps it may allow me to return to my home world." The patrons of the tavern stood with puzzled looks, for they knew not of other worlds.

Sheathing his blade at his belt, he descended the stair into the cellar, and upon lifting a rusted grate, entered the vaulted stone sewers.

VI

The crumbling stonework of the sewers was lit by shafts of low light from the gaps in the streets above. The water in the center of this long passage was not high, but bore the remnants and refuse of the city. Rats crawled in darkened corners, scurrying at the sound of the warrior's footfalls. Long did he wander in the sewers. Their corridors wound as a chaotic maze throughout the bowels of the city. His course was guided by the appearance of age in the stonework. He found that crudely hewn stone lay at the outskirts of the city, and as he entered the older structure, the walls around him became more refined, as if the newer work was completed more hastily.

Just as the Earth Warrior became sure that he was lost, he came upon a section of wall which was in ruins. The large stones which held up the streets above had been smashed away by some cruel intruder, perhaps a grave robber set upon raiding the catacombs which lay yet further still in the cold earth. The chasm in the sewer wall led into an excavated tunnel which was not part of the sewer complex. The warrior stepped over the crumbling stone into the opening, which was barely lit by the moon above. Upon the earth in the tunnel was an unlit torch, dusty with age, yet it carried the heavy scent of rancid oil. He produced his flint from the pouch which held all he owned. He struck the flint with his sword, throwing sparks onto the torch, lighting it with a flash. He descended down into the earth, walking upon the unsteady footing of the earthen tunnel until he reached the opening on the other side. Beyond lay the walls of the catacombs which he sought. Leading with his torch, he stepped over the massive block opening into the halls of the dead.

Meanwhile, high aloft in his tower, Vael peered once more into his scrying pool of black, watching as the warrior entered the catacombs, ever nearer to his tower.

VII

In the distant past, a council of high wizards set Ardona as the center of civilization; a kingdom meant as a hub to all nine great realms of Eyrn. Nine great sorcerers were they, led by Ryndir, chief magician to Eldrin the Wise. The wizards made a pact to serve the race of man set upon the world, and to keep an age of peace for all time. Vael did not find this to his liking, and sought to take what power he could for his own. He pitted the wizards against each other, and one by one, took both their power and their lives, leaving himself the sole ruler in the Tower Keep. For a thousand years, Vael prolonged his life with the powers he had usurped, and held the far reaches of his dominion in an icy grasp. Far beyond the boundaries of Ardona could the dark magick be felt, into the wilds of Eyrn. The very trees surrounding the walls of the kingdom grew twisted and malicious in appearance.

It was in this realm that the Earth Warrior fought great foes of legend, and sought the riches which they guarded. Now he sought the tower that held the source of all this evil.

The chamber he stood in was covered by the dust of a thousand years. The walls were of smooth stone, carved with expertise by a forgotten culture, long before the burial of the dead who rested here now. The crypt held the remains of several generations of noble lords, and the bones of their servants lay about the corners of the room. Several skeletons lay on the floor in a manner which seemed entirely out of place in a tomb, being dressed and outfitted in the garb of adventurers and raiders. These were surely the men who had excavated the tunnel by which the warrior had entered. What could have ended their adventure here? What beasts of the dark had taken their lives? He silently thanked them as he passed by.

At the far end of the room was a heavy wooden door bound in iron. Beyond this ominous door lay horrors heretofore unknown, which perhaps were the doom of the fallen raiders. The warrior grasped the iron ring bound to the door and opened it with some hesitation, holding his torch in the growing gap as the door swung open. The room before him held several stone sarcophagi, with relief carvings of their human occupants upon their lids. The warrior looked down at the images of the dead as he walked past.

The depictions of long dead warriors in bizarre armor stared back in blank archaic silence.

Colonnades cast strange shadows on the alcoves at the edges of the tomb. Bronze figurative statues stood watch over the bones of the dead. At the far end of the room, a large archway led the warrior further into a winding hallway. The warrior followed the hall as it carried him on a shallow slope downward, descending further into the earth beneath Ardona. The torch lit his way, yet did not reveal the end of the hall, which snaked downward past many tombs of the same design as the first one he had entered. The air filled his lungs with the dust of bone meal: it had not passed into the lungs of a living being for time untold. The warrior walked for a distance before the hall widened and opened into a large gallery. A faint glow could be seen about the stonework ahead, and his torch sputtered out in an unexpected gust of wind. As his eyes adjusted to the new dim light, he became aware of the endless hall of bronze statues, which now towered above him in height. As he wandered through the high vaulted corridor, the statues became more grotesque, now not simply human warriors in armor, but men with the heads of beasts and the look of arcane races of times long past. As he continued, the once faint light grew stronger, coalescing to form the visage of a man in the rich, flowing garments of a king, yet decayed to the point of being nearly skeletal. Beyond him, a massive stone door loomed, upon which was placed the green glowing sigil of Vael.

VIII

"Here, in the roots of the Tower Keep, I have lingered, doomed and cursed for all time to keep the path shut to all who would dare the wizard of my unmaking. I was Eldrin," spoke the glowing phantasm. "I have always been here, and here I will remain."

The warrior studied the ghastly appearance of this once-king who hovered eerily before him. His form had suffered the decay of flesh and the remnants of mummified skin clung to the skull beneath, even in his ghostly, translucent state. Hollow eyes peered from beneath a golden coronet at him in tired malice.

"Beyond the door begins the spiral stair which ascends to the Tower Keep," said the specter. "Warrior, be warned! Though the sword of steel you wield is of ancient origin, it poses no threat to the dark magick that lurks at the zenith of this tower. You are as the dead! Go and lie with the bones and turn to dust!"

The warrior with no name reached for the Eye and held it forth. The dull blue glow of the crystal grew brighter at once in the presence of Eldrin the Wise. At once, the specter was taken aback by this light in his dark existence.

"See now, O Eldrin the Wise: the Eye of the Kings has entered your burial hall!" the warrior called out to the specter.

The visage of the king changed suddenly as his gaze fell upon the glowing jewel. "Long have I waited for one who is chosen by fate to return to the Keep with the Eye. Prophecy has told, long before I was reduced to the wraith you see before you, that a warrior with no name from dimensions unknown would lift the curse of black magick which would befall this kingdom. We ruled a land of peace for a thousand years: the council of high wizards and the line of my fathers. In our ignorance, we did not see the power which sought to dethrone and conquer. Now, as you have undoubtedly seen, the land is cursed. Men seek their fortune at the slight of others, and demons roam free within the shadows to take the lives of the pure in sacrifice. I am trapped here, bound by Vael with this green sigil, for all time. The years bring naught but madness and torment to me. Yet, as prophecy has brought you here, I find the lost hope that I may rejoin the line of my fathers in the great halls of the dead. Beyond the seal which binds the door before you, I cannot follow. Go now, warrior, you have found and trodden lost roads. Now ascend the Tower Keep to your fate!"

The ghost of King Eldrin turned and raised his arms. He spoke words of an archaic language, unknown to the warrior, and the seal slowly began to fade. As this happened, the ghost writhed in pain and dissipated slowly into the air, vanishing with a shriek. The warrior replaced the Eye in his pouch, and walked forward to push open the stone door leading up into the Tower Keep.

IX

The warrior struggled against the mighty slab of stone until he began to hear a rumble, and with no small amount of effort, the door slid open enough for him to enter the great tower. He had no need for torchlight, he saw, as the spiral stair was alight with torches of its own; the light which they produced was of a sickly green hue, flickering and casting watery glimmers onto the smooth stone walls. A continuous carved relief coiled its way up into the tower, depicting men and gods in the time when this planet of Eyrn was young. The warrior did not linger, and began his ascent.

The Tower Keep was laid out in a series of chambers, connected by a spiral stair. Each one of these chambers held an altar and a ritual space, once used by the council of wizards who sought to serve man, now corrupt and defiled by the demonic servants of Vael. The Earth Warrior climbed the stairs for what seemed like a long span of time. There were no windows as he made his way, so he had no way of knowing whether he was still beneath the earth, or high above the city of Ardona. All that guided him were the glimmering torches of magick fire which had burned since this was a place of honor and reverence. The carved relief, not unlike the friezes of antiquity of his home planet, depicted the battles before time in this world began. Men and women battled with beasts unfamiliar to the Earth Warrior's eyes, until other beings arrived on the battlefield. The wizards arrived to turn away the wild creatures which besieged the races of men, back to the dark places of shadow whence they had come. As the relief coiled upward, he saw the carving of the Tower Keep, depicted in its once glorious state. It was beneath this image that he came to the first door, inscribed with arcane sigils of protection. The warrior took hold of the heavy golden ring at its center and pulled open the door.

The chamber was lit by torches which threw red light onto a white stone altar at its center. Intricate stone shelves lined the walls, each filled with magickal tomes and vellum scrolls. The remnants of melted candles adorned all surfaces. As the warrior passed through this chamber to the doorway opposite its entrance, he felt an unearthly breeze which carried with it a ghastly whispering in a language different from the one spoken by Eldrin, yet also of ancient origin. This chamber seemed to serve as a library of sorts, housing knowledge of men and wizards of old. Upon the smooth white stone of the altar lay a human skull. Upon every surface of the skull were red runic inscriptions. Undisturbed for centuries, the knowledge contained within this chamber had indeed fallen into legend and myth. What secrets were held here, lost to this world? The warrior passed to the opposite side of the room and continued his ascent.

The stairs spiraled up as before, lined again with torches bearing pale violet light. The friezes along the walls depicted the Council of Wizards signing treaties and overseeing public works of infrastructure and technology. It showed them turning toward the wilderness, finally setting their gaze upon the forests of Eryn above the door to the next chamber. The warrior took hold of the massive horn which served as the handle for this door.

Yellow torches lit the second chamber, which had an altar formed from the trunk of a broad petrified tree. The walls were adorned with the skulls of animals, whose howls and cries could be heard in the mind and spirit of the warrior. Heavy animalistic energy seemed to linger about this ritual space, and the warrior felt the fury of nature in the core of his being. This was a room of sacrifice, and each skull bore runic inscriptions, binding their power to this place, and to the keeper of the tower. At the center of the altar lay a bow of some alien tree, with leaves still green in the passing of time. The warrior passed through and continued up the spiral stair.

The torches now shed an orange light and seemed to align with the imagery within this section of the tower. Carven in relief were the images of troops armed and marching for battle. As the stairs continued their ascent, the downfall of humanity was shown plain. The warrior puzzled at his place within the tower, certain he was now high above the streets of Ardona, and yet, he felt that he had not moved anywhere at all, and that all was swirling around him. As he climbed, the depictions of warfare had grown fierce and bloody. Finally above the door to the next chamber was a scene of triumph over a conquered people. Great detail was given to the expressions on the faces of the victors. It was not an expression of joy or relief, but one of sorrow. The Earth Warrior reached out to the door handle, which was the hilt and pommel of a sword.

The third chamber held an altar of forged iron, and the walls were bathed in blue light from torches bound to the walls. Armor and weaponry lay in great heaps and upon racks around the room; they seemed to vibrate with the intensity of a thousand warriors. The many cultures and peoples of this planet, still a mystery to the warrior with no name, were represented by the weaponry which filled the room. Great cruel axes of the men of the north, the curved swords of the horse-riders far to the east, pikes and savage bill-hooked spears of the warriors of civilized birth: all these things painted a picture of violence and conquest. At the center of the altar was placed a chalice of blood. The lives of men were ever troubled, and yet, one could compare this ferocity of the kingdoms of men with the kingdoms of the beasts. Man was naught but a beast of the wild, and let all cower before the wrath of nature. The futility of conflict was apparent within this room, and with glory came great sorrow.

The warrior exited this final chamber to ascend once more the great stair spiraling up the Tower Keep. The torches were now bone white and the walls obsidian black. There were no markings on these walls as before. The door which he approached next was one which carried on its stone surface the markings and sigils of evil magick, similar to those at the entry which Eldrin the Wise had once kept. Affixed at its center was the face of a beast in bronze within a nine-pointed star. The warrior pushed open the door to find a wide room, with no altar but a monumental statue of a demonic creature at its center. There were no other doors exiting this chamber, as in the rooms before. He would have to find another way to continue his ascent. This chamber was not a remnant of the great wizards of old; this was a shrine to an old god, forgotten with willful intention by those with good in their hearts.

The statue's head was that of an eagle, with the body of a wolf, and the tail of a great lizard, which encircled its clawed feet. From the statue emanated a strange glow, and as the warrior stood, he felt a great heat from his pouch of supplies. As he reached for the Eye of the Kings, his hand began to burn. He threw the stone to the floor. A great arc of electricity crept from the eyes of the demonic statue, which opened now to reveal hot white fury, and met with the Eye of the Kings. The warrior reached out toward the glowing jewel and a deafening crack rang out through the tower. Blinding light burst forth from the Eye of the Kings and the warrior shielded his eyes.

X

The great commotion ceased, and the warrior withdrew his hand from his eyes only to find that he was no longer in the chamber within the Tower Keep, but in a land unknown to him. A cool, alien breeze enveloped him in acrid sulfurous air. As he looked around, he found himself in the center of a ruined necropolis: a city of the dead dotted with pyramid-like tombs and sturdy rows of columns supporting mighty pediments and sturdy arches. The familiar aspects of these ruinous structures did not disguise the fact that something seemed drastically wrong in this plane of existence. The physics of this planet were different from the worlds he had traveled to before. The mountains which dotted the horizon were cruel and crooked. It seemed that the horizons here did not line up with his notion of reality. His body felt heavy; he felt oppressed by the very air, which was thin and depleted of suitable oxygen levels. While he stood on what seemed to be flat ground, the angle of the earth beneath his feet and of all which surrounded him seemed to be desperately wrong. The breeze which swept through the stonework monuments felt as if its origins were from all places, stagnant and active at once. The very geometry of the pyramids and temples was very off-putting. The sky itself had an inky blue-violet hue to it, and restless clouds swirled along the mountainous horizon. This was a place of gods forgotten by people; he had heard stories of this kind of place in his own time, but never once dared to dream of the truth behind the myth.

He wandered the strange land for some time, pausing to gasp at the thin air in attempts to catch his breath. Rounding the corner of a large temple ruin, he entered a centralized square, lined with brutishly large cobblestones and surrounded by a colonnade. In the middle of this architectural arrangement, towering above the surrounding columns was a great fiend of a form: perhaps the deity of the inhabitants who labored over this ghastly work of cast metal. It seemed a companion to the creature which guarded the portal to this land in the Tower Keep. Three curving horns jutted from its forehead above eight wide eyes. It stood upright on two legs, with four muscular arms rising from its torso. The metallic sheen of its construction disguised what appeared to be a skin of scales. Behind it there arose a reptilian tail with a large, boney club formation about its end. Whether this creature was dreamed up by doting worshippers at the dawn of time, or of a race of interdimensional conquerors feared by distant planets, the warrior could not be sure. The stone near the base of this figure was stained with what the warrior could imagine was the blood of sacrifice, although it bore not the red hue of human blood.

The warrior approached with some level of caution; this was a new planet, and he was careful to ensure the monument's dormancy. As he walked toward it, he saw what appeared to be a talisman of sorts about its neck, cast in gold. When he stood in the shadow of the beast, the attention to detail of its makers shocked him. Every scale covering its horrible body was raised with the utmost care, and its gaping mouth, filled with cruel teeth, appeared all the more terrible, and of a size which could devour a man. He looked up at the curious golden talisman, and saw that it was the clawed foot of a winged predator unknown to him, with four talons seemingly clasped onto the thin sulfurous air.

The warrior with no name knew that he must not linger in this realm long if he were to continue his quest. Surely there were no means to sustain his life in this desolate world. Reaching into his pouch, he produced the Eye of Kings, pondering at how such a small thing could hold such power, and why it had drawn him here. He felt his hand magnetically drawn nearer to the talisman, which began to twitch as it dangled from the neck of the beast. His gaze fixed on the talisman, the warrior fell into a hypnotic state. In his daze, he climbed up the bent knee of the dreaming god of the past, and plucked the talisman from its neck as one plucks fruit from a tree. Leaping down to the stony ground below, he took the blue jewel in hand, and studied both it and the golden talisman as he regained control of his mind. The magnetic draw once again forced the two pieces toward one another. As they moved closer in his hands, the talons of the talisman slowly moved apart, making room to fit the crystal within their grasp. Once more, a trance fell over the Earth Warrior as he ritualistically raised the Eye of the Kings and the talisman above his head and slowly placed the Eye between the talismanic talons. As he did so, the talons quickly closed upon the crystal and a surge of energy burst forth from the talisman, nearly knocking him from his feet as the artifact fell to the stony ground.

After some time, the warrior with no name came back to his senses, and retrieved the fallen talisman. As he tied it onto his belt, pondering the power it now held, he noticed in his peripheral vision a slight movement. He immediately turned again to face the behemoth statue, only to find its gargantuan head was lolling back as it stretched out its hideous jaws, beginning to drool. Its clawed fingers and arms twitched, then flexed, as it lifted its feet from the stone base on which it was set. It loomed over the warrior, and with outstretched arms, let out an ancient howl of horrible revival.

Reaching for the warrior with both hands, it lurched forward as he leapt back. Hastily he tied the talisman around his belt, then he unslung his shield from his back and unsheathed the ancient blade which rested at his belt. Bracing himself behind the iron shield, the warrior received an initial blow from the demonic beast of antiquity, and heard a loud metallic ring: this creature, while now fluid in motion, was indeed composed of unearthly metal. The warrior swung his sword at the grabbing hands which assailed him as the creature bounded forth, cracking the stone cobbles beneath its massive feet. The blows had no effect on the beast whatsoever, and sparked as the ancient sword clashed against its heavy metal.

The warrior edged backward towards the columns which encircled the ritual ground where he had awakened the demon from an untold past. Soon he felt the cold stone of one of the columns press against his back. He dodged the lunging beast and it shattered the hard stone, sending chunks of it flying far off and landing at the feet of a great pyramid. The warrior, knowing that he would only damage his sword should he attack, continued his retreat up the adjacent steps ascending one of the pyramids in the otherworldly necropolis, buying himself some time. The thin, oppressive air made him gasp in fury, disorienting him in his flight. The demon ascended after him with sluggish, deliberate motion, stone crumbling under foot with a metallic clamor.

The warrior neared the apex of the strange pyramid as the heavy metal demon lurched and hulked ever nearer. As it came nearly within striking range, the warrior looked behind him to find a white stone altar atop the pyramid, with strange lingering stains reminding him of the sacrificial sites of his home world. In the center of the altar was a smaller raised stone pedestal with the carved imprint of the very talisman he plucked from the throat of the demon who now assailed him. Approaching the altar with quick caution, the warrior removed the talisman from his belt. As he did so, the demonic creature reared up with two of its arms raised, ready to crush the Earth Warrior upon the stone. Without knowing what would happen, the warrior raised the talisman high above his head and slammed the clawed form into the hollow within the pedestal. The beast paused and let out a terrible shriek as the talisman began to emanate a faint blue light. A low hum and vibration began to rattle the pyramid. The hum grew into a deep roar, and the dust which lay upon the stone began to levitate as the vibration grew to a great shudder. The demon struck down at the warrior in vain, and began to lose its balance: wild arms franticly reached for him as he dodged their grasp. The pale blue light grew from within the Eye of the Kings, enveloping the apex of the pyramid in an orb of blinding light. The demon shielded its eight eyes, and as it did so, a widening crack grew beneath its feet, sending the demon into the depths of this strange world. The warrior peered into the chasm to see the beast fall into molten stone and cry out in agony. Lifting his shield against his own eyes, he edged into the spherical light and reached towards the talisman. As soon as his fingers touched the surface, he heard a loud electrical crackling boom and everything went dark.

XI

With eyes still closed, the warrior sensed not the cool otherworldly breeze, nor the oppressive thin air he felt a moment sooner. As his eyes adjusted to the darkness, he found himself on a dark winding stair, with an ironwood door bound in bronze before him. Looking behind him, he saw that the spiral stair fell not only into darkness, but out of existence. The stonework melted into space as smoke or mist, as if the shadow had truly engulfed and dissolved the physical realm. Upon the door before him were inscribed runic curses of evil sorcery: beyond this door, the Wizard of the Tower Keep made his spells.

The warrior reached for the bronze ring in the center of the door, and as he did so, the massive door creaked on its hinges, opening before him by its own power. The room which lay before him was impossibly large, for this was the chamber of magick at the top of the tower, and it had no reasonable creation at the hands of men. The room of yellow stone was lined with rows of fluted columns lit by fiery torches, below a high vaulted ceiling of intricate crystalline geometry. In shadowy alcoves, black onyx statues of heavily armored beings guarded the empty room. The warrior proceeded down the hall, sword and shield at the ready, talisman again at his belt. Sneaking past the onyx statues which seemed too lifelike, the warrior considered that they were likely prisoners of Vael, turned to stone over the course of a thousand lifetimes. He passed many such statues, several with bizarre arms and armor, some resembling the cultures of his home planet, and some which seemed altogether alien. All of these creatures were once mighty warriors, now reduced to their helpless state.

As the warrior approached the far end of the corridor, three large stone archways led into a final chamber. A white marble altar, draped in cloth of royal purple silk, stood in the center, and a massive, empty throne of black could be seen at the far end of the room. The walls were covered in rich woven tapestries, depicting the histories of this world and interlaced with golden thread. On each side of the throne were piles of gold, jewels, and fine weaponry left as tribute to the tyrannical wizard. Upon the altar were placed two large candles alongside an unadorned human skull.

As the warrior began to feel the unease of emptiness which lay upon the room, the candles upon the altar crackled alive with a sickly green flame. Coiling smoke seeped into the room, and gathered upon the black throne in a curling mass. The smoke rising from the candles thickened and took on the form of the wizard himself, and with a flash, Vael appeared sitting upon the throne as the candlelight returned to a familiar orange hue. He sat stroking his black beard and arose suddenly.

"Warrior!" cried the ageless wizard. "I have sought the Talisman of Kings for eons, and you, a barbarian, a wanderer, a thief, have recovered it despite the odds! You have no conception of what you carry at your belt as a trophy of plunder! With the powers of dimensional travel, it calls to me now, as it had before it was cast into forgotten realms. The Eye had lain dormant in the belly of the Demon of Evermorn, hidden from my sight for a thousand years, and the talisman given to the guardian in the world of death and dreams beyond this reality. You have destroyed the guardians of both the talisman and the Eye of the Kings, and have now delivered them to me as prophecy has foretold. Place this Talisman of Kings upon my altar, that I might be the master of all time and space! I will not patronize you and say that you may earn back your life by doing so, and I will make you no offers of truce: you will not leave this tower alive. My warriors now guard the hall which you entered by, and to exit here means to battle with hundreds of the greatest warriors throughout all time and dimensional birth. There is no escape from the magick which now binds you here."

The warrior took the talisman in hand and faced the wizard, standing in front of the altar. A vision passed before him, and in his mind he returned to Earth, his home world. It was a cool autumn afternoon. He was arriving home from the record store on his bicycle with several newly purchased albums clasped under his arm. As he dropped his bike in the front yard, he leapt up the stairs and through the screen door. Padding across the living room floor towards the turntable, he unsheathed the LP which would be first: *Demons and Wizards*. The needle dropped.

"He was the wizard of a thousand kings, and I chanced to meet him one night wandering...." The words echoed in his mind, reverberating through space and time, and he arrived back in the Tower Keep.

He looked down at the talisman of the kings who had passed long before in this distant world. He wondered what great legends were still unknown to him in this realm, and in all the others. He had found the spaces between these dimensions, and strode their lost roads with little ease until this time. Staring at the talisman, he knew that this was the key to return home, if somehow it could be preserved, but no matter. He now lived the tales which had inspired him to dream on Earth. This was now his home world.

"Sorcerer! I have trodden the sands of time, and leapt through portals between worlds. I tire of these things, and present you now with the Talisman of Kings," shouted the warrior, a secret in his heart.

The warrior held the talisman high above his head, looking directly into the eyes of the wizard. He lowered the golden claw clasping the cerulean jewel onto the altar. The grinning wizard spoke, too pleased with his fortune to question this action.

"So, you have chosen to betray your fate and side with darkness.

There is a place for you among the great warriors of the past who have sought my destruction. You shall remain as living stone for all time within the halls of the Tower Keep. Your life shall end, and you shall never die." Thus spoke the wizard, not seeing the warrior reach for his blade. The heavy metal warrior now raised his sword over the talisman, and with a mighty swing, crushed the golden claw and azure jewel upon the altar, sending shards of the relic to all corners of the room in a blinding blast.

Standing aghast, the wizard shouted frantically, "Fool! Now hast thou doomed us both to lie in the rubble for a grave!"

"No, I have doomed you to rot where you stand, and become as the dust of the earth! Vile betrayer of man and usurper of the Tower Keep: now unravels your eternal life!"

The tower began to rumble, and the wizard lunged forth with a twisted obsidian blade, unsheathed vengefully from his side with a howl of hatred. The warrior drew back his sword and thrust it through the chest of the wizard as he leapt down from his throne. The blade pierced through his ribcage, and black, oily blood spewed forth, staining his robes of crimson. His beard now drained of color, turning white, as his skin dried and shriveled, revealing the skull beneath it. Eyes sinking back into his face, the dying wizard gasped in a final rattling breath. The warrior looked about him, as cracks appeared in the crumbling walls of the Keep. He watched in horror as the stones of the vaulted ceiling did not crash to the floor, but rose up into the sky above, revealing a swirling vortex of blue and violet hues.

The warrior turned from the throne to run back through the entry hall from which he had come. As he hurried in his flight, he noticed that the onyx statues were beginning to shift from their pedestal bases. They jumped down from where they once stood and began to give chase. A once great warrior of onyx neared his side and he turned, maneuvering his sword to deflect a lethal blow. With a crash, the warrior swung down hard on the onyx helm of the warrior, shattering him down through his torso. Shards of black flew into the air, cutting the warrior, as they rose up into the growing vortex above. Several more onyx warriors charged in, one with a pole axe and two with short swords. The Earth Warrior swung at the haft of the pole axe, splintering it and sending the head skidding across the rapidly disappearing floor. He then made a great sweeping strike across the midsections of each onyx fighter, splitting them in two, and sending them in pieces to rise up into the air.

The vibration of the hall grew to a great tremor, and as the warrior looked over his shoulder, saw that huge blocks of stone began to rise up and separate from the tower, ascending into the vortex in the sky. The onyx warriors, too, were lifted from their feet, hovering upward into unseen oblivion.

The warrior reached the ironwood door which he pulled open, for it had no magick left within it, and began his descent. The tower was disappearing behind him, and it was all he could do to remain ahead of the crumbling stone. He ran down the spiraling stair for many turns; as the wizard's magick had left the tower, the once ethereal stairs had now solidified in their crumbling state. Finally, the warrior accessed the chamber with the stone chimera creature through a widening crack in the walls of the Keep. This portal which had initiated his travel to an archaic dimension lay dormant: its eyes were now closed for all time. He paused once to watch as this statue crumbled to pieces and flew up into the sky, now a whirlwind of stone leading up until it were but dust. The warrior passed through each of the three ritual spaces, torches now roaring violently black. He reached the final door at the base of what was once the spiral Keep. He opened the door and looked back once at the galaxy of stone and rubble which rose into the night sky beyond what was left of the stairs leading into the earth. He entered the door to the catacombs, slamming it behind him and sliding to the ground in exhaustion.

The warrior heard a voice, ethereal and noble. "The dark wizard, Vael, is no more. The Tower Keep is gone. The Eye of the Kings is lost for all time, and yet, you remain," spoke Eldrin the Wise. "You have forsaken your home planet, for what purpose? You may never return now, and you are in fate's cruel hands."

"I have chosen my path, once-king, after fate has chosen it for me time and again," the warrior responded in short breaths.

XII

The Earth Warrior with no name breathed a heavy sigh, and rose to his feet. It was done. He sheathed his sword, and slung his iron shield about his back. Eldrin the Wise hovered before him, restored beyond his wraithlike state, emitting a powerful azure glow. The ghost of the king gazed upon the warrior and made a secret sign as he grew transparent and dissipated, finally to enter the halls of his fathers.

The warrior made his way back through the catacombs and sewers; finally climbing back through the rusty iron grate in the cellar of the tavern from where he had begun his journey. As he ascended the stair and entered the tavern hall, all but the bard had left the fireside to stand in the streets, gazing at the vortex in the sky hurling stones up into the unknown. The bard sat and played a strange song: both mournful and triumphant. The tower which once stood at the center of Ardona was now razed to the ground, leaving only the remnants of the last of the spiral stair within the foundation. In future times, a monumental block would be placed over this, to seal in the demons which lurked in other parts of the catacombs.

The people of Ardona stood in the streets in awe, watching as the ancient tower which had stood for longer than anyone truly knew ascended piece by piece into the vortex. As the last stone entered the abyss, the swirling ceased, and the night sky returned to its former state. A great roaring cheer could be heard through the city, as the people knew that the reign of Vael had come to an end. A new age was upon them, and this was its genesis. Long would fathers tell their children of the days when darkness cloaked the realm of Ardona, and of the warrior who ascended the Tower

Keep, only to send it up into the sky to an unknown end.

As the Earth Warrior walked across the wooden floor of the tavern, he saw that it was empty of travelers. They were all outside, watching the great tower ascend into the sky. He approached the deserted bar and drew a mug of ale from one of the casks which lined the wall. He sat down by the fire, and the bard began to play a new song. The warrior closed his eyes to gather a moment's rest.

The needle slid into the fallout groove, and the familiar sound of dust and scratches from another time filled his ears. The needle lifted with a pop and crackle, but the warrior dared not open his eyes for what he might find.

***D.R. Lackner** is a multi-instrumentalist and oil painter. His creative output can be seen and heard as the guitarist, vocalist, lyricist, and cover artist for the epic heavy metal band **Legendry**. His work in all mediums revolves around fantastical realms of sword and sorcery, and takes inspiration from Robert E. Howard, Manilla Road, and Frank Frazetta, among countless others. "The Wizard and the Tower Keep" is a prequel to "Beyond the Mirrors of Faellnoch," which appeared in the* Swords of Steel Omnibus.

The Dead God's Spell

by Howie K. Bentley

Saxon steel shall drink its fill,
And the wheeling kites shall sate,
When the Franks rush us from yonder hill,
We'll leave what's left for the Raven's plate.
And this was the augury,
A mistaken prophecy…

Swords and bucklers, setting sun,
Now ownerless steel still gleams,
And all that can be heard from afar,
Are the women's wails and the children's screams.

And an old man lies dying,
Engulfed in a fever dream,
Running on all fours… wolfen giant.
He gnashes his bloody fangs in hate,
And breaks the Cross-Curse in defiance,
Where swords lick out but can't penetrate.

Wraith-like, Lycanthrope doth rend,
Reversing the Dead God's spell.
Those who embrace foreign desert gods,
You can all go straight to Hel.

Dying man saw from Beyond,
One-eyed warlock wanderer.
He said to the man, "Don this wolf skin,
I'll cast the Runes. You'll live forever!"

Now, Lycanthrope, he doth rend.
Tramples cross beneath his feet.
Savaged corpses of Charlemagne's men.
He rose from his deathbed a ravenous beast!

Dragonslayer's Doom

Written and illustrated by Sarah Kitteringham

The sky was blanketed with a milky array of stars when Agnes regained consciousness. Ache pervaded every limb; the enveloping silence held no sinister intentions. The first thing she noticed was the metal chinks of her rerebrace digging painfully at the wrong angles into a throbbing arm. The coppery scent of metallic ichor was discernible, but its source felt irrelevant. She struggled to rise as the pounding in her skull raised to a fever pitch. Stupor prevailed.

Much time passed. Agnes opened her encrusted eyes: the vivid sunset revealed varying shades of crimson dancing amidst the sky. Two sounds were now evident. One was the rustling of her squire Valencia as she stripped the surrounding corpses of their finery and goods. The other was a distinctive clanking that grew louder as it approached.

Gathering her senses, Agnes turned her head to the latter sound. Figures were approaching from the east, outfitted in the dress of the slipshod underground village that sat roughly ten score furlongs from her last outpost. Valencia stopped her pillaging and stood still, eyes narrowing as the distant figures' heads bobbed on horseback in the distance. Their heraldic flag depicted the vivid Stargazer, resplendent with bright shades of royal purple, vivid pink, and cheery yellow. Set to the backdrop of a glowing sky, it was identifiable from a league. The buckets slung over the flag bearing horse's back clanked oddly with customary offerings.

Agnes already knew the request they fielded.

It was always some variation of the same: Kill the ancient, bloodthirsty serpent Campe that plagued the once bountiful land. The monster resided somewhere on the scraggliest peak to the north, and had for a millennium past. Its unrelenting presence damned all to a simmering malaise. Progress was swiftly dismantled by the viciousness of Campe's wrath as the mighty dragon assaulted emerging settlements and roasted humans and herds of animals alike. Its cruelty necessitated that all who remained dwell in a series of hovels.

Pocketing the land like patchwork, these hovels were occupied by small groups of fearful hunters, minstrels, warriors, pedlars, sheepherders, and healers alike—thrust together by necessity. Agnes had dwelled within a handful of these collectives, resolving what small-scale skirmishes arose. More often she'd ensnare rabbits to feed the orphaned children after adorning them in the unfortunate beasts' warm skins. She had assisted with building underground shelters that were invisible to the dragon's watchful eye and granted the inhabitants some protection from the unforgiving northern climate. Alongside the healers, she'd cleaned wounds and set bones. It was in these hovels that she'd met Valencia. The young girl was ferocious and filthy; Agnes had assisted in setting and splinting Valencia's broken femur, watching dumbstruck as the girl refused to shed a single tear.

For these actions, Agnes had received a warm reputation of some acclaim. Some of the particularly enthusiastic among them had even dubbed her Queen, although Agnes suspected the title was inspired by her more ruthless actions. After all, the pounding war drums called her endlessly to roads where armored captains ride. She had sold her sword to the highest bidder and been rewarded handsomely for the efforts. However, her true pleasure came from vengeance. Recently, she had beheaded the malefic wizard Roldand. The dark eyed brute had conquered and pillaged the village where he reigned without remorse. After slowly whipping his skin raw, lash by lash, she chopped off his head. To die screaming, soaked in his own carnage, was just what the murderous rapist deserved. The memory of his pathetic cries brought a grim smile to her lips. She had left his head on the highest pike overlooking the village as a grim reminder to those who wished to recreate his deeds. As she and Valencia had left the village, they noted with grim satisfaction that the crows had already eaten his eyes.

It's this violent creed that accounted for Agnes' current state, struggling to regain consciousness on that hillside. She had been recruited by one particularly persistent hovel to defeat a pernicious group of bandits who'd ransacked the living quarters nearby and murdered two of its magickal inhabitants. The community residing there mourned the deaths of the Elder Cantatrix and her young apprentice, demanding the bandits' blood in compensation. Enraged by the crime, Agnes was happy to oblige. She'd refused any physical payment. Their deaths would be plenty.

She'd stalked the dozen-strong company for three days alongside Valencia, gathering information on their whereabouts and various aptitudes. Agnes then swiftly cut down all but one via arrow, axe, sword, and dagger. She was dragged from her horse by the final bandit and rendered unconscious after striking her head on a rock below. Valencia intervened, stabbing the assailant directly between the eyes.

Valencia was increasingly brutal in her enactment of justice. It triggered in Agnes a deep, albeit complicated, sense of pride. Valencia had grown much throughout the years they had spent in one another's company. They loved each other intensely, quietly, and unreservedly. The timid young girl who had been orphaned by a gang of marauders was now an intelligent, strong, competent, and battle-scarred young woman capable of greatness. Agnes' wary pride was courtesy of the environment that necessitated Valencia's brutality. She did not want Valencia's savageness to match her own. Instead, she longed for Valencia to have something better than what she'd been given, and feared that the young warrior would be unable to reconcile her ever increasing body count with her humanity, should she ever happen to have the opportunity to exercise it. Valencia was headstrong and brilliant. She was also consumed with barely suppressed rage. She was a worthy squire, even if Agnes was no knight.

Countless warriors had been recruited for and failed at the task which the flag bearers predictably requested of Agnes now. The list began with a keenly overconfident knight appropriately dubbed Mallory. The braggart was resplendent in rich clothes and had trained with sword masters since he was old enough to lift steel. The tale reiterated that he'd been swiftly and promptly consumed by the serpent before landing a single blow. Next came the General from the East; his prowess in military combat was renowned and he had spent a lifetime making adept warriors out of mere children. After that came an almost comical array of sell swords, knights, and warriors from both near and far. Every last one failed.

It was then rumored that even a mighty albino king with a soul drinking sword had arrived to kill the beast. Agnes thought this rumor laughable, all the more so when she found in his place a stunningly handsome woman with shimmering silver hair. They had become fast friends one raucous night, swapping battle tales and drinking deeply of ale in a warm corner of a hovel before unexpectedly engaging in the deeds of darkness. Perhaps it was a sense of fatalism, and perhaps they each saw their reflections in the other. Agnes felt a resigned sadness upon hearing the news of the death of the woman she later learned was named Ilian.

Last came the legendarily competent dragonslayers who had previously defeated wyrms in lands near and far: Făt-Frumos, the E Bija e Hënës dhe e Diellit, Prâslea the Brave, and Dietrich von Bern. As far as Agnes was concerned, their names were all now the same: dead, dead, dead, dead.

Many years passed and the stream of willing warriors had dried up. Now devoid of both heroes and monarchs alike, a heralder of magick known as the Stargazer had recently grown in prominence. This Stargazer seemed benevolent, but Agnes instinctively dismissed the spellforger. It was a fool's errand to engage with hope. After all, the true ruler was the ancient wyrm of the mountain.

Nevertheless, hope percolated amidst the hovels. The Stargazer was wise and powerful, claimed the hunters. This heralder of magick trained in casting spells and incantations that could one day cunningly defeat the beast, chanted the minstrels. The learned wielder would infuse strength into the sword of the victorious one, whispered the warriors. The once bustling markets of spices, fruits, and cloths would return, yearned the pedlars. Beasts of burden would accompany them, hoped the herders. The sick and aging could once more be justly treated, dreamed the healers. These beliefs were persistent and gave a sense of purpose to many who had been without hope for a long time. Agnes could not begrudge this hope, despite feeling none of it. She, too, yearned for a world without this ancient menace. Meanwhile, the mere whispering seemed to fill Valencia with spite.

Perhaps it was this foolishness that allowed her to even entertain their proposal. After Valencia had collected the final spoils, she built a blazing fire alongside a flag bearer. Together, warriors and heralds prepared the generous offering of food and drink provided by the Stargazer's party. They drank ale, feasted on rabbit, and voraciously consumed a rare treat of candied plums that Agnes had only heard of in stories. Stomachs filled as they encircled the fire amidst the dying rays of the setting sun. It was here they made their official offer.

After a decade of trial and error, claimed one heralder, the Stargazer had finally achieved what was necessary to aid only the purest-hearted warrior in slaying the beast. One spoke of an incantation to obfuscate the warrior's entry to the cave where the dragon resided; another spoke of a potion to increase the strength of the warrior; another of the most fantastic gift of all: the ability to infuse a sword with the same unquenchable energy that would occasionally flash across the sky exclusively during the peak of only the most violent storms.

With deep suspicion, Agnes listened silently. All of it sounded obscene, daring, and wild. The excitement of the group was infectious. Even Agnes' characteristically silent young squire seemed entranced.

Finally, a member of the party who had not yet spoken made the request: Would Agnes return with them to the village? There, she would train alongside a legendary sword master and receive instructions from the great Stargazer. Her squire would do the same. Were she and Valencia successful in the quest, they both would be granted a customary host of treasures and acclaim. Should she choose to refuse, she was welcome to remain here as Queen of the Hovels.

Agnes noted that the title was tinged with respect and a slight sense of envy rather than malice. This motley crew clearly believed in their Stargazer and in the Stargazer's choosing of her. It caught Agnes off guard, but she did not show it. As the moon lazily rose into the night sky, their leader offered Agnes the night to consider. If she acquiesced, the party would begin the journey to the Stargazer's realm at daybreak.

After a fretful sleep plagued by indecision, Agnes found herself on the road alongside the flag bearers. Oscillating wildly between fatalistic and hopeful, she found herself lost in thought. Their leader granted Agnes a respectful distance as she considered what the coming days would bring. Meanwhile, her young squire seemed quietly enamored with one of the particularly rugged flag bearers who proudly held aloft the Stargazer's insignia.

Riding side by side, the two engaged in quiet conversation, eyes darting at each other infrequently. After many hours of feverishly stolen glances, Agnes recognised something long dormant in Valencia: attraction. It was odd, this shift. Now not only was there the possibility of attraction, but of a future where romance could bloom. Seeing Valencia's bloodstained, grey eyes made bright via hope, Agnes grimly committed to the task. Perhaps, just maybe, this time would be different.

Perhaps Agnes would die screaming in agony.

Many moons passed before the company arrived at the Stargazer's hovel. Whenever the company took respite from the road and took shelter in a local hovel, ghastly night visions appeared to Agnes. Scales and talons gave way to violence and force as howling flashes of the ravaged hovel dwellers appeared. After being raided by the vicious wyrm, their pathetic dying squeals reverberated throughout the community. Valencia appeared, dead-eyed and haunted, stained with her mother's putrid, rotting blood. Agnes would awaken with a start, dismissing these visions as mounting tension associated with the impending quest. She did not inform Valencia of these grim harbingers, instead returning to her horse, and the road, with a fresh determination.

Despite having resided in the area in her childhood, Agnes noted a perceptible shift as the company approached the Stargazer's land. Hope had lightened the air, infusing it with a sense of vibrancy and brightness. While much of the land that lay between here and the dragon's lair was ribboned with parasols of fungus dotting the half-felled trees, here the air smelt fresh, even fertile. Fragrant lilacs emerged from between the leafed trees. People were infrequently witnessed on the road. Agnes hardly trusted the notion, but even the sunshine seemed warmer, the grass lusher, and the company itself seemed oddly invigorated. This obvious juxtaposition infused Agnes with distrust. Campe was known for assaulting areas of warmth and growth. She passed the observations along to Valencia, who immediately concurred. Valencia shyly added that the same hard-to-perceive lightness seemed to emanate from the core of her flag bearer. After many discussions, the flag bearer had revealed that the Stargazer's magick had cast protection over these grounds and over their subjects.

This bizarre reality was instantly confirmed when the party reached the hill where their host resided. Within moments of dismounting their horses, the mystical and magickal Stargazer came into view, as if via apparition. Adorned in royal purple robes and a bevy of amulets and trinkets that hung from their limbs haphazardly, the Stargazer shined. Agnes didn't quite know how to perceive them; it was as if magick emanated from their very being. Their aura shimmered with a radiant light, its spectrum similar in color and tone to the bands of light that emerged in the sky following a rainstorm. It was unnerving and admittedly bizarre to be engaging with a stranger that felt both warm and otherworldly. Agnes could not pinpoint much about this stranger and knew it was not relevant to inquire. In the presence of someone with a nature so different from her own, she instinctively extended her trust.

Approaching with familiarity and purpose, the Stargazer immediately embraced Agnes and sincerely thanked her for making the journey. In a rare demonstration of solidarity, they offered the same appreciation to Valencia, who stood agog, tensing at the intimacy and violation of custom. The band of heralds dispersed and the warriors were invited to the Stargazer's inner sanctum.

Weaving throughout the dirt tunnels beyond the cave mouth as she followed the Stargazer downwards alongside Valencia, Agnes' mind again anxiously brimmed with questions. The Stargazer answered them willingly, albeit the responses provided little clarity.

"What is your true name?"

"Stargazer."

"Is this land protected by your magick?"

"Yes."

"How long have you been able to protect these lands?"

"As long as I am living."

"Could you cast these same protective spells over all the lands and protect them from the beast?"

"No, I am not strong enough to extend my magick that far."

"Why do you not journey to kill the beast yourself?"

"I lack the necessary brute force and health to make the long journey. Magick has depleted my life essence and I do not have the strength."

"Where does your magick stem from?"

"The stars."

"What does that mean?"

"The stars up above grant all stargazers magick; I am one in a long line of stargazers whose magick stems from the otherworldly forces of the cosmos."

"How do you harness the power of the stars?"

With that, the Stargazer stopped. A door stood before them.

"Would you like to see for yourself?"

They entered the Stargazer's sanctum. Scrolls were stacked from floor to ceiling, falling over each other along one wall without any sense of order. In the hearth, a supernaturally hued fire with mystic flames roared, licking surreal shades of turquoise uncharacteristically reminiscent of the sea. Its flames constantly transformed, abruptly shifting into an earthy brown, then a metallic silver. Dried herbs and plants hung in overlapping bundles from floor to ceiling, emitting strange scents. Stones of every conceivable shape and color seemed strewn haphazardly amidst the meticulously drawn symbols that held precisely placed items both macabre and whimsical: in one, a neatly tied wisp of curled hairs, another contained an unnaturally large canine tooth. Everything collected within this room was in strange configurations that felt surreal and outlandish. Agnes' eyes raked over the abundance, unsure of how to respond. The Stargazer motioned for Agnes and Valencia to join them at the simmering black cauldron perched above the fire on a thick iron chain. Trepidatiously, Agnes and

Valencia approached.

Inside the cauldron a liquid of strange intensity simmered. Its color and form were unknowable, as if they'd come from somewhere not of this earth. Oddly disfigured purples, molten blacks, and subtly shifting blues percolated and transformed. Agnes and Valencia stood, transfixed. Their pupils reflected strange events not physically present in the cauldron as shimmering scales manifested and slowly shifted against a backdrop of gold and stone. The women stood, mouths agape, watching as a horrifying creature manifested on the surface. The serpentine creature was gargantuan and terrible, winged and horned. It turned, hissing, and opened its ancient jaw as a flickering flame belched out from its bloodstained teeth.

The Stargazer disturbed their stupor. The warriors gasped as their awareness of their surroundings returned.

"You witnessed Campe in its lair?"

Both women verified they had.

"This potion contains the essence of the stars and its power draws from the same power as the wyrm. It can be used to butcher the ancient beast. If you drink from it, you will be infused with the might of my ancestors. It is the same might that compels the wyrm. To kill the beast, you must drink from the potion, then thrust your sword directly into its heart. I have gifts which will aid you in your quest. The power of magick is indispensable. With it, you will prevail."

With grim determination, Agnes locked eyes with the Stargazer.

"Present your sword master."

* * *

The new moon passed through three cycles while Agnes and Valencia trained with the hoary old sword master. His stony disposition did little to dissuade Agnes from taking a liking to him—and perhaps even had the opposite effect. He was thorough, battle-scarred, and tenacious. He respected their talents and demanded improvements. Accordingly, Agnes spent endless hours feinting, thrusting, locking, and lunging alongside Valencia before collapsing, exhausted, onto the warmly packed straw in her sleeping quarters.

Despite training at the same frequency and intensity, Valencia seemed comparatively energised. She had stolen excursions with her flag bearer; she was discreet, but the smile hidden behind her eyes told another story. Agnes did not interfere. Truth be told, it filled her with a simple sense of pleasure to see someone she loved be loved in return.

Over the waxing and waning moons, Agnes rarely saw the charismatic Stargazer. A thick fog rose from their underground sanctum at odd times; elsewhere, unusual tendrils of sparks seemed to be summoned in the surrounding skies. Agnes and Valencia did their best to endure these remarkable premonitions with grace, but they were unsettled. This world of magick was one they did not know.

Agnes longed to return to the hovels. There, life felt simpler, albeit more tenuous. Valencia may have found a lover, and perhaps with that lover somewhere to call home, but this place left Agnes with an empty yearning. She longed to undertake their quest, if only to hear the familiar grunting of an embattled foe. Whetting her sword with methodical precision, she swore that her steel would soon draw blood.

One night, the full moon rose, soaked in an unusual shade of blood red that hung suspended in a cloudless sky. Agnes had been lying sleepless in her chambers; moon shards danced in the reflection of the dagger she was flippantly twirling betwixt her fingers to calm her mind. The birds were unusually restless as the ravens cawed and the owls hooted. A falcon screamed in the far distance. The trees were oddly still. Hair rose on Agnes' neck.

It was then that the Stargazer appeared.

"Go to the wyvern's lair before the blood moon!"

With a supernatural intonation that seemed both unearthly and ancient, they summoned Agnes to the sanctum before their prismatic visage instantly evaporated. Agnes rose quickly and bounded through the tunnels, knowing that she and Valencia would soon leave this place.

Arriving at the chaotic sanctum, Agnes witnessed the depths of the Stargazer's exhaustion. They'd clearly spent countless hours casting spells and incantations, and now were discombobulated and intense. They thrust two glowing vials and a simple whetstone into Agnes' outstretched hands, explaining the purposes of each. The items were meticulously presented and had required many sleepless evenings to prepare. The Stargazer's erratic and weary behavior simply reinforced this truth.

First, they offered an incantation to obfuscate the warrior's entry to the cave where the brute resided. Despite the wyrm's decrepit state, its hearing and vision were peerless. The incantation must be chanted as the sun set directly prior to the next blood moon, and would grant her invisibility and silence, enabling her to survive the approach of the beast and strike the fatal wounding blow. The Stargazer explained that the words had been snatched from a cruel grimoire, plucked from the tumulus of a forgotten queen. They closed their eyes, and reopened them.

The Stargazer's pupils suddenly showed a milky black. As if hypnotised, their voice dissolved into a baritonal chant.

"Al da hab, dash de hab!"

Agnes murmured the incantation endlessly, imprinting its strangely lulling syllables in her brain.

"Al da hab, dash de hab!

"Al da hab, dash de hab!

"Al da hab, dash de hab!

"Al da hab, dash de hab!

"Al da hab, dash de hab!"

Next was the purple potion to infuse the warrior with strength. Agnes was granted two vials, one for her and one for Valencia. They were attached to simple strands of rope that hung from the neck. The Stargazer stressed that they must be consumed shortly after reaching the beast's lair. The effects of the potion would last only hours and would grant the consumer unearthly brawn.

"Al da hab, dash de hab!"

The final gift took Agnes' breath away. It was but a simple whetstone, but its underside revealed the truth: The stone crackled with the same celestial energy as the light flashes that zigzagged across the sky during the peak of violent storms. Before entering the mountain, Agnes must sharpen her weapon with the whetstone. She must strike hard, and strike true. The power infused in the sword would last but a single battle and would grant the wielder the power of the Stargazer and their storied lineage. This gift had come at a great personal cost to the Stargazer, and now it was hers. Agnes was then told she must leave in the morning and embark with Valencia on their perilous quest. Again, the Stargazer's eyes glazed black.

"You must go to the wyvern's lair before the blood moon!"

Back in her bed, Agnes quivered with anticipation and wonder. The same anticipation she had recognised in Valencia moons prior now resided within her. Many of the greats had failed at this quest, and now she would prevail. Before closing her eyes, she chanted the incantation.

"Al da hab, dash de hab!

"Al da hab, dash de hab!

"Al da hab, dash de hab!

"Al da hab, dash de hab!

"Al da hab, dash de hab!"

Comforted by the offerings she scarcely understood, Agnes fell asleep, ascending into dreams of victorious bloodshed. She woke up the next morning refreshed. Opening her eyes to the bright rays peeking through the slants in her hovel roof, she lay silently for many moments. Possibility. The Stargazer had granted her the gift of possibility.

Reflecting on this newfound joy, Agnes packed and embarked to the stores. Valencia was waiting there with their stallions already bridled, eyes shining with a profound sadness. Unable to meaningfully address what Valencia would be leaving behind in such a moment, Agnes instead fixated on the provisions. The sword master joined in the preparations, offering unlimited access to all possessions and occasional advice on necessities. Despite hardly needing the assistance, Agnes and Valencia were grateful for the presence of their battle-scarred teacher. It may be the last time they gazed upon him. As he quietly held each of the items aloft, Agnes looked into his eyes, acknowledging their—and by extension, his—value.

Flint. Tinder. Ten yards of thick cloth treated with animal fats. Bows. Arrows. Slings. Axes. Knives. Swords. Whetstone. Cooking pots. Forks. Bowls. Cups. Rope. String. Fishing line. Rough woollen blankets. Long, clean fabrics for wounds. Tunics. Goat-leather capes. Furs. Wool bridles. Spurs. Hauberks. Shields. Dried meat. Hardened cheeses. Dried barley. Dried oats. Dried rye. Leather flasks. Wineskins. As each item was carefully placed in their saddle bags and rucksacks, Agnes revealed the Stargazer's gifts to Valencia: the glowing vials, a small bag of stones, salves, and the whetstone.

Entranced, Valencia gazed deep at the oscillating amethyst hues of the vials. Her demeanor changed, both strengthening and hardening. The sadness left her eyes, replaced with a grim determination. Placing the vial around her neck, Valencia slipped it beneath her tunic, embraced the sword master, and returned to her horse without uttering a single word. Agnes followed.

Al da hab, dash de hab!

* * *

They spent many of the following moons on the road astride their two plucky stallions. Valencia had been uncharacteristically optimistic despite the uncooperative weather that alternated between torrential rain and sleet. They missed the warmth and comfort of the Stargazer's home; the fragrant lilies, the lush grass, and the warm people had been a mighty privilege. Here, the barren, rocky landscape was unforgiving. Often, the sky darkened with ominous hues of grey and blue, unleashing a walloping maelstrom. Predictably, Agnes and Valencia were cold, wet, tired, and frequently hungry. They occasionally spent the night in friendly outpost hovels along the journey, huddling close on the straw beneath rough woollen blankets to ward off the rapidly chilling air. One particularly cold night, the wind howled and sleep was fitful. The same vision that plagued Agnes on the journey to the Stargazer's sanctum returned to her in flashes of fitful intensity, but this time with a new ending: Scales. Talons. A flickering flame. Valencia stained with gore. Teeth. Molten purple potion bubbling in a cauldron. The Stargazer's harried visage howled, *"Go to the wyvern's lair before the blood moon!"* Celestial energy poured from her sword. Blood. The Wyrm screamed. Violence. Force.

Agnes awoke with a gasp next to a snoring Valencia. They had but five nights to reach the peak where the dragon resided and kill the beast: The blood moon was coming. After Valencia awoke, the warriors prepared to leave. Thank the gods that their next and final outpost would be the hovel that hired Agnes to dispense of the bandits just a season prior. There, they could fill their bellies, sharpen their weapons, and maybe even drink some ale. They cleaned and prepared their belongings, ensured their horses were well fed, and rode.

Al da hab, dash de hab!

A full day and moon of riding passed before Agnes and Valencia arrived. Craggy, blackened trees jutted from the rocks, which were marked with stains of rotting brown. A single torn yellow flag marked the location; it fitfully flapped in the wind.

Something was wrong.

Very wrong.

The warriors dismounted from their horses, drawing their swords. They moved swiftly towards the hovel entrance, cautiously awaiting death. A putrid smell greeted them. Within the entryway, a corpse lay curled in a fetal position. Enraged, Agnes and Valencia ventured further into the hovel with their swords drawn and shields in a defensive position, meeting nothing but silence, bodies, and blood.

The hunters had died upright with quivers in their arms. They were shot through with arrows and their dried blood was a feast for the flies. The minstrels' throats had been cut and they lay slumped over the tables of the tavern. Their stench was overwhelming. The warriors were scattered throughout the hovel and had died violently while protecting the pedlars and herders. Then they entered the infirmary.

An arrow flew past Agnes!

Gathering her wits, Agnes rushed towards the assaulter, who fumbled to nock his bow for another round. She shoved her sword into his guts and held it firmly in place as he howled.

"Who are you?" she screamed, slowly twisting her steel.

The brute spit in Agnes' face and laughed. His eyes displayed no humanity, instead reflecting pale pools of light not of this world.

"My master was the mighty Roldand."

Agnes removed that malefic wizard's head from his body not so long ago alongside Valencia. They had seen some of his weaker subjects had been entranced by a strange combination of magick, cowardice, weak will, and lust for power. After the death and beheading of the murderous rapist, it seemed the enchantment had lifted. Agnes now knew it was her failure to address that the brute's magick was not fully squashed. Before she could say another word, the pale-eyed coward died in spasms.

Wiping her sword on his tunic, Agnes turned back to Valencia. Her squire stood akimbo in the doorway, an arrow protruding deeply from her thigh. It had missed her shield by a hand's width. Through locked teeth, Valencia looked Agnes square in the eye. Blood was slowly seeping through her trousers.

"Would you extract this arrow from my leg?"

Agnes prepared the infirmary, removing the long, clean fabric. Once they had left this place, the wounds would need to be treated with boiling water and wine, then stitched. For now, they removed the arrow and tightly wrapped the wounds. Mercifully, the weapon had penetrated entirely through Valencia's leg. Both women had completed arrow extractions before, knowing that if the arrow had remained lodged in the thigh, Valencia would be doomed to death or amputation. In this lonely place, the latter would mean death as well, albeit a slower and far more painful one. It was no small mercy to discover this was not the case. With cautious gratitude, Valencia remained still and scarcely made a sound.

Agnes laid out their woollen blankets and clean fabrics for bandaging, then awkwardly placed Valencia's punctured leg on a wooden bench at the best angle for the arrow to lay flat. As Valencia grimaced and contorted her body, Agnes took out her aged whetstone and sharpened her blade. She bid Valencia to be still, then quickly severed the arrow head with her sword. Agnes twirled the shaft to ensure it had not punctured Valencia's femur bone, finding to her immense relief that it had not. She then put her weight on Valencia's leg to apply pressure to assist with reducing pain, firmly gripped the arrow shaft, and wrenched the remainder of the arrow out.

Blood immediately poured forth from the wound as Valencia's face drained of color. Agnes wrapped the long, clean fabrics around

Valencia's leg tightly. It went around her thigh one, two, three, four, then five times before running out. Binding it, Agnes sighed deeply in relief. She felt profoundly exhausted after a full day of hard riding followed by close combat. Shutting her eyes, the Stargazer's visage immediately appeared.

"Time is running out! Go to the wyvern's lair before the blood moon!"

The Stargazer howled the words in a vortex of swirling colors.

Gasping, Agnes opened her eyes and steadied herself. She knew she must leave Valencia and continue the journey alone. There was no battle to be fought or won with an arrow wound, especially one against an ancient wyvern. Little time was left. The incantation, the potion, and the whetstone would ride into battle alongside Agnes. Valencia could not and would not.

Al da hab, dash de hab!

After preparing a small fire far away from the wretched stench of death that emitted from the hovel, Agnes grimly readied herself for the days to come. Before she could clean and suture Valencia's wounds, they must give the blood time to coagulate. Valencia rested silently, conserving her energy. Her face had grown surly. She knew her part in this quest had ended and mightily resented that it was instigated by the cowardice and cruelty of a bewitched, simpering fool.

As the night began to fall, Agnes explained to Valencia the visions she had seen of the Stargazer and the urgency of the quest. She sharpened her axe, her dagger, and her sword. She plucked the barley, meats, oats, hard cheeses, and cooking pot from the saddlebags, then poured the water she and Valencia had collected from the closest stream into the pot. She suspended the pot over the fire. After preparing and consuming their hearty meal and setting up their camp for the night, Agnes cleaned the pot and filled it with a mixture of water and wine. Valencia watched the process warily, knowing the pain to come was necessary for the healing process. Any potential infection must be burned out.

Before Agnes commenced, Valencia raised her hand, halting Agnes momentarily. With a strange smile that was half grimace, she grabbed Agnes' hand. She was silent for a moment.

"Is now an appropriate time to inform you that I'm with child?"

Flabbergasted, Agnes' face burst into a smile. She embraced her old friend and protégé, knowing instantly that Valencia's flag bearer was the father.

"Let's make sure you are healed before the birth."

Agonising minutes passed as Agnes poured the mixture over Valencia's wounds and washed the hardened blood from her leg. Once complete, Agnes sutured the twin puncture wounds. Together, they decided that Agnes would proceed and Valencia would remain here for the next three moons to give the wound time to completely close. Riding immediately would quickly force it back open and would endanger them both. As such, when, and if, Agnes returned, they would return together to the Stargazer's hovel.

Al da hab, dash de hab!

Nightfall crept in. Both women enjoyed a deep slumber devoid of visions. As the sun rose over the horizon, Agnes embraced Valencia.

"Goodbye my friend. I cherish you. I cherish your offspring. We will see each other again in three days."

Valencia looked into Agnes' eyes, then removed the vial of potion hanging around her neck from beneath her tunic. Valencia placed it around Agnes' neck.

"You will kill the wyrm. I will see you in three days."

She paused.

"I love you."

"I love you."

Without a backward glance, Agnes rode toward the mountain. It was a long, solitary ride. She arrived at the rocky base of the peak around midday. Agnes dismounted her horse and departed on foot with only her sword, her shield, her dagger, the whetstone, and the two vials. Scanning the area for clear signs as to where the wyrm's lair would be, Agnes eventually found a stream and followed it upwards.

Al da hab, dash de hab!

The calming cadence of the babbling water was a pleasant companion to the enormity of her impending mission. After filling her belly many times with its cold, clean sustenance, the dark, beckoning mouth of a cave eventually emerged in Agnes' vision. The sloppily discarded carcasses of horse, man, and goat bleakly scattered amidst the area confirmed her suspicions: She was close to where the wyrm resided. Instinctively flitting her eyes towards the soon to be setting sun, Agnes gritted her teeth and removed the whetstone from her pocket. It was time.

Agnes was spellbound as she sharpened her sword. The blade was possessed by the radiant energy and it was unlike anything the warrior had ever seen. Fantastic light bands danced along the edge, oscillating bizarrely like some mystic storm. The Stargazer's magick and radiance resided within and were expelled from the blade.

Agnes' hair stood on end. Her eyes glazed black as she chanted the incantation in a baritonal voice completely unlike her own.

"Al da hab, dash de hab!

"Al da hab, dash de hab!

"Al da hab, dash de hab!

"Al da hab, dash de hab!

"Al da hab, dash de hab!"

It was as if time increased in speed. The sky darkened surreally within moments and the blood moon shone in all its vermillion glory.

Agnes entered the cave. She was instantly surrounded by nearly translucent dolomite stones, including raggedly beautiful stalagmites and stalactites. Barely having the time to appreciate the stunning alien surroundings, Agnes looked down and realised she could no longer perceive her own limbs. The incantation had indeed obfuscated her entry to the cave. All that was visible was her steel, whose very edge sizzled in a frankly foreign fashion.

Agnes' senses were considerably heightened. She noted with pleasure that it was as if darkness did not matter. She witnessed and perceived every nook and cranny. Her eyes followed the surroundings and it was clear that she must follow the cave into the depths of the mountain. The air grew musty, and the acrid smells of death and decay filled her nostrils, increasing with each step. Agnes must be swift. Who knew how long the effects of the incantation would remain?

Scampering swiftly downwards while avoiding the jagged rocks, Agnes knew she must soon consume the potion. She put it out of her mind to focus on the task at hand. Down, down, down she went, noting the widening cave and the faint trickling of water. Rats and various scaled slithering creatures fled, screeching in outrage as Agnes interrupted their routines.

After some time, the stench began to subside and a colder, fresher air took its place. It was then that Agnes came upon the subterranean lake. As she traversed the shoreline towards yet another fissure in the mountain, a low rumbling sound became discernible and suddenly, a sulphuric scent joined it. Warmth pervaded the air. The wyrm was here. It was undeniable. She stopped, instinctively, and pulled the simple strand of rope from below her tunic. Gazing deeply at the oscillating purple concoction, Agnes breathed deeply and kissed the vial. She pulled the stopper from it and poured the contents down her throat.

Withdrawing her dagger, Agnes realised her entire body was radiating with a ferocity not unlike the heat of battle. The heat pulsated from her fingertips down into her toes. Her sword suddenly felt no heavier than a feather. Nothing felt real. The air was static. She closed her eyes and the Stargazer visited her for the final time.

"Go to the wyvern's lair. Harness the magick of the blood moon!"

Their magick pulsated through Agnes' eyelids.

The wyrm was near.

Very near.

The heat increased substantially, but Agnes hardly felt the effects of it. The rumbling and growling were growing in volume. As she came upon the mouth of the sub-cave, the first glimpse of incandescent scales was visible. The wyrm was gigantic, its tail alone the thickness of a stallion. The visible lower half of its body slithered slowly and deliberately as it traversed its lair. Agnes knew she must get much closer to its torso to plunge her sword directly into its heart.

Squeezing up against the dolomite to avoid disrupting the stones and alerting the beast, Agnes gazed all along the mouth of the cave. Everywhere lay shimmering objects of various lengths, widths, and sizes.

Coins! Riches! *Goblets!* Bones. Strangely brilliant stones. Glassy remains. Armor. *Pearls?* It was shocking to behold this array of items so carelessly discarded.

Perceiving the vast riches that lay strewn about, a bizarre fanaticism rose to a fever pitch in Agnes' chest: She must kill the malignant wyrm who had pillaged her land. Walking directly towards the wyrm, she felt as though she had exited her body—as if she were in a dream. The mighty beast had massive, browning teeth that protruded from above and below its lip. Its head alone was elephantine. The horns that jutted from its head were long and textured, and their tips appeared to have cracked against the cave mouth. Its muddy color oscillated between earthy and rocky tones that embodied the very same magick of the Stargazer. Its eyes were reptilian with a rapidly closing inner lid, reflecting a cold indifference so like its kind. It felt otherworldly. It felt malignant. It felt evil.

Stepping forward with delicate precision in her invisible state, Agnes appreciated the vein-laden wings of the dragon. Stretching the length of at least two human men, they folded elegantly along the beast's massive body. Translucent and strange, they outlined its grandiosity. It was almost time.

Agnes hesitated. This encounter felt too quiet, too simple. Too easy. Raising her sword to striking position with assassin's precision, she waited for the beast to bow lower. Agonising moments passed…

Almost there…

Go!

She leapt into action and struck hard with the enchanted sword, completely severing the revolting beast's head at its elongated neck. Hardly able to whimper, let alone roar, before its blood sprayed across the cave, its wretched body collapsed, shaking the ground. The magick that had possessed the blade no longer danced along the sword edge; it had dissipated. It was over.

Wiping her sword on her tunic, Agnes uttered a grim goodbye to the beast she knew as Campe. As an act of revenge, she spat on its remains. Mallory, the General from the East, Făt-Frumos, the E Bija e Hënës dhe e Diellit, Prâslea the Brave, Dietrich von Bern: They deserved better. Well… maybe not Mallory.

She laughed, and that quickly transformed into a sob.

The silver haired Ilian had deserved so much better. Agnes uttered a final goodbye to them all.

Another roar pierced the silence.

It was as if the very air was being sucked into a void.

High, loud, and piercing.

So very, very loud.

Freezing in place, Agnes desperately pulled the whetstone from her tunic, and began sharpening her steel once more. The magick forces that had dictated its agile movements had tragically faded into oblivion. The Stargazer's gift had already been used. There was no more to be extracted from this. Dropping the whetstone, Agnes opened the second vial of potion and felt a secondary surge of power and violence as she threw it back.

The ground rumbled as the second dragon smelled the blood of its counterpart and lunged forward from the darkness. The cave was roaring with the impact; the roof overhead oscillated and rumbled as deadly stalactites plunged from overhead and shattered on the ground below. Had she killed Campe's baby?

Despite her heightened senses and strength, Agnes was forced to cover her ears as the mighty wyrm roared in anger and pain at the discovery of her slain counterpart. As Agnes withdrew her hands from her head, she realised in horror that her visage was reappearing before her eyes. The magick had faded. Agnes turned and ran from the sub-cave towards the lake.

Perhaps she could trap the gargantuan beast.

Perhaps she could hide and escape another way.

Perhaps Agnes would die screaming in agony.

Gasping as she fled, Agnes heard the dragon inhale sharply and unleash a torrent of molten fire. Licking at her heels, it instantly melted the blade of her steel. Screaming at the unbearable heat, Agnes dropped the useless hilt.

Turning to fight, Agnes withdrew her dagger. Campe unleashed a roar so ferocious that Agnes staggered backwards. As the serpent drew its head back, Agnes sprang into action, leaping directly at the wyrm with all her remaining power. She plunged the dagger directly into the mighty beast's eye. Its howl shook the depths of the cave and blood poured forth. Falling from the height, Agnes ducked and rolled. She could not allow the wretched beast to win.

The wyrm's massive foot pinned Agnes to the ground.

Agnes' gurgling screams echoed on the whistling wind of the

cave. Inhaling one last breath, the mighty wyrm spewed forth molten spittle, leaving nothing but a mess of charred flesh and blood.

Her ashes scattered—lost on the wind.

***Sarah Kitteringham** is the vocalist and lyricist of epic heavy metal band **Smoulder**. She is an acclaimed music journalist whose byline has appeared in Banger Films,* Decibel Magazine, Invisible Oranges, Iron Fist, *Bandcamp,* Exclaim!, Unrestrained!, BeatRoute Magazine, *and her own annual metal zine,* Last Fanzine Before Doomsday. *She has written album liner notes for Pagan Altar, Reverend Bizarre, and Cirith Ungol; her mixed media artwork has been published via Grendel's Sÿster, Smoulder, Zine-Obscura, and more. Her story "Dragonslayer's Doom" is based on the final track from Smoulder's 2023 album* Violent Creed of Vengeance.

ALSO AVAILABLE

Want to get an e-book for free? *The Infernal Bargain and Other Stories* is available exclusively for DMR Books mailing list subscribers. This collection contains 10 tales, including some you won't find anywhere else. Go to www.DMRBooks.com and get your copy now!

The Chronicles of Caylen-Tor by Byron A. Roberts – The Wolf-King of the north, Caylen-Tor, does battle with imperial armies and sorcerous serpent-men in three exciting novellas! Spectacular sword-and-sorcery by the lyricist of Bal-Sagoth.

The Chronicles of Caylen-Tor Volume II by Byron A. Roberts – The Wolf of the North returns! Caylen-Tor, the mightiest warrior of a savage, time-lost age surges back into the fray in a new collection of thrilling sword & sorcery tales by famed Bal-Sagoth vocalist/lyricist Byron A. Roberts.

The Chronicles of Caylen-Tor Volume III by Byron A. Roberts - From a time-lost age of arcane legendry, the barbaric warrior-king Caylen-Tor rises once more to hack and hew his way to blood-spattered glory! In this, the third pulse-pounding volume of sword & sorcery tales by renowned Bal-Sagoth vocalist/lyricist Byron A. Roberts, the iron-thewed Lord of Wolves voyages across pirate-thronged seas in search of an ancient treasure, leads a warband of ferocious clansmen into battle against malefic sorcery, and ultimately faces his vengeful nemesis in the blighted depths of the netherworld itself!

Renegade Swords – This anthology contains eight fantastic tales, each of them obscure or overlooked in some way. Includes stories by Robert E. Howard, Clark Ashton Smith, Manly Wade Wellman, and more!

Renegade Swords II – Once again DMR Books delves into the vaults of the past to unearth tales of swords, sorcery, and mighty heroes. *Renegade Swords II* contains stories by Michael Moorcock, Robert E. Howard, Karl Edward Wagner, and more!

Renegade Swords III - DMR Books makes another foray into the realm of time-lost tales and returns laden with treasures! *Renegade Swords III* contains stories and novellas by Adrian Cole, Brian McNaughton, and more—not a single one of which has been reprinted before!

Necromancy in Nilztiria by D.M. Ritzlin - The world of Nilztiria is an ancient one. Beneath its brilliant crimson sun and demon-haunted moons wondrous treasures lay buried, waiting to be uncovered by intrepid adventurers. Yet peril abounds as well, in the form of nefarious sorcerers, grotesque beasts, and inexplicable phenomena. If you crave stories of adventure and wonder with a touch of gallows humor, look no further than these thirteen tales of Nilztiria!

Vran the Chaos-Warped by D.M. Ritzlin - Vran the Chaos-Warped is a man who will never break an oath or drop a grudge. When he discovers the despicable wizard Foad Misjak has committed the most foul of crimes against the population of Nilztiria, he swears to slay the evildoer or die trying. Vran confronts Misjak, who learns how the cursed swordsman earned the name "Chaos-Warped" when he casts a spell which has drastically different effects than intended. As a result of the uncontrollable magic, the pair of nemeses are swept away from Nilztiria to another dimension!

Swordsmen from the Stars by Poul Anderson – Three classic novellas from the pages of *Planet Stories*. Heroic science fantasy at its best!

Dark Dreams of Nilztiria by D.M. Ritzlin – Nilztiria! An ancient land where daring swordsmen and unscrupulous sorcerers alike strive against unfathomable monstrosities in their personal quests for glory. Nine tales of this fabled land can be found in this new collection, detailing the exploits of infamous heroes such as the cursed warrior Vran the Chaos-Warped, the freewheeling barbarian Avok Kur Storn, and the enigmatic wizard Xaarxool the Necromancer.

Samhain Sorceries edited by D.M. Ritzlin - Just in time for Halloween, DMR Books presents ten haunting tales of swords and sorcery. On Samhain, the dead will rise, dark rituals will be performed, and gateways to the afterworld will open. One of the more notable tales in this anthology is "Night of the Burning Ghost" by Keith Taylor, which features Felimid mac Fal, hero of the classic *Bard* series. *Samhain Sorceries* also includes stories by Adrian Cole, Matthew Pungitore, Harry Piper, and more.

The Ship of Ishtar by A. Merritt – When John Kenton uncovered an artifact from ancient Babylon, he was transported to a new world beyond time and space: one which offered pain and the near certainty of a bloody death, but also brotherhood, vengeance, and the most entrancing woman he ever laid eyes on—Sharane, flame-haired priestess of Ishtar! This special Centennial Edition of *The Ship of Ishtar* includes the author's preferred text, as well as nearly two dozen vintage illustrations and previously unpublished ephemera from the Merritt estate.

The Empress of Dreams by Tanith Lee – Sixteen tales of swords and sorcery by the Crown Princess of Heroic Fantasy!

Made in the USA
Monee, IL
08 April 2025